IMPERFECT ALIGNMENT

KATHERINE NICHOLS

Black Rose Writing | Texas

The author grants the final approval for this literary material.

First printing

This is a work of fiction. Names, characters, businesses, places, events, and incidents are either the products of the author's imagination or used in a fictitious manner. Any resemblance to actual persons, living or dead, or actual events is purely coincidental.

ISBN: 978-1-68513-674-1
LIBRARY OF CONGRESS CONTROL NUMBER: 2025937971
PUBLISHED BY BLACK ROSE WRITING
www.blackrosewriting.com

Printed in the United States of America
Suggested Retail Price (SRP) $21.95

Imperfect Alignment is printed in Minion Pro

*As a planet-friendly publisher, Black Rose Writing does its best to eliminate unnecessary waste to reduce paper usage and energy costs, while never compromising the reading experience. As a result, the final word count vs. page count may not meet common expectations.

Praise for
Imperfect Alignment

"Nichols captures the struggle between mother and daughter and past and present."
–**G.A. Anderson** author of *South of Happily* and *Dream a Little Dream*

"This fast-paced suspense story had me sneaking in chapters throughout the day until I finished."
–**Kim Conrey** author of *Ares Ascending* and *Nicholas Eternal*

Finalist in American Book Awards
Named Top 25 Mysteries of 2024, Strand Magazine
Nominee for Georgia Author of the Year

American Legacy Book Award
2025 Finalist

This book is dedicated to single working mothers everywhere.

IMPERFECT
ALIGNMENT

CHAPTER 1

Past Becomes Present

Whenever I see a horoscope—in the paper or on a desk calendar or in an Internet pop-up—I crave a cigarette. Strange, since unlike my chain-smoking mother, I've never had a thing for nicotine, and I have never believed the alignment of the stars played any role in the determination of my future. Still, I want to hold an unlit Virginia Slim between my lips and imagine a world where every day of my life is written in predictable black and white. A world where my shortcomings can be explained away by my date of birth. After all, those born under the sign of Cancer are moody and pessimistic by nature. Not my fault.

Most people my age get their news online. But I love the way my fingers slide over the porous paper and the soft crackle of the pages as I turn them. Or possibly, I'm becoming more like my mother than I care to admit.

Unlike Mom, who never planned her day without checking her horoscope, I rarely even look at the column with its ridiculous predictions and advice.

Generally, my job with a Los Angeles-based production company keeps me too busy to think about what the stars have in store for me. But after a night of restless dreams filled with flying crockery in a smokey kitchen and driverless pickup trucks chasing me down the road—images that are both unfathomable and familiar—I experienced the irresistible urge to turn to the occult.

With my last project, a complicated spot for a major airline, in the editing bay, I had nothing pressing on the schedule. So, I made a cup of coffee, sat at my kitchen table, and turned to the page featuring the daily horoscope.

Be prepared for when past becomes present, and the future walks through shadows.

Now I remembered why I stopped reading that crap. A fortune cookie would offer as much wisdom and rarely was it as stale.

I headed for the shower, stopping to unplug my phone from the charger. It immediately vibrated, then emitted the two-note theme from the movie *Jaws*.

My stepfather's name, Barry Winters, popped up. If he was calling, I would most definitely be stepping outside my comfort zone. Bracing myself for his booming baritone, I answered on the fifth ring.

"Hey, Lizzie. Hope you're not in the middle of something important. But, honey, I've got some bad news. It's your mother." His voice broke.

I collapsed into my chair and held my breath.

"Mom? Oh, God. Is she . . ."

He cleared his throat and continued. "No, not that." His tone negated the hope his denial implied. "But not good. She had a stroke this morning, and she's unconscious. They've got her in intensive care. The doctors haven't determined the extent of the damage but advise we get you here as soon as possible."

It had been almost two years since I'd been back to Barry's estate in Roswell, Georgia, the house he casually referred to as my home although I only lived there for a year after they married.

"The earliest flight I could get was the red eye tonight."

Despite his distress, my stepfather had assumed control. Growing up in a fatherless house—I have only vague memories of someone who smelled like motor oil hoisting me in the air—made it difficult for me to deal with male authority figures. So, it was no surprise

Barry's need to take charge drove me crazy when I was younger, sticking his nose in everything from the clothes I wore to the boys I dated. As I approached thirty, I became more tolerant. What had once been infuriating only mildly annoyed me. Today, it was oddly comforting.

He provided me with flight details and informed me he would have his daughter pick me up at the airport. The idea of being trapped in Atlanta traffic with my stepsister behind the wheel made the vein in my forehead throb.

Four years younger, April had come with the package when Mom and Barry united. At the already difficult age of twelve—or, as she would insist, almost thirteen—she was no more thrilled to become a member of a blended family than I was. We spent our parents' brief courtship exchanging hostile glares and snippy remarks. A lifetime of pretending to like my mother's latest love had given me the capacity to hide beneath a thin veneer of fake goodwill. April's dislike for my mother, however, was openly hateful, and I did nothing but observe, and occasionally even encourage, her blatant disrespect.

The thought of seeing her brought with it shame for my past behavior, and I insisted I'd get to the house on my own. But Barry wouldn't have it, and I wasn't up for fighting.

After promising to update me on any changes in Mom's condition, we ended the conversation with his standard "Love you, kid" and my awkward "Uh, uh. Thanks."

The ever-present LA sun streamed through the brilliant purple and gold bougainvillea thriving on its own outside my window. Beams of light struck the framed photo sitting on the sill. The dusty eight-by-ten shot of me and Mom at my college graduation was the only picture I had of us together. I swiped a paper towel over our faces and studied it.

My long, dark hair is unnaturally flat, a result of the cap I hold in my hands. Next to my petite mother, I appear much taller than five four. Underneath my billowing blue robe, I'm frighteningly thin from black market diet pills that got me through all-night study binges.

Despite her diminutive frame, my mom is curvy in a tasteful, feminine way. We had the same deep brown locks, but over the years, hers grew increasingly lighter. The last time we were together, I discovered her desire to blend the gray in gracefully had culminated in a startling Marilyn Monroe platinum blonde.

Her smile is wide and toothy. Only someone close to her might spot it as forced. Except for a slight upturn at the edges and despite the urging of the photographer, my lips form a straight line. The resemblance is noticeable, but not remarkable. Our strange silvery-gray eyes give us away. The shade is difficult to capture in a photograph. Something in the pigmentation creates a ghostly glow in the irises, giving them a hazy, other-worldly look. No matter how bright our camera-ready smiles are, we don't exude warmth.

I replaced the picture and made a mental list of what I needed for the trip. Preparing for late March in Atlanta, especially since I had no idea how long I would be there, was a challenge. I spent the next hour filling one large suitcase and a carry-on, before I realized I had forgotten to let my boss, Russ Young, owner of Young and Younger Production Company, know my plans.

I dreaded the call and considered avoiding an immediate conversation with him by leaving a message with the firm's office manager. My reluctance had nothing to do with worry he might object to me taking time off. No, my boss would, if anything, be overly conciliatory because he wasn't just my boss.

When we met, I was between relationships. I worked freelance, and his company had just started to take off. I came in to help with some of the overflow, and late-night work sessions led to late-night play sessions.

A little older than anyone I'd been with, he was muscular with thin silvery threads of gray in his hair and a perpetual tan. I was aware of his well-earned reputation as a player, but he had a way of saying what a woman wanted to hear. When he told me how sexy smart women were, while trailing kisses down my neck, I believed him. Once we completed the project, he found another one for me and then another. Eventually, he made me an offer I couldn't afford to refuse, and I broke my cardinal rule of never dating the boss.

I also broke my rule about going out with married men. In my defense, Russ insisted he and his third wife were separated when I agreed to go out with him. Later I discovered *separated* meant the latest Mrs. Young was in Brazil getting some *work* done. His marital status seemed irrelevant—not because I was some kind of husband-stealing hussy—but because he was the kind of man who cheated. It was as much a part of him as his strong jaw or capped teeth. If not me, he would have been with someone else, and since I had no intention of becoming the fourth Mrs. Russ Young, I presented no threat to the current one. For me, he was a temporary love interest—heavy on the temporary and light on the love.

Not his fault he didn't realize my relationships came with a pre-stamped expiration date. I never explained to him that, unlike my mother, who lived to orbit around the man she loved, I was more cometlike in my approach—coming dangerously close to the sun before striking an elliptical path as far from it as possible.

Despite my obvious lack of interest in discussing a future with him, he remained blissfully unaware his most appealing quality from the beginning had been that he was totally unavailable. Recently, he had begun to hint at an unwelcome willingness to leave his wife, something I wanted no part of. The trick would be to get out of the relationship without getting fired from a job I liked and needed.

He answered on the first ring. "Babe, are you okay?"

Shit. I had completely forgotten about our lunch meeting. I could picture him now, sprawled out on the hotel bed watching the stock market report on TV.

I apologized for standing him up and explained my situation.

"You shouldn't be by yourself. What flight are you on? I'll come with."

Irritated by his offer, a nagging sensation tugged at me. Maybe Russ wasn't quite as manageable as I'd believed. The idea of spending four and a half hours on a plane with him while he droned on and on about starting a new life together brought me close to hyperventilation. I assured him I would be fine alone. He protested and refused to back off until I promised to call in the event I needed sustained comfort.

After acknowledging his declarations of love and concern with as much enthusiasm as I could muster, I got him off the phone. While scanning the kitchen one more time to ensure the toaster and iron were unplugged, I grabbed the picture of Mom and me.

I sat on the bed folding clothes and wondered how I had missed Russ's growing attachment. Apparently, he let himself believe great sex must be an indicator of something more. I saw him as incapable of the depth required to be bothered by rejection. Angry, yes. Hurt, no. Now I realized getting out of this relationship would be much more difficult than with my last two. One of my coworkers called me a serial monogamist who makes piss-poor choices in men. I didn't tell her those were exactly the kind of men I wanted.

• • •

I planned to follow the universal packing light protocol and laid out multiple outfits on the bed, intending to eliminate half of them. But springtime in Georgia requires layering. After fifteen minutes of removing and replacing the same sweatshirt three times, I gave up and stuffed everything in my suitcase, including the picture of me and Mom.

Then I headed down the little path behind my unit to the apartment of my closest neighbor and amateur therapist, Charles Cartwright. I met him two years ago when I came home from a late night at work. He was walking an overweight French bulldog who whined as I passed.

My move from West Hollywood to Santa Monica didn't prepare me for the unwritten laws governing pet owners and pedestrians. Growing up in the South, I was familiar with the names of all the neighborhood dogs before those of my neighbors. Not so, in sunny

California. Anything more than a pleasant nod at whatever creature attached to the end of a leash might be viewed as an intrusion of privacy. Pausing to pat or otherwise touch said creature is an overt act of aggression.

Even if I had been aware of how egregious my display of affection could be considered, I doubt I could have resisted the doleful little face gazing up at me that evening. So, without so much as a glance at his owner, I kneeled and began scratching behind his ears.

Whining turned to grunts of ecstasy, and he rolled over, exposing his chubby belly. I indulged his request and rubbed in a circular motion that brought about an immediate leg spasm.

"Truman, you naughty beast. Have you no shame?"

At the sound of his name, he moaned softly and pulled his lips back into a doggy grin. I continued the massage.

"You are about the cutest thing I've ever seen. Yes, you are," I crooned in the voice animal lovers employ.

"I'm going to assume you're addressing my companion."

I snapped to attention and explained I'd lost myself to the power of canine charm.

"It's okay. I'm used to it. I mean, I am not without a level of cuteness myself, but this boy is totally adorable." Illuminated by the glow of the streetlight, he flashed straight white movie-star teeth. The lenses of his tortoise-shell glasses magnified bright blue eyes, and slightly receding reddish-brown hair accentuated an already dominant forehead. The comforting sound of his voice with its leisurely pace and the slight softening of syllables made me forget all about stranger-danger.

I laughed and introduced myself. After eight years away from home, I lost most of my accent, but he recognized a fellow Southerner immediately. He invited me to join him and Truman for drinks and dog biscuits, and we bonded over our status as outsiders.

A web designer from Montgomery, Alabama, he had been living in LA for almost twenty years. We fell into what I expected to be a onetime encounter—like when you're at a party and find yourself wishing you were somewhere else. And you catch the eye of a stranger who looks as miserable as you are. You strike up a conversation and because there are no expectations of future hangouts, you unburden yourself. I told him about my conflicting emotions over working for the boss I also dated.

He commiserated with me on the difficulty of finding the right person and shared his romantic woes regarding a recent break-up. And instead of saying goodbye and going our separate ways, exchanging distant pleasantries when we passed each other, we ended the evening with a plan to meet for lunch, making that night the beginning of our friendship.

Recently, he had become involved with a much younger Hollywood make-up artist and, despite the age difference, seemed happier than I'd seen him. Fearful of the perils of trusting in the lasting nature of love, I worried he might get hurt but kept my doubts to myself.

The bluesy sound of Janis Joplin lamenting the loss of Bobby McGee wafted from within. Charles came to the door, unshaven with ruffled hair, but smiling. The smile faded when I told him about my mother, and he pulled me close. Truman wriggled between us. And for the first time since hearing the news, I broke down.

The little dog stood on his hind legs pawing the air while Charles held me. My sobbing eventually turned to sniffling. I declined his offer of coffee and asked him to collect my mail. He agreed and promised to keep an eye on my apartment.

Another bout of weeping threatened to wash over me. Not because of my stepfather's call, more at the simple comfort of having a neighbor to depend on. My charming but troubled mother believed isolation was the key to surviving. She didn't trust the kindness of strangers, especially ones who lived next door. Other than a brief time during my college years, I accepted her paranoia as my legacy until I met Charles. Unlike her, his concern came with no strings attached.

I got home before three. That gave me under seven hours to kill before leaving for the airport. I planned on spending one of them cleaning my two-bedroom apartment, determined not to get sucked into my obsessive ritual where—like a fugitive on the run—I work to obliterate any trace of my existence. But after dusting every possible surface, mopping the kitchen and bathroom floors, and running a damp cloth along the baseboards, I noticed the windows needed cleaning. Then I cleared out my almost-empty refrigerator and scrubbed the inside of my seldom-used microwave. I changed my sheets, tossed the dirty ones in the wash, and collapsed onto my freshly made bed.

While staring at the ceiling, I halfway convinced myself Russ might have had a point when he suggested I see a therapist for my inability to stop once I got started. But then I noticed an intricate pattern of cobwebs and hopped up to find the extender for my duster.

After showering, I went to the closet, dug out my airplane pants—the ones with a wide elastic waist—and threw on a loose-fitting top before applying powder, blush, and mascara.

I made three complete reconnaissance trips through the entire apartment, looking for devices to unplug and windows to lock before calling for a rideshare.

I forgot all about Russ's unwanted advice and ardor. I concentrated on the billboard with ads for movies and alcohol and plastic surgery. I counted red cars and filed my nails—anything to keep my mind off what could be waiting for me.

My reluctance, unlike my cleaning frenzy, was totally rational. After all, I would be returning to a house I didn't consider home, a stepfather who still felt like a stranger, and a mother who might not recognize me.

CHAPTER 2

Walking through Shadows

Most people find the redeye from Los Angeles to Atlanta exhausting if not downright demoralizing. I've only flown it a handful of times, but to me the sensation of skipping an entire night of sleep is invigorating. It's one less evening of finding ways to keep terrifying bedtime thoughts at bay. And it allows me to play with other people's lives.

I can transform the bored businessman in the aisle seat into a corporate spy stealing trademark secrets. Or make the sweater-vested lady on my left, mumbling what I think are prayers as we take off, the mastermind behind a pyramid scheme involving high-end household cleaners. The tired woman in sunglasses covering half her face is an heiress returning from an illicit liaison back to an unsuspecting husband.

Occasionally, if I'm in a daring mood, I scan the aisles for someone whose features suggest we might share a bit of DNA. This pathetic habit would provide hours of fodder for the counselor I will most likely never see, but it's obvious I have a daddy thing. Whatever happened between my parents shortly after I turned four left my mother with a quiet, but unquenchable, rage. She refused to discuss him with me, saying only that he deserted us, and we were better off without him. Eventually, I stopped asking about him and for months, sometimes years, I never thought about him. Being suspended thousands of feet in the air triggered my interest in the man who had shown none for me.

After an hour or so of rewriting the lives of strangers, I usually drift into a sort of half-sleep, where I hear bits and pieces of conversations or the pilot announcing turbulence, safe in the understanding that my level of slumber won't be deep enough for my dreams to turn ugly. By the time we land, I'm surprisingly rested.

But tonight, I remained in a state of wakeful edginess. I gave up on reaching my pleasant travel trance and scrolled through the movies. I rejected the one about a boy and a dog because I was pretty sure the dog wouldn't make it to the end of the movie and a romantic comedy because I wouldn't make it to the end. That left me with a thriller that wasn't.

Outside my window clouds rolled past and reminded me of the prediction of future shadows. My mother's face emerged through a cluster. She wore red reading glasses, making me think of all the times I'd been late to school while she finished reading her horoscope.

I woke to the sound of the pilot announcing our approach. I once read that half of fatal crashes occur during take-off and landing, so I always pay close attention to the pilot's tone and exact wording. If I hear the word *final* paired with *descent* in his pronouncement, I prepare for the worst. When he used the less ominous version, "starting our descent," I exhaled and obediently waited for permission to get out of my seat.

A quick glance at my messages revealed three texts from Russ. He had forgotten or willfully abandoned the rule he established early in our relationship: leave no digital trail.

In the first, he reminded me how sorry he was to hear about my mother and repeated his sentiment urging me to take as much time as I needed. Not bad. The tone was one of a caring boss expressing concern for a valued employee. The problem was that Russ wasn't known for his compassion toward employees or anyone else. I hoped his wife wasn't aware of this shortcoming.

The second was intense, but still open to interpretation.

Call when you land. We have to talk.

Easy to make the case any boss might urgently want to speak to an associate.

His last message, however, shot a bolt of dread through me.

Can't stop thinking about you. Admit it. We need each other.

This set off warning bells. It was impossible to view it through the impersonal lens of employer and employee. And where the hell did *needing each other* come from? Not the Russ I knew, for sure. One of his most appealing qualities had been what I perceived as self-reliance. When I shared the thought with Charles, he pointed out that what I called self-reliance was more self-absorption.

"I've known lots of guys like your boss," he said. "They're perfectly lovely until you disturb their world view, the one where the planets and everything else revolves around them. Throw them out of orbit, and they can get nasty."

Since Charles had more experience with men than I did, I hadn't dismissed his opinion. But I attributed it more to his own unfortunate choices in partners than to any resemblance to my situation.

After rereading Russ's last communication, I began composing a break-up text in my head. My thumbs were poised over the keys, but I considered ending a relationship via phone to be the ultimate in tacky, so I suppressed the urge to tell him we were over. A vague uneasiness hung over me, but I pushed it aside and read my next message. It was from April.

Hey, Sis. See you soon.

I gritted my teeth. I hated it when she called me *Sis*, but I had to hand it to her. The girl was an expert in hitting a nerve. I lined up behind fellow bleary-eyed passengers as we started and stopped our tedious trek off the plane. On the way to the luggage area, I wondered which April would be waiting for me.

My stepsister was known for her chameleon-like social ability to blend in with whatever company she happened to be keeping. During the brief time we lived together, she morphed from a gangly pre-teen to the alpha in her pack of mean girls. Her curly brown hair had been tamed to cascade down her back, sparkling with both high and low lights. A testament to the powers of dermatology and orthodontics, her skin was clear and her smile almost overpowering in its brilliance. Unlike her less blessed peers, she grew smoothly into her willowy frame and fully comprehended the power of her blossoming body. I suspected she understood it a little too well, in fact, but the pretty, rich Aprils of the world got away with a multitude of indiscretions.

On one of my rare visits from college, the summer after she turned sixteen, the police brought her home dead drunk in the back of a squad car. She swore someone drugged her because she absolutely did not drink, and Barry believed her. Only my mother's skepticism kept him from filing a complaint against the host of the party and his parents. Other than what I hoped was a truly killer hangover, however, my lovely stepsister suffered no consequences.

This episode was the first in a series of events that formed the texture of her teenage years. I graduated college and headed to the West Coast about a year before she finished high school. Mom sent updates about the sorority April joined and her frequent changes in majors, but I made it a point to ignore them.

I found my mother's eagerness to befriend Barry's little beauty painful to watch. And although I resented any maternal intrusion into my own life, I resented her interest in my stepsister more.

The last time I saw her was the two Christmases ago. Her latest transformation was into a law student at Georgia State. She wore her hair in a sleek chin-length bob and was dressed in Givenchy jeans and a navy blazer, the picture of privilege and sophistication. She ate quietly and left before I did to meet with a study group. I remember remarking how dedicated she was to spend her break studying and being surprised when she simply smiled at the dig.

Since then, she passed the bar and accepted a position in a law firm in downtown Atlanta. Other than Facebook posts, the only way either of us kept up was through Mom.

I reached baggage claim and stood at the carousel, dividing my attention between searching for April and watching for my suitcase to roll out. I caught sight of a slender young woman with smooth, shoulder-length brown hair waving to me from across the room.

She arrived the moment my bag passed by. I lunged and missed, torn between chasing it or waiting for it to make the long circular journey back. April made the decision for me when she stepped in front of me and stood there smiling.

Neither of us were huggers. Whenever a relative trapped her in an embrace, she remained rigid. I empathized with her discomfort and noted this aversion to close contact might be the only thing we had in common.

She must have overcome her distaste for the practice, or maybe her legal training included how to fake human emotion.

"I'm so sorry about Ginny." Her dark brown eyes clouded with what seemed actual concern.

"Thanks for picking me up. I told Barry I could make it home on my own."

"You don't have to thank me."

Dressed in black yoga pants with a lightweight striped sweater, she could have been a fitness catalogue model. It's not that I'm not in decent shape. I walk and work out on a semi-regular basis and keep my curves in control. But I've never had my stepsister's easy put-together thing going on. I tugged at my sweatpants, spared from additional self-scrutiny by the reappearance of my bag. She watched as I snagged it, then hurried to my side.

"Let me." She wrenched the handle from me. "You must be exhausted."

And suddenly I realized I was tired, very tired, barely able to keep up as she led the way through clumps of travelers, then to the parking deck and her shiny black Lexus SUV. She stowed my bags in the back, and we exited the lot into the sluggish morning traffic.

I kept my foot on the imaginary passenger-side brake, bracing for impact as she maneuvered her way to the HOV lane. While she threaded through narrow gaps between slower moving vehicles, I tried to distract myself from the certainty of annihilation by focusing on the skyline.

Like most big cities, the view from a distance never tells the whole story. Rays of sunlight provided back light for the taller buildings, creating what could have been the cover of a brochure—so long as the camera stayed fixed on the city proper and remained tilted upward.

On the other side of the highway, closer to the road and reality, ugly industrial areas hinted at the presence of even uglier pockets of poverty. Ramshackle apartments reinforced the concept.

We passed the exit for Turner Field, the former home of the Atlanta Braves. I could see the top of the entrance to the stadium where I had gone to watch the team on random weekends. Rather, my friends stayed focused on the game for hours at a time. I drank beer and waited for fireworks.

"Look out, asshole!" April blasted the horn at a car drifting into our lane. She glared at the offending driver as we passed. I kept my eyes straight ahead.

"Did Daddy give you any details about what happened?" she asked, unfazed by our brush with death.

"Not really. Just that Mom had a stroke, she's in intensive care, and the doctors are assessing the damage."

It was surreal talking about my mother as if she were a vehicle being scrutinized by an insurance company—a cold but accurate analogy.

"That's right, except they moved her out of ICU into a private room, which is really good news." She checked her side mirror and switched lanes. "She was working in the garden when she fell. Thank God, it was cleaning day. Otherwise, who knows how long she might have been there."

Something about her story struck me as odd, but a slight break in my stepsister's voice and the wave of guilt I felt at not being there distracted me. I recently worked on a pharmaceutical ad about the prevention and detection of strokes, so I knew how crucial an element time could be.

I turned to the window, marveling at the vibrant greens of Georgia after living with the drought-induced beiges and browns of large portions of California.

"Daddy left to take a shower and, hopefully, a nap. He wasn't sure whether you would want to go by the house first or straight to the hospital. I'm your chauffeur for the day. Your wish is my command."

Suddenly, the urgency to see my mother—touch her face, her hair—was overwhelming.

"To Mom, please."

My stepsister continued to weave in and out of mid-morning traffic seeming to understand my need for silence. I expected her to be different, some new incarnation, but this April—considerate, compassionate even—didn't fit into any preconceived category. Had she evolved into a better version of herself? And why was the prospect of a kinder, gentler April so unappealing? Maybe it was my aversion to the idea my shallow step sibling might have become a better person than I was. More likely, however, it was just another example of her consistent inconsistency.

We pulled into the hospital parking lot. She slowed the car, reached across me, and removed a handicapped sign from the glove compartment.

"It's your mom's," she explained, hooking it over the rearview mirror. "From her knee surgery."

Knee surgery? When had my mother had knee surgery? The dread I might have forgotten something so serious was replaced by the certainty I hadn't. That left me with a sickening realization: Mom never told me about it at all.

I considered protesting taking up a handicapped space, but the fact Mom kept her infirmity from me to avoid bothering me, or worse, didn't think I'd care—kept me from assuming a morally superior stance. I slinked from the car, faking a limp on the way to the hospital entrance.

The moment I stepped inside, my right elbow began to ping, muscle memory of the time when I was fifteen, and Tommy Lee sent me to a different emergency room. With my mother by my side, I stuck to the story of catching it in between the wall and the banister during a fall. I still remember the doctor's expression when he announced I had a spiral fracture, requiring both a special splint and a cast for a minimum of four weeks.

This modern building with its shiny tile and floor-to-ceiling windows was nothing like the small facility with its dingy countertops and stained floors. But the walls covered with expensive art and the vast gleaming atrium didn't change the fact it was still a place no one really wanted to be.

"You okay?" April asked.

I nodded, and we took the elevator up to the fourth floor. More shiny tile, this time with a colorful contrasting pattern, ushered us past the nurses' station to an adjoining hallway and into my mother's room. A tall, ebony woman in bright blue scrubs stood at the threshold. I stepped in front of her.

"I'm Liz Tucker, Mrs. Winters's daughter."

I wanted her to be aware it was my mother she had been poking and prodding, to make her understand I had gotten there as soon as possible and wasn't a totally reprehensible excuse for a child. But the words wouldn't come. If she noticed my inability to speak, she gave no indication. I speculated dazed and confused was the usual state of family members of the stricken.

"I'm afraid we haven't any news for you yet, but the doctor should be by shortly. You can go in and sit. We recommend approaching her as if you were having a normal, although one-sided, chat. We aren't certain of her level of consciousness. She might be completely unaware. But it's possible she hears everything we say."

She bustled away before I had the chance to ask her to be more specific about the parameters of an ordinary conversation. I thought how awful it would be to be lying there while people talked over you, speculated on your recovery, or discussed your appearance in unflattering terms.

"I'll get coffee," April said, reminding me she was still there. For the first time in my life, I didn't want my stepsister to leave my side, but she was right. I needed to face my mother alone.

Hissing whispers greeted me, as if a serpent kept guard over the childlike figure lying in the bed. Not whispers at all, I realized, just the mechanical sound of the machine keeping her alive.

A rubber tube jutted from her nose. Instead of the Gwen Stefani-blonde she had last sported, bright crimson curls fell across her pale face, an experiment with a shade-gone-wrong in the auburn color family. The contrast between her pallid skin and the vivid hue was jarring.

"I like your hair," I lied gamely. "It's very, uh, very. . ." Come on, I thought, you make a living misleading the public. Surely, you can spin this.

"Striking," I blurted. I bobbed my head up and down. "It really suits you."

The ventilator marked time with its relentless wheezing, and I scooted my chair closer to the bed. I took her hand and automatically turned it palm-side up, then traced her broken love-line to the spot between her thumb and forefinger, where the shallow crease ended in a jagged red scar.

Once again, my elbow throbbed with a ghostly pain, and I released her to rub my own battle scar. Not visible like hers, but just as real. Both marked us as survivors, but I have never been sure whether we had won or lost.

CHAPTER 3

Running from the Past

I can't be certain, but I don't think my mother checked her horoscope on the Saturday morning Tommy Lee sent me to the emergency room.

The night before, Mom worked the late shift at the diner. He invited a group of guys from the gym over to play poker. They usually set up in the den and created a thick fog of cigar smoke and testosterone that slowly spread throughout the house.

I'd taken the necessary steps to avoid running into any of his Neanderthals by stocking up on the essentials—soda, chips, and Oreos—and hunkering down in my room. By seven, I was locked in, lying on my bed reading with music blasting.

Halfway through my second stack of cookies, Tommy Lee began pounding and shouting. "Get your skinny ass out here before I come in and drag you out."

When I opened the door, he was standing there with one of his buddies. Tommy Lee looked angry, but Glen or Gus or whatever his name sported a slack-jawed grin on his fat face.

"Where the hell did your dumbass mother hide that bottle of Jim Beam? Find it." A man of few words, Tommy Lee turned abruptly, leaving me to solve the mystery of the disappearing bourbon. Good old Gus-Glen, however, remained behind.

I became aware of how sheer my T-shirt was and folded my arms across my breasts. His grin stretched into a full-fledged leer, and I stayed close to the wall as I sidled past him to the linen closet where Mom had stashed the liquor after Tommy Lee's last bender. The goon stumbled after me.

Rather than reach for it myself and give my escort more to ogle, I pointed to the top shelf. "It's under that stack of sheets, toward the back." I moved as far from him as the narrow hallway allowed.

"Mmmm," he murmured, inhaling laundry softener. "Smells good," he said and tossed them to the bottom of the closet, then retrieved the bottle. Bourbon in one hand, he lifted a strand of my hair with the other and came close enough for me to see the stiff bristles inside his nose. He made a snorkeling sound as he sniffed and backed me up against the wall.

"But you smell better." He closed his eyes and parted his lips.

I tried to side-step, but his thick-barreled chest pressed against me. The stench of stale beer and garlic oozed from his greasy pores, and I gagged.

His eyelids sprang open, and he stepped back, holding his hand against his mouth. Luckily, my attacker was a sympathy-gagger. I used the opportunity to stomp his foot and bolt to my room. I heard him alternating between dry heaving and cursing as I slammed and locked my door.

I flipped off the lights and crawled under the covers but didn't fall asleep until long after my mother came home from work.

Around eleven the next morning I dragged myself out of bed. The house was quiet, the kitchen empty. While pouring dry cereal into a bowl, I sensed movement behind me and turned to find my mother's boyfriend standing there, staring into the distance. His eyes were no more bloodshot than usual, but he had a faraway look, as if he couldn't quite place me.

"So, no good morning?" he snarled. "No how ya doing? No kiss my ass?"

Unable to come up with an acceptable answer to his multiple-choice question, I eased toward the door. He grabbed my shoulder and whirled me around, sending cereal flying and the bowl crashing to the floor.

"Don't you walk away when I'm talking to you, you little bitch." He pulled me closer and gripped my chin, making it impossible to avoid his hot, sour breath. "Think you're too good for me and my friends? I'll teach you some manners."

More surprised than frightened, since he'd never gotten physical with me, I pushed against him, and he loosened his grip. Stumbling backward, I fell against my mother, who had slipped into the kitchen without my noticing.

"That's enough, baby," she said to him. "How about I fix you some eggs?"

I took advantage of the distraction and made for the hallway.

"*How 'bout I fix you some eggs*?" This mocking tone sounded more ominous than his angry one.

I turned in time to see him smile as he backhanded Mom, knocking her to the floor. I had seen the evidence of his handiwork in purpling bruises and split lips, but never had he struck out with such vicious intent in front of me. My mother lay amidst the broken shards of my bowl. I wanted to run from the room, call the police, do something. But the sight of her, lying on the ground, blood streaming from her wounded hand, paralyzed me. I stood motionless as he loomed over her.

"Why don't you *fix some eggs* for your boss? I bet he likes them *over easy*, just like you."

She said nothing as I tried to pinpoint the origin of Tommy Lee's fury. A few months earlier, Mom had taken a job at Barry's Buffet. The owner, my current stepfather, was remarkably unremarkable.

No way was he talking about him. He was old, skinny, definitely not my mother's type. She hadn't even mentioned his horoscope sign.

Regardless of what set Tommy Lee off, it was clear his level of violence was escalating. He leaned over my mother, hand raised.

I flung myself at him, clutched his arm, and held on. He flicked me off, but I came from behind him, wrapped my arms around his neck, and dangled in the air when he straightened.

His guttural roar rang in my ears, but I hung tight. For a few glorious seconds, I was the attacker, and he was the victim. My fifteen-year-old hands, however, were no match for his, and he peeled me off like a sweater. He grabbed my arm and twisted it. I screamed.

Keeping my eyes squeezed shut, I heard, rather than saw, the cast-iron skillet bounce off his head with a satisfying *thunk*. I opened them in time to see his face slam against the corner of the kitchen table. Then he was the one on the ground, my mother hovering over him, weapon still raised.

Disappointed when she lowered the blood-streaked pan, I found comfort in his deadly stillness. She wrapped a dish towel around her wound, then turned to me.

"Are you okay?" she asked, the imprint of Tommy Lee's palm an ugly blotch on her cheek.

Until then, I hadn't registered the throbbing pain. It took my breath away, and I was unable to speak.

She grabbed her purse from the counter and gave me a gentle push.

"Come on, honey. I'm afraid it's broken."

Although the searing spasms in my wrist made it difficult to focus, a flash of elation came over me as I stared at the lifeless body of our tormenter. Between gritted teeth, I could feel my lips begin to turn upward despite the fiery sensation coursing through my injured arm. Even with the burden of pain, my step was lighter.

I cradled my arm and passed through the door when a groan— more of a growl, I suppose—sounded from the floor. The weight of my life dropped down on me as I realized Tommy Lee wasn't dead.

•   •   •

Hypnotized by the steady rise and fall of my mother's chest, I found myself thrust back in hospital time—a zone all its own. Hollow-headed jet lag overwhelmed me as I studied my mom's face, searching for the warrior who felled Tommy Lee with one blow. But there was no hint of the woman who had finally put me first. I eased onto the chair and closed my eyes, intending to rest them for only a few seconds.

Instead, I dropped into a dreamlike state and returned to that night in the emergency room. I was lying on the examination table, high from whatever drug they gave me. Outside the room, voices drifted in and out, my mother's agitated and tearful and another, muffled and male. At first, I thought it was Tommy Lee and tried to call out for help. Too addled to form a coherent sentence, I turned my head toward the door where I saw Mom begin to cry. A man, not my assailant, spoke to her in a comforting, vaguely familiar voice.

As I fought to escape from my dreamlike memory, my stepsister interrupted from far away. "Are you okay?"

I struggled upright and wiped at a damp spot on my chin.

"I would have let you sleep, but it sounded like you were having a bad dream." April stood over me. "Sorry it took so long, but work called." She set two cups of coffee on the tray table. "I couldn't remember if you take yours black, so I picked up cream and sugar." She pulled a paper bag from her oversized Michael Kors satchel. "And I got donuts." She scooted a chair closer.

"Chocolate for you, but we can save it until you're feeling better."

Still groggy, I was slow to recognize she was talking to the unconscious woman on the bed, making natural conversation—something I seemed incapable of.

She took a sip from her cup before continuing. "Daddy said he'll be back before dinner." She bit into a plain donut. "And Carmela says to tell you the house is too quiet without you."

A twinge of jealousy came to me at the ease of this one-sided intimacy. When had my stepsister's relationship with my mother gone from barely concealed hostility to what sounded like affection? The answer was simple. It happened sometime while I was on the other side of the country avoiding them.

The rising pressure in my chest surprised me. I've never been the kind of person who dissolves into fits of sobbing. Not in front of people. Not alone. I'd been an athlete training for a triathlon, hardening my feelings and increasing my capacity for emotional pain to the point I rarely experienced either. But nothing had prepared me for the rhythm of the breathing tube in competition with the steady beep of the heart monitor.

"I can't think of anything to say to her," I gulped before waves of sorrow broke over me.

"It's okay." She plucked tissues from the box on the bedside table. "It doesn't matter. Being here is enough."

The nurse rushed into the room, interrupting our moment of sisterly bonding. She dashed straight to the wall of monitors. I realized the staccato beeping had quickened and jumped to my feet, heart racing.

"Is she okay? Is something wrong?"

She held up one hand to silence me, then took Mom's blood pressure.

I fixated on her slender mahogany fingers as they flitted over my mother, resting lightly on her forehead and pulse before traveling to her toes. Her steady movements seemed to slow both my mother's and my heartbeat.

She adjusted tubing and checked the IV, then said, "Nothing to worry about. Everything's back to normal."

"Why would it speed up like that? If it does it again, will she have a heart attack?"

She smiled and touched my shoulder. "That's always a risk with stroke patients. But your mother isn't in distress. The doctor's been delayed by an emergency surgery. Now would be a good time for you to rest." On the way out, she added, "We'll take care of her."

"So, what do you say?" April asked. "Let's pick up some food and go home. And seriously, Sis." She wrinkled her nose. "You might consider a shower."

"Thanks." An intense desire to get out of the room, away from the reminder of my mother's fragile condition, propelled me toward the hallway.

"First, I have to call Daddy."

I returned to Mom's side. This serene, empty stranger could not be the woman who had once held so much power over my life. Was it possible she was the same person who began every day eagerly reading her horoscope in search of the perfect forecast, one that would take her out of her ordinary existence and propel her into a world of adventure? Her shining beacon on the hill was the pronouncement romance was on the horizon. Sadly, she had trouble distinguishing between the light and the darkness.

•   •   •

The image of that other woman settled over my sleeping mother like the ever-present haze of smoke. Instead of lying motionless here, I saw her back at our cluttered breakfast table grinding out a butt in an overflowing ashtray, holding a cup of black coffee. She placed the mug in front of her, lit another cigarette, and picked up the paper. Paying no attention to headlines or ads, she went straight to the daily horoscope.

The *Marietta Gazette,* now defunct, was her favorite because it included both the current astrological forecast and the blurb from the previous day. This gave Mom the chance to review the role the heavenly bodies played in her immediate past, then find a way to apply the present prediction to her imminent future.

On good days, the pink foam curlers she threaded through her dark hair would begin to unwind as she nodded in approval and read aloud.

You have an interesting energy about you. It's as if you are an electromagnetic field pulling people toward you.

And she became more energetic and hopeful.

On other days—ones where she was cautioned against raising her hopes or disappointed because the previous day's reading was a flop—stillness descended. Then she would light another cigarette, take a deep drag, and run her finger down the page to my sign. I always held my breath, hoping for a lackluster prophecy. If I were lucky, there would be nothing exciting in my future, and she would pass the paper to me and point to the passage.

"You ought to check this before you make any big plans for the day," she might say. And I would read cryptic warnings—like how I shouldn't trust my instincts or should be careful not to reveal my true emotions.

If I were not so lucky and the stars were in perfect alignment for me, she would slap the paper down in front of my cereal bowl and exit the room, leaving a cloud of smoke and despair. I never bothered to read the pronouncement. I knew the force of my mother's will had the power to rewrite whatever happy prophecy Fate tried to send my way.

CHAPTER 4

Being an Electro Magnet

I rubbed my eyes and, once again, found myself staring at a beautiful stranger. I kissed her cheek and slipped out of the room.

April was leaning against the wall, sipping coffee and talking on her phone, approximately two feet from the *no cell* sign. When she saw me, she wrapped up the call.

"I tried to talk him into resting, but he insisted on coming back right away. I said it wouldn't do anybody much good if he wore himself out, but you know how bull-headed he can be."

I agreed with her in principle but appreciated that he would be with Mom.

When we reached the car, I glanced at my watch, 9:35 in California. But I was on East Coast time now, which meant I'd lost three hours. I've always resented this disappearance of random segments. It would be different if I could choose specific moments to toss into that cosmic time warp. I knew exactly the events I would discard like used tissue and precisely the words I would erase with a sweep of the minute hand, possibly changing the course of my life.

"I've been going on and on and haven't even asked about LA." April merged onto the highway. "Tell me what show biz is like."

I laughed. "I wouldn't exactly call it that."

"Ginny's been keeping me updated. It sounds glamorous." She changed lanes, cutting off a tractor-trailer.

"Mostly it's about scheduling and organizing."

"But you must meet lots of celebrities."

"Not really. We book talent through agencies representing struggling wanna-be actors." She looked disappointed, so I switched to her favorite subject. "Enough about me. What's going on with you? Are you dating anyone special?"

She spent the next few minutes telling me how challenging it was to find a man "at the same social and intellectual level who isn't a total bore."

"What about *your* love life?" she asked, catching me off guard. "Ginny mentioned you'd been seeing someone on a regular basis."

In a moment of weakness, to pacify my mother, I alluded to my relationship with Russ, omitting the part about him being married and me not really liking him all that much.

"We broke up," I lied, thinking it didn't count as a lie if you meant to make it the truth.

"Too bad. But it's interesting, since I talked to an old friend of yours the other day, Daddy's financial planner. Grant Albright. I remember him from when you went to school together. He hung out a lot whenever you were on break. Unless he changed a lot, he is not the kind of man a girl would forget."

She was right. There was no way I'd forget him.

"Oh, that Grant Albright. I wouldn't say we hung out all the time. He was more my roommate's friend." A little truth mixed in with the story always makes it more believable.

The appearance of an *Eat Mor Chikn* billboard provided a welcome distraction.

"Chick-fil-A! That's about the only thing California doesn't have too much of. Could we stop here, please?"

"No problem." She turned into the lot and steered past the giant cow. The line of cars in the drive-through lane snaked around the building. She headed toward it, then swerved and pulled into a parking spot instead. "It'll be faster if I order inside. Tell me what you want."

I ordered my usual number one combo with a diet lemonade, the same thing I had at the UGA campus where I first met Grant Albright. He and a friend asked if they could join me and my roommate Whitney, not realizing the two of us were dead drunk and that he would end up being our chauffeur for the evening and for many evenings after, throughout the next three and a half years.

He was one of the few people I brought to my stepfather's elaborately decorated home. Both Mom and Barry loved him, and if he had faked his affection for them, he was a better actor than I was.

My past with him was complicated, and at the end of college, we found ourselves standing on that precipice between friend and lover. And with one act of self-preservation, I shoved him off the ledge.

• • •

My first day at UGA, Mom and Barry insisted on helping me set up my dorm room. He dragged boxes and suitcases from the car while she made my bed with the yellow and green floral comforter she selected. She wanted to help me unpack, but I lied about going to a freshman mixer and shooed them out.

I stood at the window watching to make sure they were really gone and experienced the same lightness of being I had when I thought Tommy Lee was dead. Only this time, I was truly free. There would be no Lazarus-like groan to keep me captive. No overly solicitous stepfather shadowing me throughout the big, beautiful house I couldn't wait to escape. No disappointed glances from Mom when I failed to appreciate Barry's generosity or enjoy my newly acquired sibling.

I was too young to understand that freedom was less a physical condition and more a state of mind. I discovered it was far easier to unshackle myself from the chains of family than it was to throw off the gossamer threads of doubt and distrust lingering from my past.

Mom had been surprisingly reluctant to let me go away to school, probably because she would be on her own with my terrifying stepsister. It was Barry who advocated for the University of Georgia. And it was Barry who paid for it all. Instead of being grateful, I saw his generosity as a desire to get me out of the way and behaved accordingly, thanking him politely with absolutely no enthusiasm.

I debated between unpacking or taking a walk around the campus when a tall, slender girl breezed in, effortlessly pulling an enormous hot pink suitcase behind her. She stopped for a second to survey the room, crinkling her straight little nose in what could have been interest or distaste. Her long dark hair was pulled back in a red headband, showcasing high cheekbones and clear, lightly freckled skin. If the information in my introductory packet was correct, this was my roommate, Whitney Harris.

"Can you give me a hand with my bags?" she asked.

Without waiting for an answer, she disappeared into the hall. Obediently, I shoved the bag toward the closest of the two matching dressers, letting the door close behind me. Within minutes, insistent knocking announced my roommate had returned.

I took my time, irritated at her expectation I was there to serve at her pleasure. After April, I was more than done with haughty princess types.

Weighed down with two medium-sized shoulder bags and numerous brightly colored canvas ones covered with names of expensive make-up companies, she looked like a refugee from Beverly Hills.

She stumbled in, dangerously close to careening into the sink on the wall. I reached out to steady her, and she dropped a bright purple bag, spilling its contents onto the floor. We stooped down at the same time to retrieve a rolling lipstick and cracked heads, hard.

"Shit on a cracker!" Whitney exclaimed, rubbing her smooth forehead.

"Shit on a cracker?" I echoed. And we both burst out laughing.

She wrestled out of the straps and handles and rummaged through the pile.

"Ta da" She held up a bottle of wine, uncorked it with a fancy corkscrew in one fluid movement, and poured it into a yellow Dixie cup that had appeared from her magic bag.

"I don't normally drink red before lunch, but desperate times, right?"

I learned Whitney Harris was from Buckhead, a prestigious section of Atlanta. Until three months ago, she had been expected to attend the same school her fraternal grandmother had, Agnes Scott, an all-girl's college known for its strong feminist views and, more recently, for its sexually diverse population. A population most likely not quite so open when her grandma went there.

"It's not that I have anything against lesbians," Whitney explained, refilling our empty cups. "I've been to tons of coming-out parties." She touched her cup to mine. "Here's to lesbians. Because they have good taste, and they taste great."

I burst into a spasm of giggles and wine shot from my nose. The burning sensation and my uncontrolled laughter brought tears to my eyes. Whitney reached into yet another bag and handed me a tissue.

"So, how did you get here?" I asked after composing myself.

"I drove, duh."

"Not *here* here. How come you didn't go to Agnes Scott?"

"It turns out their admissions people weren't impressed by my essay. One of the topics wanted me to explain what I would bring to the student body. I said I could offer hope to my sisters who were confused about God's plan for them to marry and procreate and subjugate themselves to their husbands."

"Jesus," I whispered.

"I know, right? But when my name wasn't even on the waitlist, my mother contacted someone she knew on the board, and, well, let's just say my writing did not receive rave reviews. Dad wasn't a fan either, but he was never as dead set on me going to an all-girls school in the first place. And he sure as hell didn't want me staying home. So, he talked Mom into letting me come to Georgia."

Rendered speechless by the sheer force of Whitney's personality, I took another drink, surprised to discover my wine was almost gone. She dug out a second bottle, opened it, and poured refills.

"What about you? How did you get *here* here?"

"The regular way. My mother and my stepdad wanted me out of the house, but not too far." I swirled my cup, watching the burgundy stain spread up the sides, hoping she wouldn't press for details and was pleased when she changed the subject.

We discovered neither of us was in a serious relationship, and we both thought coffee houses were stupid. I also discovered the room had begun to spin.

"You don't look so good," my roommate announced. "I'm starving. Come on." She unfolded her long legs from underneath her and rose gracefully.

I offered no resistance when she pulled me to my feet. Once upright, I stumbled to the sink and splashed water on my face. A glance in the mirror confirmed my suspicion: I looked almost as bad as I felt. Whitney's reflection appeared beside mine—unaffected by our booze-soaked afternoon and just as lovely as before.

She steered me down the stairs to the quadrant. All around us, students moved with the frenetic pace of convicts in the final stage of a prison break. Like me, they were heady with new-found freedom. Unlike me, they were not throwing up into an enormous pot of geraniums.

Whitney stood by patiently, holding back my hair. When I emptied my stomach of its liquid contents, she produced another tissue and a piece of gum from her purse.

"I know exactly what you need," she said, grabbing my hand and leading me to the multi-level parking deck. Instead of heading to the elevator, however, we veered to a side door marked *Do Not Enter*. She opened it.

I've never been one of those mindless rule-followers, but I also don't believe in calling unnecessary attention to myself—like getting hauled in by the campus police on my first day at school.

She shoved me forward. I pushed back, refusing to move, but when the sound of laughter signaled the approach of a group of students, I obeyed. After the bright sunshine, it took several seconds for me to adjust to the darkened hallway. A narrow passageway snaked ahead of us.

"What is this place?" I asked as she searched through her purse.

"Not sure, but it probably leads to a storage area. I found it when I visited my cousin last year before he flunked out." She produced a small plastic baggie and waved it triumphantly, then removed a tightly rolled joint and a lighter from the bag.

"Holy shit!" I smoked my share of pot in high school, but usually in a secure spot, like some boy's basement when his parents were out of town or the heavily wooded area behind the baseball field. Certainly not in an off-limits passageway in the state university, but she already had the joint to her lips. After sucking in the skunky sweet smoke, she held her breath and passed it to me.

What the hell, I thought. I might as well be stoned riding in the back of a cop cruiser. I took a hit and waited for that first gentle swell. Instead of a slow-moving stream, I got sucked into a raging current.

"Wow," I whispered when I was able to speak.

"Damn straight." She grinned. "You don't need much of this stuff. I snatched it from Granny's stash before she finished her last round of chemo." She inhaled again and passed it back to me.

"Oh, God. I'm so sorry." But the euphoria descending over me made it difficult to regret smoking marijuana pilfered from a sick old woman, and I took another hit. Whitney was right. You didn't need much.

She laughed. "It's okay. Granny's in remission. She still likes to get high every now and then, though. Drives Mom crazy." Pulling a pair of manicure scissors from the baggie, she snipped off the end of the joint, tossed it to the ground, and crushed it with the heel of her Calvin Klein boot. After a few seconds of waiting to make sure it was out, she returned the remaining weed to the plastic bag.

Miraculously, my nausea had disappeared.

We slipped back out to the main lot where she had parked her car, a bright red BMW convertible. I tried to look cool and indifferent as I eased onto the plush leather seat and leaned against the headrest of the most luxurious vehicle I'd ever ridden in.

She lurched toward the exit. Normally, the thought of riding with someone in her condition would have terrified me. But Granny's medication gave me a sense of invincibility. Besides, this was my first day of college, and, by God, I would enjoy it if it killed me.

CHAPTER 5

Resisting Magnetic Forces

My reckless disregard for staying alive wavered as we raced along the highway. Too terrified to check to see how fast we were going, I shut my eyes and tried to enjoy wind against my face. When I opened them, I saw the way it rippled through the golden leaves of the trees lining the street. Heat shimmered on the sidewalks and reflected off the students, surrounding them in a Monet-like haze.

The earlier elation of independence returned. Not only was I free, I was in a magical place where youth was the currency and, for the first time in my life, I had a full line of credit.

Whitney slammed on her brakes and turned into the Chick-fil-A lot, scattering a bevy of long-haired girls in tattered jeans. The tallest girl in the group shouted, "Bitch" and flipped us off.

With no indication she heard the angry young woman, she cut the wheel hard and squeezed into an impossibly tight spot. I suspected she had become inured to obscene words and gestures flung at her by less beautiful creatures. My new roommate reminded me, while I might be loaded in the youth department, I was lacking in the power of privilege. Without it, I was still at the mercy of people who never worried about those left in their wake.

I moved with the exaggerated precision of someone impersonating sobriety and followed her into the building. The comforting aroma of fried food wafted over me, but I was disheartened by the long lines.

"Grab us a seat and I'll order," Whitney commanded.

I had been sitting on the booth side of a two-seater table for a few minutes when I realized she hadn't asked what I wanted. Once again, she impressed with her capacity to transform the mundane into the extraordinary. In her hands, an ordinary college essay turned into a missile; the entrance to a storage closet, an exotic den of iniquity; and now, a fast-food order, a mystery.

I was eager, excited even, when she approached with a tray full of the unknown. Other than the overflowing fries, I had no idea what the containers held.

"I got two number one combos and extra boxes of nuggets, plus lemonade and chocolate mint shakes."

She attacked the feast with a passion that suggested I was wrong about her being anorexic. Of course, she might have plans to purge after polishing off her share of the food. The thought threatened to dampen my enthusiasm, so I pushed it aside. There would be plenty of time to uncover any unpleasant details about my roommate.

I was in the middle of a break between sandwich and fries when someone dropped onto the seat next to me, brushing a hairy leg against mine. I listed to the right like a boat thrown off course, then caught a whiff of vanilla and musk in the air. Before I pinpointed the source, a tall boy with deep blue eyes stood behind my roommate. His loose-fitting shorts and oversized black UGA T-shirt made him seem gangly and a little clumsy, a colt growing into his body.

"Excuse me." He cleared his throat. "Is anyone sitting here?" His voice cracked the tiniest bit on "here" before he smiled, revealing perfect white teeth and two disarming dimples.

Whitney peered at him from beneath her thick lashes. Mouth still full of fries, she gave a look I would later come to think of as her pin-the-butterfly-to-the-board stare. She took her time chewing, then inclined her head toward the boy next to me.

"Just your pushy buddy."

Without a hint of social discomfort, the friend extended his hand to her. "I'm Chad Parker."

She ignored him and popped a nugget into her mouth.

He grinned and withdrew the hand. "The guy hovering over you is my cousin, Grant Albright. You'll have to excuse him; he doesn't get out much."

Grant's face turned beet red.

"Sit, boy," Chad commanded.

Grant sat, the blush extending and disappearing under thick, dark curls grazing his forehead.

Whitney swallowed, took a napkin, and dabbed at her mouth. The boys watched closely as she completed her cleaning ritual by touching the tip of her pink tongue to the corner of her lips.

Grant knocked his tray with one elbow, and Chad, seemingly unaffected by my roommate's performance, steadied it and tipped his head toward Whitney.

"And you are?"

"Getting bored." She stifled a yawn, leaned back in her chair, then stretched her long arms catlike.

Chad laughed and turned to me. He was handsome in the carefully orchestrated style of an Abercrombie and Fitch model. He wore a red plaid cotton shirt over his khaki shorts. His light brown hair was combed back, and his scruffy beard was sculptured perfectly so that he exuded just the right blend of ruggedness and sophistication.

"What about you?" he asked. "Are you bored, too?"

"Not yet." I answered, turning from him to Grant. "I'm Liz Tucker and this is my charming roommate, Whitney Harris."

Grant's dimples flashed in his clean-shaven cheeks.

"Well, Liz and Whitney," Chad began. "We're headed to a keg party at the Kappa house. Would you lovely ladies like to join us?"

He leaned closer and brushed an imaginary crumb off my shoulder. His touch left a familiar tingle that spread southward. I'd done my research and found out the Kappas were among some of the wealthiest boys at the school. I looked at Whitney, who shrugged her indifference.

"I've heard those parties are wild." I rested my fingertips lightly on his knee and watched his eyes widen.

"That depends." He began tracing his index finger along the inside of my arm.

I put my hand over his, stopping his progress. "Let me guess. I bet it depends on how wild we like it." This time I ran my fingers up his firm bicep, pleased at his responding shiver.

"Right," he half-whispered. "So how wild would that be?" He scooted closer on the narrow bench until most of his leg pressed against mine. I broke contact.

"I guess we'll have to see." I smiled but kept the distance between us. "If it's okay with Whitney, that is."

"Why not?"

Grant beamed at her.

I gave Chad's knee another squeeze before standing. I could already tell he was just my type. Sexy with enough money and status to be in one of the top frat houses on campus. And precisely the correct amount of bad boy vibes. A perfect contender for becoming the love of my life—for freshman year.

I didn't sleep with Chad that night. We did, however, log at least a half hour of passionate kissing with a bit of over-the-clothing groping in a darkened room of the Kappa house. Then, I hadn't been aware my behavior wasn't governed by any sense of propriety or even some moral code. It was a repeat of the pattern I unconsciously adopted at the beginning of my sophomore year in high school.

From the start, I was drawn to the kind of guy nice girls were afraid of—players with smooth lines and rich parents who went out of town a lot. I needed someone fun, popular, preferably with a decent car. Once I found a promising candidate, I'd engage him in a bit of provocative conversation, testing his reaction to casual, but potentially arousing subjects like the advantages of a slow bubble bath over a hot, soapy shower. If his pupils dilated and he squirmed, I might touch his arm while we talked or lean into him while giggling at something he said.

On our first date if he headed for some well-known make-out spot, I acted shocked and a little hurt, I might even shed a tear or two before insisting he take me home. If he was appropriately sorry, I forgave him and let him kiss me once at the door. When he asked for the second date, I might hesitate, then say I had a problem with trust. After listening to frantic promises of how trustworthy he was, I would lower my voice to a whisper, then explain it wasn't him I didn't trust. It was me; I couldn't trust myself with him. Then it was game on.

There was usually a little gentle sexual exploration, not teasing— just setting and then extending limits, withholding myself until I was sure the boy really cared about me. I understand now that for me, sex had little to do with it. I needed those urgent declarations of love because of the power they gave me.

I ended up having three boyfriends in high school, one a year starting when I was a sophomore. Each was a graduating senior, which made the break-up easier. I pretended to be broken-hearted, but insisted he deserved the chance to enjoy the entire college experience, free of the encumbrance of an ongoing romance.

I feared older boys would be more challenging. As it turned out, they weren't all that different.

A little after three, I left Chad unsatisfied and unconscious on the dingy sofa and went to find Whitney. I followed the sound of pulsating music to the basement where somebody had set up a make-shift dance floor. A dense film of smoke created an exotic filter over the gyrating couples, giving them an air of romance. There was, however, nothing remotely romantic about the smell of stale beer and vomit emanating throughout the room.

I weaved my way past a couple locked in a slithery kiss and a threesome with the lucky guy sandwiched between two grinding coeds before finding my roommate, slow dancing with Grant. Unlike me, she had not stopped drinking once we arrived at the party.

"Whitney," I said, tapping her lightly on the shoulder as they drifted by me. "It's pretty late."

She opened her blood-shot hazel eyes and stared at me before exclaiming, "Liz! Grant, it's Liz, the best roommate a girl could have." She took my hand. "Come dance with me," she shouted above the music.

I slipped out of her grasp. "I'm really tired. Can we please go home?"

She stuck out her bottom lip and crossed her arms over her chest. "But we're having such a good time." She hiccupped loudly. "Grant, tell her what a good time we're having."

"We are having a good time," he admitted, his grin disappearing when he saw the look on my face. "But Liz is right. It's late." He slipped his arm around her waist and guided her toward the front of the house. "I'd volunteer to drive you, but I'm over the limit. Let me call one of the campus cabs."

"That's not necessary." I tugged Whitney's keys from her pocket while she continued moving to the music.

"Okay, text me when you get home, though." He held out his hand, and I gave him my phone so he could punch in his number. "I mean it. If I don't hear from you, I'll be coming over."

Outside the frat house, moisture clung to the overgrown holly bushes in heavy droplets from rain we'd been too busy partying to notice. Steam rose from the pavement as I led Whitney to her car. Luckily, she put up the top to avoid the possibility of finding some drunken couple making out in the backseat. I helped her in and sat behind the wheel, realizing I'd never driven a car that cost more than the first place where my mother and I lived.

My roommate snored in the passenger seat as I drove home through the same streets that bustled with student activity only a few hours ago. Without their frenzied masses, the landscape was alien— vast and empty. I sped up, filled with the need to be back in my cramped dorm room.

I found a parking space near the elevator, roused my sleeping passenger, and walked to her side, expecting dead weight. But she rallied. Apparently, the same metabolism that allowed her to eat mass quantities of fried food and drink milkshakes while staying slim also processed alcohol faster and more efficiently. Once we were in the room, she brushed her teeth and washed her face before passing out, still fully dressed, on top of her naked mattress.

I followed her example, brushing and washing, before dragging my suitcase onto my bed to find a pair of pajamas. When I removed a stack of neatly folded jeans, a sheet of newspaper flittered to the floor. Picking it up, I saw that it was my horoscope from yesterday.

Sometimes refusing to make a choice is the most dangerous choice of all.

Underneath this piece of non-advice was a note in my mother's flowery handwriting.

Don't be afraid to be happy. Miss you already. Love, Mom

I crumpled the paper and tossed it toward the wastebasket where it rebounded off the side and landed in front of the closet. Too tired to retrieve it, I stripped to my underwear and slipped on an oversized tee before getting under the covers and turning off the bedside light.

I recalled the sensation of Chad's soft, tickly beard brushing against my neck. I pictured the two of us cheering at football games and tossing Frisbees across the quad. But when I fell asleep, those consciously summoned images dissolved, and I didn't dream of a short, bright future with my latest bad choice.

Instead, I spent the entire night on the edge of a dance floor illuminated by jewel-like splashes of color from an overhanging crystal disco ball. In the center of the room, spotlighted by glittering patterns of light, Whitney and Grant appeared. Her flowing gown sparkled against his perfectly tailored tux as he twirled her around and around.

CHAPTER 6

Dangerous Choices

April opened the car door, and I returned to the present.

"Did I wake you up?" She situated our drinks in the cup holders.

"Just resting my eyes. It's easier to adjust to the time change if I power through."

"As I remember, powering through was your thing."

Before I could ask what she meant, the Eagles began singing "Life in the Fast Lane" from within my purse. Russ's ringtone. I saw he had left five text messages.

"Hey."

"Thank God!" he exclaimed. "Are you okay? Is your mother better? I've been worried sick. When you didn't return my calls, I assumed the worst and got totally freaked out."

My mother's stroke isn't about you, and what grown man says "freaked out"? I took a deep breath and remembered this wasn't just some boyfriend I was ready to break up with. Russ was my boss. I assured him I was fine and hoped my mother would be, too.

"We're waiting on the doctor's latest report, though."

"That's it. You don't have to deal with this by yourself. I'm coming out there. I've been looking at flights and—"

"No!" I said, loud enough to cause April to whip her head sideways and stare. I smiled and shrugged. "I mean it's insane here.

You'd be a distraction." I lowered my voice. "A welcome one, of course, but I have to stay focused on Mom."

The last thing I needed was to have Russ hanging around reminding me just how badly I screwed up my life. In past relationships, I always managed to end things in a final but congenial manner. I let them think the break-up was their idea, and we'd go our separate ways. But with Russ, going my own way wasn't ideal. I needed to keep my job.

"Okay but stay in touch. When I don't hear back from you, I go crazy."

I tried to picture what that might look like with someone who rarely lost control. Hopefully, it didn't involve telling his wife about us, needlessly hurting her. But I promised to be more responsive.

"I love you, babe," he said.

"Uh, uh. Thanks," I replied and hung up.

"That did not sound like ex-boyfriend talk." April smiled and kept her eyes on the road.

"It's complicated."

"Complicated as in hot make-up sex or complicated as in tactfully pointing out someone has toilet paper stuck to the bottom of her Louis Vuitton's?"

Complicated like trying to keep your job after telling your boss the party's over.

"Just complicated," I repeated, relieved to see we'd reached our destination.

She slowed the car as we turned onto the long, curving drive of the home where April had grown up. All angles and arches, it stretched on top of a small hill. The combination of gray stone with cream trim contrasted perfectly with the immaculately groomed pink and red azaleas.

My mother balked at coming to live in the house decorated by Barry's long-dead first wife. Not until he agreed to let her redo the interior, did she acquiesce. He seemed to understand that for Mom it was more a security issue than a matter of taste.

For most of her life, she had nothing worth stealing. Now she had expensive clothes and shoes and jewelry and handbags, and she wanted to keep them safe. So, she started by assigning her fancy-pants decorator a redesign of the master closet. She doubled the size by removing the wall between it and an adjoining area that had been the first Mrs. Winters's sewing room. Next, she installed specially designed doors that could be locked inside and outside.

Satisfied that her belongings were safe, she gave the decorator free rein. They succeeded in transforming the place into something out of the pages of *House Beautiful*. But it was almost too perfect—a showcase that would never be the kind of home where people enjoyed hanging out. Or maybe that was me.

April parked next to the bright red Ford Fiesta belonging to our Colombian-born housekeeper, Carmela. She and her family had fled her country in the nineties, but she never discussed specifics and, as a typically self-absorbed adolescent, I never pressed for details.

She had been cleaning Barry's house since long before his first wife died and had her own ideas about what was and wasn't part of her duties. I smiled at the thought of how she pretended not to understand whenever my mother tried to give her special instructions. Mom referred to it as high-handedness.

"She thinks she's too damn good to learn our language," she would say on the many occasions the cleaning woman ignored Mom's broken-Spanish attempts to tell her to polish the floors or sweep the deck. I never told her about the times I caught Mela in front of the TV totally engrossed in *All My Children* or *The Guiding Light*—English versions. And she never mentioned the times I snuck in after curfew.

"Can you grab the drinks while I get the food? I'll come back out for your bags," April said.

I carried the lemonades to the arched front door and unlocked it, calling Mela's name as I entered.

"Miss Liz," the plump little woman scurried to the foyer. She still wore her dark hair pulled into a tight bun, but more silver threaded through it than the last time I saw her. The soft-sharp scents of cinnamon and Pine Sol wafted over me as we hugged.

"It's so good to have you home. Your mother will be so happy you're here."

"I'm glad *you* were here." I kissed her powdery cheek and stepped back just as my stepsister came through the door.

"Miss April," Carmela greeted her. "Let me set a place for you both. The kitchen, right?" She had sensed how uncomfortable I was, sitting at the antique dining table the decorator had chosen.

We followed her to the sunniest room in the house. My stepsister put the food on the counter and went back to the car.

"Here," I said, making a move for the silverware drawer. "Let me help."

Carmela told me to sit. I tried to tell her we'd eat from the boxes, but she ignored me, setting up plates and cutlery as if we were having a five-course meal instead of chicken sandwiches and waffle fries.

When April returned, she said, "I took your stuff to your old room." Then she turned to Carmela. "I bought three of everything, so there's plenty if you'll join us."

"Thank you, but I ate earlier. I still have some work upstairs."

"We're not going to eat unless you sit." I pushed a chair away from the table with my foot. "I mean it, Mela."

"For only a few minutes."

"Can you tell me how you found her? How long she'd been lying there?"

Carmela sighed and looked out the window. I remembered April's account of Mom passing out while trimming the roses. That strange feeling I experienced when hearing about her fall returned, and I realized why. My mother hated any form of yardwork, but she especially disliked the rose garden because it had been planted and nurtured by Barry's dead wife. She might have been picking flowers for an arrangement or shooing the neighbor's cat away. But tending the garden? No.

"Your mother and I often go for hours without running into each other."

Ever tactful, Carmela alluded to what we were all well aware of. As much as she hated yardwork, Mom also had a natural antipathy toward housework. In the little house we lived in before Barry, I could always find her at the end of a trail of magazines, cigarette butts, and plastic coffee cups. When the clutter threatened to close in on us, I tracked the breadcrumbs and ashes, then retraced my steps with a broom and dustpan. Within a day or so, Hurricane Ginny would cut another swath, and the cycle began again.

Carmela continued, "But if she's home at lunch, we often sit together to discuss her schedule, sometimes just to talk." She stood and walked to the linen closet in the hallway. Pulling two napkins from a drawer, she returned. "Your mother prefers cloth."

I covered my smile with my hand, thinking how absurd it was to think of my mother insisting on fancy linens. Even more surprising, however, was the thought of Mom and Carmela sitting down for a chat. In the early days of their marriage, she played the role of unstoppable force with Barry's housekeeper serving as the immovable object.

Whenever Mom left a room upended with her brand of domestic chaos, her nemesis followed with vacuum cleaner blazing. Over the hum of the machine, pure Hispanic fury filled the air. The smattering of Spanish I retained from high school hadn't prepared me for the sheer speed and invective of her tirade. I picked up references to pigs and cattle, as well as a few popular curse words.

My mother ignored her and kept on puffing.

Not until our housekeeper threatened to quit did Barry intervene. It was one of the few times I felt genuine sympathy for the man. His relationship with Carmela dated back to his first marriage. She had been the only constant in his and April's lives, and her ability to restore a sense of order after the loss of his wife had been invaluable. But his relationship with my mother included sex, which pretty much tipped the scale in Mom's favor.

In what I considered an act of true courage, he initiated a sit-down with the two women. Neither April nor I witnessed what took place, but the resulting cease-fire restricted my mother's smoking and coffee drinking to the deck and sunroom while allowing her free rein with magazine scattering. Carmela agreed to continue her three-day per week schedule and to let my mother live.

"Before the accident, I brought the mail to her as I always do. She likes to go through the bills before giving them to Señor Barry." She smiled, possibly because we both knew my mother suffered from financial insecurity despite having married a very wealthy man. The fact she seemed to care enough about Mom to understand her need for a sense of control over the household revenue spoke volumes about the evolution of their relationship.

"Normally, she sorts through it, then stacks it on the desk in the library. On my way back to the kitchen, when your mother—what is it called?" She touched her hand to her forehead. "Sheiked?"

Carmela's English is near perfect, but stress sometimes results in linguistic confusion. "Sheiked?" I repeated, conjuring the image of a handsome Arab sashaying through the room.

April, who had seemed too engrossed in her fries to be paying attention to our discussion, asked, "Do you mean shriek?"

"Yes, thank you. She gave a little shriek, and I ran back. Your mother was holding an envelope. She was shaking and pale—so pale. I rushed to her side. She said she was okay. But I knew she was not. I should never have let her go outside alone." She used the end of her apron to dab at her eyes.

The realization that Carmela, once Mom's sworn enemy, seemed to know her better than I did, made me feel suddenly out of place.

"Do you remember how long she was in the garden before you found her?"

"I'm sorry, but a deliverance came to the door, and I lost track of time."

"A delivery man?" This was the first I'd heard of any visitors the day of Mom's stroke.

"Yes, in a very dirty van, but he had come to the wrong house. Poor man, not so very smart."

"Did you see the company name?"

She shook her head.

"What about the letter?"

"I don't like to be nosy," she said with a look that dared me to contradict her. "And there was so much confusion after the ambulance came. They wouldn't let me ride with her to the hospital." Her voice broke.

I got up and put my arms around her. "If you hadn't been here . . . " My throat constricted.

She leaned her head against my shoulder. "I will bring the letter to you." She walked from the room.

"Since when did those two get so close?"

"It happened gradually. Remember how careful they were around each other after Daddy negotiated the truce?"

I did. She and I placed bets on which one of them would break. I said no way Mom would limit her smoking to two areas of this big old house. My stepsister predicted Carmela would explode within a week. As it turned out, we were both wrong.

It hit me this might be our first truly honest discussion. Had she really changed for the better? I didn't want to think about how I had changed.

She gathered our dishes. "Wonder what kept them from going after each other?"

"Maybe the moon was in the seventh house, and Jupiter was aligned with Mars."

She laughed at my reference to Mom's unshakeable faith in astrology. We shared a disdain for her reliance on the stars.

"And peace will guide the planets," she responded, using an oversized spoon as a microphone. "And love will steer the stars."

I joined in on the chorus. "This is the dawning of the Age of Aquarius . . ."

We continued until somewhere in the part about trust abounding before trailing off.

"Dear God. Your mother must have played that song a million times on that dreadful trip."

I had tried to forget that vacation. It was right before Christmas my senior year after Barry got Mom and Carmela to cool it. The first day of the break, they dragged me and April out of bed and forced us to join them for breakfast. He announced our big present was a Bahamian vacation. The prospect of spending the next ten days pretending to be a happy family was less than thrilling.

"We were pretty awful, weren't we?" I winced at the memory of our teenage bitchery.

"That mix-up about the date didn't help much either."

In the midst of our moaning and groaning about not wanting to go to what Barry called "a vacation in paradise," we encountered a problem with the departure time. During their shaky truce, Mom and Carmela discovered their mutual interest in the art of prognostication. Both had checked travel forecasts for Libras and Capricorns and the advice from every source—including Mom's psychic and Carmela's great aunt with the evil eye—was traveling before December 19th would be a very bad idea.

"Hard to believe they both bought into all that fortune-telling crap," April said.

"Don't let Mela hear you cast aspersion on the supernatural," I warned.

"Poor Daddy. He ended up losing a chunk of cash changing the flight to the next day."

My stepdad doubted astrology and prophecies but had no interest in going against either one of those women.

"And after all that trouble, our little getaway was far from blissful," she added.

I had to laugh at the understatement. It had been a nightmare. But the plane hadn't crashed, and nobody contracted any communicable diseases, so by our family standards, we deemed it a great success.

More importantly, it gave Mom and Carmela something to focus on other than how much they despised each other. And somewhere along the line, their hatred dissolved and eventually disappeared.

Seeing how upset Carmela was made me understand they didn't just not hate one another. They cared about each other.

I took a sponge and began wiping crumbs from the table. She returned, holding an unsealed manila envelope.

"I found it beside your mother in the garden. She was holding the letter."

Her assumption the mysterious communication required a high level of secrecy indicated she might know more about its contents than she was willing to reveal. The first thing I noticed was the lack of a postmark, which suggested someone had stuck it in the box. Not shriek-inducing but disturbing. The sender had neatly printed Mom's name and address in the proper format. But the upper left-hand corner contained only three letters: *TLF*. Tommy Lee Fagan. I understood why my mother had cried out and turned pale. I stared in horror, reluctant to open it in front of them.

April asked Carmela to show her again where Mom fell in the garden.

"We won't be long," she said before following my stepsister out of the room.

My hands shook as I removed the sheet of unlined paper.

Someone had cut letters from magazines and newspapers, making the message look ominous and childlike at the same time. I read it and sank back into my chair.

I haven't forgotten—Tommy Lee.

I held my breath, as if any sound or movement other than the soft whir and artificial breeze from the ceiling fan might bring disaster. I watched its blades slash through the air, circulating the comforting aroma of disinfectant. Clouds of cigarette smoke never threatened to suck the oxygen from this room. And it had never reeked of fear— until now.

CHAPTER 7

No Choice

No whirling ceiling fan moved the stale air in the kitchen we shared so briefly with Tommy Lee. We had to depend on a rusty stand-up model, and it was working overtime the last time I saw my mother's boyfriend. It was on one of those rare occasions when we gathered for a sit-down dinner. The blades squeaked and squealed in protest as they tried to usher out the tomato smoke from Mom's meatloaf.

Secretly pleased she had burned what I considered mystery-meat-best-left-unsolved, I forgot how much Tommy Lee loved her recipe. Mom had been on a tear about the three of us sitting down together to share a meal and talk about our day and had used the promise of her special dish to lure him in.

Something distracted her, and her gourmet dinner went south. Possibly his unusual silence worried her. Being near my mother's latest boyfriend, in this quiet mood, reminded me of a newscaster description of being trapped in the eye of a deadly hurricane.

We had been existing in that eerie calm ever since his last explosion over two months ago, the one that resulted in a broken arm for me and a concussion for him. Apparently, Mom accepted his sad sack act—hanging his head as he passed me, even helping around the house. But I knew it would only be a matter of time before he hurled us back into the vortex.

"Well, this is just perfect," he whispered, poking at the brick-like concoction she placed in front of him.

"Liz, why don't you go get me my chainsaw from the garage, and I'll slice off a hunk for you?" He chuckled softly.

Neither of us smiled or even moved.

He slapped his hand on the table, knocking my glass of water onto the floor where the plastic cup bounced before rolling away. Without a word, he shoved back his chair and stood by Mom, leaning within an inch of her face.

"Do you expect me to eat this cement shit?" he asked in a voice terrifyingly soft and low.

"Of course not, honey. Let me make you—"

He placed an index finger across her lips and shushed her, then moved around her and began rubbing her shoulders.

"You and me need to have a little talk."

This time, I thought, he's going to kill her.

But instead of crushing her skull, he wrapped his fingers through her hair and yanked her from the chair.

The fan caught the sound of her screams and slung them around as he dragged her from the room.

Her howls became sobs as he slammed their bedroom door shut. Then I picked up the meatloaf and threw it in the trash.

The next morning, sitting across the table from Mom, I saw the little blisters on my hands and realized how hot the pan had been.

•   •   •

April and Carmela came in from the garden, and I stuffed the letter back in its envelope. Touching the paper made my fingers tingle. I checked to see if any telltale blisters had returned to remind me of the searing power of the past.

"The good news," my stepsister began as she crossed the threshold, "is Ginny fell into a big pile of mulch."

"And the bad?"

"There's no way to tell how long she lay there before Carmela found her. Sorry."

"It's not your fault," I said, in a voice harsher than I intended. I needed to blame someone. Then I might stop feeling so goddamn guilty myself.

"I appreciate your driving me around, but I can take Mom's car to the hospital. Hopefully, they'll know more about her condition."

I wanted to be alone with my mother. April and Barry formed their own little family umbrella over Mom, leaving me standing in the rain. And while that was exactly what I'd sought for the past ten years—to be excluded from that group—now it filled me with the loneliness of an outsider in a crowd.

She and Carmela exchanged a glance, but neither mentioned the letter.

"Any idea where Mom's keys might be?"

"Usually, she keeps them in there." Mela motioned toward the built-in desk.

The granite countertop held no trace of the mother of my youth. Rather than her signature clutter, only a neatly folded newspaper marred its pristine surface. When I opened the drawer, pens, pencils, a ruler, and a stapler had been sorted and arranged inside the wooden organizer. The divider at the end—where Mom's keys should have been—was empty.

"They're not here. Any other ideas?"

Carmela shrugged. "I'm sorry, but no."

April spoke up. "We'll search for them while you shower."

Maybe it was exhaustion-induced paranoia, but I would have sworn they exchanged a conspiratorial look. If I had the energy, the implication they needed to humor or somehow manage me might have set me off. But I was losing steam, so I nodded and headed for my old room, now an elaborately decorated guest suite. Appropriate, really, since I'd always considered myself a stranger in that house.

My suitcase sat on the wooden chest at the end of the bed. When I opened it, the picture of me and Mom tumbled onto the thick rose and pink floral bedspread. She dominated the little photo with those eyes that seemed to see through a person and her lips caught between a grin and a grimace. I placed it on the dresser to allow her to keep a careful watch over me, something she had never proved to be good at.

I laid out jeans and a dark gray sweater before getting into the shower and standing under the warm water until my fingertips wrinkled. After wrapping my hair in a towel, I dressed, then sat on the bed to dry it. As usual, I gave up about a third of the way into the process and pulled it back into a low ponytail.

Like my mother's, thick and coarse, it takes forever to style. Unlike hers, it's still my natural medium brown with a few unnatural highlights. Frequently in awe of the reckless abandon with which she transitioned from dark brunette to shocking blond with a few side trips to holy-shit red, I imagined her ability to exchange one look for another mirrored the way she swapped out the men in her life.

Not that my mother was casual when it came to relationships. She had the misfortune of being a hopeless romantic. Even after my father deserted us—something she refused to discuss—she continued to believe in true love. Whenever her pursuit of it hit a dead end, she turned to astrology for solace.

Whether her early selections were unremarkable or I simply put them out of mind, the first loser I remember came along just as I entered the fifth grade. A Gemini, whose impish character purported to be an excellent match for my mother's pixie-like Libra, their union was doomed. Geminis have trouble making commitments, and Libras have no patience with reluctance.

Gone before Thanksgiving, he left my mother holed up in her room for days during which I survived on peanut butter crackers and applesauce.

Eventually, she rallied enough to pay a visit to one of her favorite psychics who brought her back to her own special brand of normal with a reading that promised heightened romance and intrigue in the coming year.

That spring, she fell for an out-of-work welder who abandoned his day job to pursue what he called his reason for being. He cluttered the backyard with half-finished projects—tortured and twisted metallic creatures—appreciated only by the squadrons of spiders who took up residence in them. His pièce de résistance, however, was an angular conglomerate of scrap metal he named in honor of my mother: "Virginia in Repose." The first in a series of nudes inspired by her, its portrayal of what she assumed was her ass did not please the subject. She tossed him and his art to the curb. As a Taurus, his departure was inevitable since everybody knows what they're like.

There had been others, but none lasted long, until the summer before my sophomore year when Mom met Tommy Lee Fagan, a trainer at her gym. She joined the club after a reading that urged her to *take care of both her physical and spiritual needs.*

Happily, she began her improvement regimen with the physical aspect of the admonition rather than dragging me to some New Age church. But then Tommy Lee came on the scene.

The first time she brought him home for dinner, he had the harmless, ambling demeanor of a goofy giant from some children's book. His bullet-shaped head sat on a neck so short and thick it was almost indistinguishable from his sloping shoulders. Ropy veins rippled on hairless, heavily ridged arms. Less defined, but still impressive, his thighs bulged from underneath tight jeans. Later, I noticed his calves were surprisingly puny, which explained his strange habit of bobbing up and down on the balls of his feet, constantly trying to develop definition.

I discovered my mother's latest love interest was no affable creature from a fairytale. He was unpredictable and dangerous. Overly active and amiable one minute, his incessant movement would come to a sudden halt, leaving him silent and sullen. He would then complete the cycle with a slash of violence.

Before Tommy Lee, the men she chose were different on the surface, but at their core, pretty much the same. Whether attributable to something lacking in them or in Mom and me, they were people struggling, but unable, to make a lasting connection. They drifted in and out of our lives, leaving us no better or worse than before them.

But Tommy Lee left physical and emotional marks. Despite, or perhaps because of, his terrifying nature, after his disappearance, my mother became even more determined to find Mr. Right. And I became convinced there was no such person.

Barry Winters did nothing to change my mind although the poor man tried. They met while she was working at a twenty-four-hour diner he was considering adding to his group of restaurants. Mom served him coffee and pie. He decided against buying the diner but was impressed with my mother. He stole her away with an offer of better pay and hours. As a boss, he was considerate and respectful.

Whenever she needed time off for physical or emotional recovery from a romantic disaster, he was understanding and generous. The few times I stopped by the restaurant, he was overly solicitous, but never inappropriate.

A little under six feet, he had the body of a former runner with narrow hips, bird-like legs, and a rounding belly. His smooth, round face and slightly turned-up nose reminded people of their favorite teacher.

Absolutely nothing wrong with him. And I couldn't stand him.

"Miss Liz." Carmela knocked on the bedroom door. "I have coffee." She handed me the oversized UGA cup I used throughout my college years.

I blew on it before taking a sip. Strong, hot, and exactly what I needed.

She shared that they hadn't found the keys, nor had they been able to get in touch with my stepfather to see if he had another set hidden away. I offered to call a rideshare. But April insisted the hospital was on her way, and she needed to check in with her dad.

My shower combined with coffee gave me—if not exactly a second wind–a little breeze. But it might be short lived, so I agreed to ride with her.

Carmela handed me my purse before wrapping her arms around me. Unlike others in my life, her hugs never felt stiff or awkward. They required nothing in return.

I was afraid April would push me about the contents of the letter or at least continue her interrogation about Russ, but she didn't. My convoluted relationship with my boss brought an unwanted comparison between it and the one with Grant. Like Carmela's embraces, it had been easy, comforting even. Until I'd screwed it all up. Before I went down that destructive line of thought, I noticed the envelope sticking out of my purse.

Had the shock of reading it triggered that silent explosion in Mom's brain, or had she been harboring a ticking bomb for months, possibly years? Could a note—even one as ominous as this—possess the power to propel her into darkness?

The more pressing question became who had sent such a hateful message and why. The most logical person would be a member of Tommy Lee's family, but other than the vague mention of a sister somewhere in South Georgia, I didn't know of any other relatives.

My origin theory about the man involved someone turning over a rock so he could crawl out from under it. But he must have started out with a mother. If the person who wrote the note wasn't part of his tribe, did it come from a friend? But that seemed even less likely.

As for the content, just remembering him hardly qualified as threatening.

It was the pesky dash that worried me.

Before I signed on as a permanent employee of Younger and Younger, much of my freelance work included copywriting for TV spots. Having been an English major helped and hurt me in this endeavor. My training taught me punctuation mattered. I discovered no one cared about the nuances of the comma or the expressiveness of the semi-colon or even the urgency of the colon. Why worry about all these subtleties when a dash would do the trick? I fought the good fight, but eventually gave in to peer pressure and hoped the godlike voice-over would correctly interpret the meaning.

The author of the note might share that lax punctuation philosophy, or he could have no conviction at all. But with no deity to serve as interpreter, details mattered. For instance, the message could be "*I haven't forgotten*—important pregnant pause dash here—*about the existence of Tommy Lee Fagan.*" Or it could be "*I haven't forgotten*—dash here attributes authorship—*Tommy Lee.*"

This was no nit-picking professorial issue. It wasn't a debate about the danger of dangling modifiers or the horror of ending a sentence with a preposition or saving infinitives from being split. In this case, attention to punctuation really might be a matter of life or death.

CHAPTER 8

Physical Needs

I awoke to the ugly sound of snorting and the even uglier realization I was the source of the snort. Apparently, I fell asleep on the thirty-minute ride to the hospital. After wiping a thin line of drool from the corner of my mouth, I glanced at the dashboard clock. It was after three, which meant either the length of the trip had almost doubled, or I'd been snoozing in our parking spot for some time.

"You snore like a fat man." April looked up from her laptop. With her seat back as far as it would go, she had set up shop in the small space.

I ignored the insult and unfolded the visor. "Jesus!" Recoiling at my reflection, I wiped at smudged mascara only to discover it was part of a dark circle of exhaustion. "What kind of asshole puts runway lights on a car mirror? I look like the crypt-keeper's older sister."

"Does that make me the crypt-keeper?" She grinned. "You zonked out about the time we left the driveway. I decided to let you sleep while I caught up on some work. You're welcome." She closed her computer.

"Thank you." I reached into my purse and grabbed blush and brush, automatically putting on my best face—a quality inherited from my mother.

The hospital was busier than before. Visitors carrying flowers and balloons stood out among blue-and-white-coated professionals. For a moment, I considered a trip to the gift shop, but Mom wasn't the teddy bear or balloon type. And I doubted if they sold cigarettes.

When we passed the nurses' station, I walked a few steps in front of April. At the sight of the two men standing outside Mom's door, I stopped so abruptly my stepsister stumbled into me.

"Whoa, there." She held onto my shoulders to steady herself. "How about a signal?" She stepped around me and saw what had brought about my sudden halt.

My stepfather stood talking to a man with his back to us. His voice echoed down the hallway. The sound of his companion's response rendered me motionless. It drifted like a favorite tune whose lyrics I couldn't quite place.

I was still trying to make the connection when Barry shouted my name. He bounded forward and enveloped me in a hug. I willed myself not to stiffen in his embrace.

His face had gotten slacker since I last saw him. Deep creases marked his expanding forehead, and drooping eyelids gave him the look of a wax figure held too close to a flame.

Over his shoulder, I recognized the second man. No longer an unidentified melody, it was Grant Albright, the best friend I ever had, even better than Whitney. I hadn't seen him since the day of my college graduation over ten years ago.

His sandy-brown hair was shorter, but still thick and curly. He was also thicker through the chest and biceps as if he'd been spending time in the gym. When he approached, I fought the urge to turn and run.

"You remember Grant, don't you, honey?" Barry took my arm and pulled me along with him. "One of the best things you ever did for me was introduce me to this boy. He's been making money hand over fist for me and your mom."

"It's good to see you, but I hate the circumstances."

My chest tightened with the desire to touch him.

April rescued me. "It means a lot to my sister to have old friends stop by."

"Yes," I stammered, barely cringing at the word sister. Was it possible she somehow coordinated the timing of Grant's visit? "I really appreciate you being here."

A burgundy blush sprouted on his neck, reminding me of the sweet boy who'd been so awestruck when he met my roommate that first day on campus.

"Ginny and your dad mean a lot to me."

I experienced a twinge of something akin to disappointment at the omission of my name.

Barry's eyes misted over as he slowly shook his head. "I'm afraid there's still not much change, but Ginny's a fighter."

A short, stocky nurse emerged from Mom's room. "You can go in now." She bustled down the corridor.

"I don't want to intrude." Grant put his hand on my stepfather's shoulder, while I silently urged him to intrude all he wanted. "I wanted to see how everyone's holding up and to be sure she got the flowers I sent."

"They came yesterday," April said. "Peach-colored roses, Ginny's favorite. How thoughtful."

He grinned and shook Barry's hand, then turned to me. "It's been too long, Liz. It would be great to get together."

My *sister* interrupted. "We're always glad to see you. Right?"

"Of course." It was my turn to blush. "Anytime."

I thanked him again and hurried into Mom's room, leaving the three of them behind.

Someone had applied splotches of pink to my mother's cheeks and lipstick in a matching shade. Her make-up artist neglected to use the expensive liner Mom employed to keep the waxy substance from feathering into the fine lines around her mouth, and it would piss her off if she saw the appearance of those tiny creases. I plucked a tissue from the box on her bedside table and carefully wiped away the offending smears.

"Don't worry. I got your back." Satisfied with my work, I ran my fingers through her hair, creating a fierce scarlet halo around her.

Hinges squeaked, and Barry slipped into the room.

"She's so goddamned beautiful," he whispered, then eased onto the bed and sat across from me.

Until that moment, I'm not sure I appreciated the truth of his words. Or maybe it was the first time I'd seen her so utterly still and devoid of pretense. Not as in a pretentious person. Mom never put on airs. But she spent so much of her life pretending to be someone other than herself—an artist's muse, a sex symbol, a devoted mother—it was impossible to determine where the make-believe ended and the real woman began.

Regardless of who she was on the inside, Barry was right. She really was beautiful with her soft skin and straight little nose, and—.

"No breathing tube!" I shouted, causing my stepfather to jump. "You didn't tell me they removed it." My customary accusatory tone with him was tempered with hopeful excitement. "That's a good thing, isn't it?"

He smiled and nodded. "Sorry, honey. I thought we told you. The doctor took her off the machine a few hours ago, and she's been doing great." His voice trailed off as he stroked her cheek.

I reacted with uncharacteristic optimism. "If she can breathe on her own, I'm sure she'll be waking up any time now."

He patted me on the back.

"Does the doctor have any idea what might have caused the stroke?" I remembered the letter in my purse. "Could it be her smoking?"

He sat upright and faced me, grinning broadly. "I forgot she hadn't told you. Your mom hasn't had a cigarette since you were here on New Year's Day. She planned to tell you, um, when she saw you." Once again, he stopped in the middle of his thought, but I understood his unspoken point. My mother planned to surprise me at her fifty-fifth birthday party last year. The one I was too busy to attend.

If only I'd come home and Mom had shared her victory over nicotine with me. That simple shift in events could have kept the glitch in her system from going awry, and she wouldn't be here now, unconscious and unfeeling. If the nurse was right, she might be aware of her surroundings on some level. She could be lying there remembering what a terrible daughter I was.

Rationally, I knew my shortcomings probably played no significant role in my mother's collapse. Even if she really hadn't smoked a cigarette in over two years, she had enough in her lifetime to bring about any number of health disasters. It was irrational to think the message she received prior to her stroke contributed to her current condition. Either way, I had to find out who wrote it. Not because I wanted somebody to blame. Because I needed to figure out what it was the author remembered and, more importantly, if that person was the same man who almost destroyed me and my mother.

The sound of April's tinkling laughter slipped through the half-open door. "Thanks for everything, Grant." The smile on her face was even brighter than the norm, and I wondered if her earlier remark about him being Barry's financial advisor had been an attempt to ferret out some clue about how I felt about him. Had she shapeshifted into a matchmaker?

If she had somehow gotten the idea of reuniting me and Grant, she would be disappointed. I had no intention of revisiting our past. And even if I wanted to rekindle that brief flame, I doubted he would be interested.

She came around to her dad's side of the bed and draped her arm over his shoulder. Then she leaned over my mother and brushed her lips across the sleeping woman's forehead.

That's when I identified her latest incarnation. She wrapped herself in a cloak of devotion and transformed into the role I'd long since abdicated—that of loving daughter. I had no way to know if her metamorphosis was genuine or if—like my mother—she had simply donned a new costume. If no one were in the room, would she be placing a kiss on Snow White's brow or hoping the apple never dislodged?

"Did you hear me, honey?" I realized Barry must have asked me a question.

"Sorry. Were you talking to me?"

"I was asking if I went too heavy on the blush. She hates for people to see her *without her face on*." He made air quotes to emphasize my mother's horror at the idea of being caught bare faced. So, my stepfather had been the make-up artist.

"She looks good," I replied, feeling like an asshole for critiquing his labor of love. The low-battery buzz saved me from more self-bashing.

He bolted upright at the sound, knocking over an empty coffee mug on Mom's bedside table.

I dug my phone from my bag and rose to find a place to plug it in. He bent to retrieve the cup from under the bed. When he stood, he held it in one hand and the letter in his other.

"This must have fallen out of your purse." I stumbled over my empty chair before grabbing it from him.

"Yes." I folded it and stuck it in my pants pocket. "It's nothing, just something from a client I forgot to take care of. Not important really, but I wouldn't want to lose it." What I intended as a dismissive little chuckle emerged as an awkward honk.

He didn't seem to notice, returning immediately to his place by Mom's side. But April stared at me with furrowed brow. I avoided her gaze by resuming my search for a convenient outlet. I settled on one underneath the wall-mounted TV, where a soundless rerun of *Friends* was playing.

"I need something cold and carbonated," I said, hoping to distract her. I grabbed my purse and rushed to the door. "Can I get anything for you guys?"

Barry requested a Mountain Dew, and April volunteered to come with me.

She took two steps, and I held out my hand, stopping her.

"Thanks, but you should stay." I inclined my head toward her dad, plastering a look of distress on my face before mouthing, "I'm worried about him."

She scowled, and I suspected I'd gone a little too far with my concerned stepdaughter act. But she moved to sit beside him, and I bolted.

Taking several deep breaths, I passed the nearby waiting room and proceeded to the elevator. I rode down to the first-floor cafeteria but headed away from the sounds and smells of institutional dining and out the revolving door into shimmering daylight.

I reached into my purse for my sunglasses and surveyed the area for a quiet place to sit. The walkway to my right led from the parking lot to a small grassy spot lined with wooden benches. Two women in scrubs sat talking. On the other side, an older couple leaned against each other as they strolled down the pathway.

The envelope made a crinkling sound when I pulled it from my pocket. Rereading it wouldn't do any good. I needed someone else to read it, somebody not so intensely connected to its possibilities and consequences.

Grant was the first person who came to mind, but while I knew he would be kind enough to overlook our past to help me, it wasn't fair to entangle him in something that could have unpleasant repercussions. Technically, Russ should have been a possibility. After all, he swore undying love to me and could offer an objective opinion since he was unaware of the way I grew up. But aside from the fact I never wanted to share anything real with him and planned to remove him from the picture, he was like most privileged men who believe in the power of authority to solve all problems. He would insist I contact the police, never suspecting that such action might have a negative impact on both my mother's and my own life.

Barry—whether he knew it or not—was too close to the issue. And April? I doubted she would be of any help at all. No, this situation called for the kind of friend who filtered everything through a concern for me.

I needed Whitney.

CHAPTER 9

Spiritual Needs

In high school, I usually knew the answers to the questions teachers asked but kept both head and hand down to avoid calling unnecessary attention to myself. It puzzled me when my classmates made simple mistakes like incorrect conjugations of irregular Spanish verbs or faulty explanations for the failure of the French Revolution or improper representations of the molecular formula for table salt. But I attributed their inaccuracies to carelessness or lack of preparation.

I was more than a little surprised when my counselor called me into her office fall of my senior year.

"Your SAT score is in the top 98th percentile." She beamed at me across her cluttered desk. "And your GPA places you third in your class. Are you aware of what this means?"

Squirming in my seat, I realized what it meant to me was unwanted attention and unrealistic expectations, but I smiled and said, "I'm not sure."

She went over a long list of possible schools I should consider, wrapping up with her recommendation to apply for the honors program at UGA. She explained I would get to live in the specially designated dorm with students of similar academic ability. She gushed about the small classes and opportunities for internships. I didn't want to spoil her scholastic high by telling her getting out of Barry's house and away from my mother was all the opportunity I needed.

Rather than let her down, I mirrored her enthusiasm and completed the application.

When she called me back to her office to tell me I'd been accepted, I was sure the admissions department had made a mistake and expressed my doubts to her.

She looked over her wire-rimmed reading glasses and frowned. "You're a very bright girl, Liz. Don't be afraid to let people know it."

I remained less than confident about my intellectual qualifications for the program, fearful my peers would quickly spot my inadequacies. It took me over a week after our foray in the frat house to recognize Whitney's brilliance. Unlike me, she never attempted to hide it. For her it was like being left-handed or having hazel eyes. But if she spotted me as a fake, she kept quiet about it.

When we were assigned to the same freshman honors seminar in a small classroom with no comforting back row where I could disappear, Whitney helped me keep my lack of brain power under wraps. Instead of the anonymity I counted on, the professor arranged long rectangular tables in a U-shape. Younger and better looking than I expected, despite the bushy beard and mustache he sported, he introduced himself as Tony Kowalski—call me Tony. He pointed to the index cards at each seat and instructed us to write our names on them, then fold and place them in front where all could see.

"Since I'll be your advisor for the next four years, I want to get acquainted as soon as possible." The combination of facial hair and toothy grin sent out a Big Bad Wolf vibe, and I wondered what might happen if I got too close. "And you need to learn the names of your classmates, so you can provide encouragement along the way."

Having a support system was alien to me and after a quick survey of the room, I decided these people would require far more help than I wanted to give. I listened politely for the next hour or so as the instructor went on about how the rigor of the program was balanced by the faculty's dedication to our success. I smiled and nodded when he outlined the requirements for the freshman project. Then he suggested that an understanding of Jung's theory of the collective unconscious would be essential to any topic we chose to pursue, and I scribbled furiously in my spiral notebook along with my peers.

My fellow captives were actually taking notes, while I was busily creating backstories. The girl sitting across from me, with a coffee and cream complexion, was the daughter of an exiled Iranian aristocrat. Her parents had no idea she was planning to elope with the pale, nervous boy beside her and bring shame to her entire family. I was about halfway through the group—which now included the love child of a famous rock star, an aspiring tightrope walker, and an underwear model—when a gentle pressure on the top of my foot alerted me to the sound of someone repeating my name.

"Miss Tucker, Elizabeth Tucker."

Heat raced up my neck toward my cheeks and I wondered if this was what caring about other people's opinions of you felt like. Before I had time to remind myself I didn't give a rat's ass, the professor continued.

"Perhaps you can elaborate on your classmate's statement about the struggle between the ego and the unconscious and why it's significant for young people in their search for identity." His lips turned up into the guileless smile of a person who either is innocently unaware he's about to humiliate someone with less power than he has or a sadist who doesn't give a shit.

"Oh, my God!"

Whitney's outburst caused me to drop my pen to the floor and the girl on her other side to emit a tiny squeal. The professor turned away from me and stared at my roommate.

I don't know what kind of diversion I expected from her—a fake wasp attack or a Bigfoot sighting—but Whitney was far too advanced for such rookie moves.

"Tony, you are not going to believe this." She widened her eyes, and he focused all his attention on her. "We were just talking about Jung's theory last night. We decided the best way to get to all those suppressed memories was to keep a dream journal. Sort of wander around in our subconscious before we had a chance to push it aside."

She nodded at me, then faced Kowalski and lowered her voice, so everyone had to lean in a bit. "Especially the sexual kind. But, of course," she laughed softly, "we can't share those in mixed company, can we?" She addressed her question to me.

I twirled my hair while searching for a follow-up to the story. "Sometimes, I get a little carried away with my, well, fantasies." I sighed and glanced at my notebook. Emboldened by the shocked expression on his face, I continued, "But if it would help in that whole search for identity thing, I could share with the class." I flipped back a few pages, picked up the pad, and waited.

The professor cleared his throat and shuffled through the papers lying in front of him. "That won't be necessary, Miss Tucker." He grabbed a stack and handed it to the student to his right. "This is your class syllabus. Please follow along as I go over the course requirements."

He spent the rest of the class answering questions and clarifying assignments before dismissing us.

As we made our way through the crowded hallway, Whitney said, "You are one cool customer. What would you have done if he'd called your bluff?"

"I guess I would have unrepressed something super nasty. It would have served that asshole right."

"I don't know." She shrugged. "I think he's kind of hot."

"Hot?" I glanced at her to see if she was joking, but her expression offered no clue. "I'm sure he'd agree with you on that unconscious thought. But how the hell did you come up with all that stuff about repressed memories and dream journals?"

"Years of therapy. And I have a dangerously high IQ."

Although Whitney loved listening to the professor go on and on about collective dreams and personal symbolism, I felt like an imposter sitting in a room filled with so many intellectually inclined people who seemed to love the sound of their own voices.

The only thing keeping me from dropping out of the program was the thought of leaving the honors dorm and Whitney. After her failed attempts to stop my departure, she called her dad. He waved a magic-money wand, and I got to stay. His daughter became my support system, and, other than the issue of Tony Kowalski's "hotness," we rarely disagreed on anything of consequence. Even at the end, when I wouldn't have blamed her for condemning me, she didn't. She just stopped being my friend. Or maybe I stopped being hers.

•   •   •

A breeze fluttered over me, sending my hair flying across my face. I brushed it and my memory of Whitney away. I secured the letter in my purse and walked into the hospital.

When I returned to Mom's room, carrying a diet soda and a Mellow Yellow—the closest to Mountain Dew that they had—April was outside, leaning against the door with her back to me, cell phone in hand.

"No, we did not agree to those terms." She tapped her foot. "I do not give a damn. There's a new sheriff in town, and if they don't like it, they can kiss my ass."

I tried unsuccessfully to suppress a giggle at the image of April saddled up on a rearing stallion, badge gleaming over one perky breast. She startled at the sound and faced me, staring as if confused as to who I was. Had she been lost in a similar fantasy?

Her expression darkened and for a second, I caught a glimpse of yet another version of my stepsister, but it vanished before I could define it.

"Call me back when they come up with a better offer."

She reached into her pocket and took out my phone. "It's not fully charged, but someone's been calling since you left. I thought it might be important."

There were multiple notifications—all from Russ. Three missed calls, one voicemail, and four texts.

"Work stuff."

The look on her face indicated she wasn't buying my lie. But she shrugged and said, "I have to deal with a situation at the office, and—."

"Please. I've got this covered."

"I promise I won't be long. Daddy's lying down. I doubt he's slept more than a few hours the last few days. Maybe he'll rest now that you're here."

It was strange to think my presence might be comforting to my stepfather, but she must have been right. When I entered the room, he was snoring softly on the narrow pull-out.

I tiptoed to the chair by the bed and watched the steady movement of my mother's chest as she inhaled and exhaled. I knew not to read too much into her ability to breathe on her own but seeing her without all that frightening paraphernalia gave me hope.

I picked up the newspaper someone left on her tray and flipped to the horoscope page.

Water signs often become lost in currents of memory. You must stop struggling against the riptides of the past and let yourself float effortlessly along the tributaries of forgetfulness. Happiness requires strategic forgetting as well as remembering.

Finally, a piece of nonsensical advice that made sense. *Strategic Forgetting* would make a great title for the memoir I would never write. Because, to do that, I had to reinstall all the memories I banished from my brain. I'd have to acknowledge what having a friend like Whitney meant to me before dealing with the loss of that friendship.

I woke with my head on Mom's pillow. Whatever state she currently resided in had smoothed the few Botox-resistant lines on her face, giving her an uncharacteristic appearance of serenity.

Barry stirred, and I glanced at my watch. It was still on California time, and I struggled to make the conversion, finally reaching the conclusion it was 6:25.

"Guess we both needed a little shuteye." He stood and walked to the other side of the bed.

I tilted my head sideways and back to ease the sharp pain in my neck.

"April will be back soon. She can give you a ride home."

I started to insist I should be the one keeping watch over my mother, but he held up a hand.

"I've got this. You get a good night's sleep."

"Only if you'll let me take tomorrow night."

"Sure, honey. But I'm betting she won't need either of us to stay. Our girl's going to wake up bright eyed and bushy tailed."

My stepsister's arrival spared me the trouble of pretending to believe in the possibility of a fully recovered version of my mother waiting for me when I returned to the hospital.

"I appreciate having a chauffeur, but it would be easier for everyone if I could use Mom's car."

April told me Carmela had located the missing keys. "She found them on a shelf in the garage right after you left and put them on the kitchen table for you. Here's the code."

I suspected the women colluded to keep me from driving in my discombobulated state of mind but accepted the explanation. We rode in a silence, not exactly comfortable but not totally awkward either.

When we reached home, April explained she had work to do. I tried to mask my enthusiasm about getting some much-needed alone time, and she took off. I entered the code, worried about disarming it before the police showed up. My mother was responsible for the system, a response to the memory of how little changing the locks at our old house did to deter Tommy Lee from entering through shattered windows or cracked door frames. I hoped this state-of-the-art fortress helped her sleep.

Beside the keys on the table was a note informing me there was arroz con pollo in the oven. Carmela's chicken with spicy rice was legendary, but I was too tired to eat. I removed the warm dish and stuck it in the refrigerator.

The prospect of being alone in the cavernous house had been better in concept than in reality. My footsteps echoed off the shiny hardwood floor, creating the eerie sensation I was being followed by my own shadow or possibly some other-worldly being. Once inside my room, I shut the door with too much force, jumping as it slammed.

Along with my dolls and diary, I set aside my belief in ghosts shortly after Tommy Lee vanished. I turned the lock and double-checked it, then remembered human precautions wouldn't deter spirits from beyond.

Roughly the size of both my bedroom and living area with a walk-in closet bigger than my kitchen, the room dwarfed me. I became a miniature display, a tiny centerpiece, among the gigantic antique canopy bed (from Pottery Barn) and stylishly mismatched chests and dresser.

From my window, the lights from the pool glowed unnaturally bright against the backdrop of the dark woods behind the house. I pulled the shades and drew the heavy cream-colored curtains before completing the unpacking I started earlier. Before placing them on hangers, I carefully color-coordinated my outfits. Then I arranged my underwear and pajamas in neat rows inside the dresser drawers. In the bathroom, I lined up cosmetics and skincare products along the countertop, in the order of most to least important. Last, I placed my toothbrush in the crystal holder with my toothpaste to the side at a perfect right angle.

This elaborate ritual of "a place for everything and everything in its place" usually soothed me. I adopted this organizational mantra around the time Tommy Lee came on the scene. He destroyed what little control I had as an adolescent girl and hurled me into a riptide of violence. Not much of a swimmer, I managed to stay parallel to the shore long enough to escape from the deadly currents.

But one cryptic message threatened to pull me back into a past I would be better off forgetting.

CHAPTER 10

Lost in the Currents

When I arrived at UGA, I was unaware of my obsessive tendencies. Even the look of concern on Whitney's face when she woke the morning after we met Grant and Chad to find me creating perfectly straight rows of pens and pencils on my desk didn't offer me a clue. A few months into our cohabitation, she confessed she considered putting in a roommate change request based on the probability I was suffering from some sort of psychosis.

My lips tilted upward at the memory of my former friend. I wiped away the smile along with the remainder of my lipstick.

Russ's ringtone sounded. I lingered over *Ignore* for a moment before I answered.

"So, you are alive," he said, his tone unusually restrained.

"I've been running all day long and just saw your messages." I tried to sound contrite.

"Well, if you had taken the time to read any of my six texts or listen to even one of the four voicemails I left, you'd know things aren't exactly great here either."

Fuck you, I said, but only in my head. The obvious disadvantage of sleeping with your boss is obscene remarks must be processed through a professional filter.

"I'm really sorry. It's Mom." I didn't have to fake the break in my voice and not just because of my concern for my mother. I also experienced a bit of shame for using her illness to placate Russ. But doubted she would mind, especially not since I learned the art of manipulation from the master—or more accurately, in reference to both my mother's talents and my current position, the mistress. How many times had I seen her use the death of her favorite nonexistent aunt to wriggle out of a sticky situation? Unfortunately, nothing as simple as a mythical relative would help her now.

If I expected to distract him from his self-pitying rant, I'd been mistaken.

"I get it, Liz, but don't I deserve a little consideration?"

No, Russ. You deserve to have a colonoscopy without anesthesia. Once again, better left unsaid.

"Of course, you do," I spoke softly as if he were some frightened creature I planned to capture and eat. "So, please tell me, what's been going on."

"As if you care."

I let his words linger, knowing he would soon fill the silence.

"Aw, baby. I can't stay mad at you, and I am so, so sorry about your mother."

Not sorry enough to ask how she was doing, I noted.

"It's just, well, I wondered when you plan to come back. I'm not trying to rush you, but the Hudson contract came through, and Denise keeps coming into the office. That woman is driving me nuts because she fucks everything up."

Despite my growing irritation, I found myself grinning. Russ's wife Denise started out as a production assistant in his company. After they married, he encouraged her to stay at home, insisting it would be better for their business if she concentrated on developing social connections. It made it better for him, as the absence of his blushing bride left him free to develop his own connections. I took no pride in being one of them.

"I'm sure she only wants to help."

"Right," he fumed. "Once that bitch gets settled in, we may never get her out." He paused, then resumed in a softer voice, the tone he used when he wanted sex at an inconvenient time. "And you know what a wreck I am without you. I can't sleep or eat. I need you in the worst way."

I resisted the urge to agree it would probably be the worst way, for me anyway. When we first started sleeping together, I found the urgency of his desire exciting. Lately, his lovemaking had devolved into a few minutes of groping before getting down to the business of satisfying himself.

"It's not easy for me being this far away from you," I said, wishing to be even farther from him—some place with no cell reception. "I promise to get back as soon as possible."

"Well, if you promise. You always keep your promises, don't you, Liz?"

The physical and emotional distance between us made it difficult to determine whether his belief in the depth of my faithfulness was genuine or somehow mocking. Or possibly, darker—something closer to a threat.

If I hadn't been so tired or so confident in my ability to control the situation, I might not have dismissed him. I'd have spent a few extra minutes convincing him I missed him even more than he missed me, throw in a little phone sex for good measure.

But I was exhausted and eager to get rid of him. So, I reassured him I did keep my promises, and he would be the last thing on my mind before I fell asleep.

"I hope you mean it, baby, because I'm always thinking of you."

His tone set off a faint buzzing in the back of my brain, but he signed off with his usual "I love you" and disconnected. I glanced at the stream of texts on my phone and the voicemail notifications and considered reading them but didn't. Instead, I ignored both the messages and the brain buzz and got ready for bed, completely forgetting about Russ.

The shrill sound of my alarm at 6:30 brought me out of a confusing dream where I was a flower girl at April's wedding. Wearing a stiff taffeta dress, I skipped down the aisle tossing roses into the laps of guests with blurred faces. The groom's face was also obscured. Within only a few feet from the altar, an engine roared behind me, and I turned to see Tommy Lee's pickup barreling down on me. Like the groom, the driver was out of focus. I hurled myself toward one of the pews just as the vehicle passed. I awoke with the certainty that the smell of diesel fuel clinging to my damp nightgown was real.

After a quick shower, I dressed and walked downstairs. The house was as quiet as it had been the previous evening, but the sunshine streaming through the windows banished last night's unease as did the comforting scent of coffee coming from the kitchen.

Carmela must have set the timer on Barry's fancy cappuccino maker. I poured a cup and drank it while rummaging through the refrigerator. I removed a carton of vanilla yogurt, taking the time to straighten the remaining flavors, before checking the expiration date: over a week from today. Unlike my mother, who had been known to stretch the best-used-by label well past the breaking point, Mela ran a tight, ptomaine-free ship. I ate standing over the sink, then left for the hospital.

Behind the wheel of Mom's Mercedes, thoughts of the puzzling note returned. Whatever reaction the sender had expected, her collapse must have changed the plan. Unless hurting Mom had been the objective. If so, hadn't the goal been achieved? If not, would there be a follow-up if—no, when—she recovered?

Before entering the hospital parking deck, a woman walking a tiny terrier set off a lightbulb in my overworked brain. Charles was the perfect person to help unravel the meaning of the note. He knew enough about my background to respect my obsessive behavior and lack of trust, but not so much that he would insist I schedule a psychiatric consultation. He would take me seriously.

It was too early to call, so I sent a text letting him know Mom hadn't improved significantly. I told him I'd be in touch later, then went straight to her room where I found Barry standing over her holding a hairbrush.

"Thank God you're here," he greeted me. "Your mother's hair has always been a mystery to me." He handed me the brush.

I laughed and said, "Join the club," before beginning the task of restoring order to the tangled crimson strands. After a few moments of fluffing and smoothing, I turned to my stepfather.

"Did you get any rest at all?"

"Slept like a baby." His dark circles suggested he wasn't being truthful.

"You should let me stay tonight."

"That's real sweet, honey, but I'm fine." He reached for Mom's hand and held it for a second. "I can't sleep unless this little lady's by my side."

My throat constricted and tears stung my eyes. A short, round man in a white coat barged into the room, saving me from a meltdown.

He greeted Barry without acknowledging me.

"I'm pretty sure she moved her right leg around four this morning." He continued holding her hand. "Doctor Mason, this is my daughter, Liz."

Ever since the wedding, he introduced me as his daughter. And every time he did, I amended his statement with *stepdaughter*. Today, I smiled and said, "Nice to meet you."

"Uh huh," He grunted, then flipped open the tablet he carried and moved to the head of the bed. He lifted one of Mom's eyelids and shined a light in it. Moving to the other end, he turned back the covers. He took a pointy metal object from his pocket and poked the bottom of her foot a few times before typing something into his device.

"I don't see any change, but it won't hurt to schedule another CT."

Barry seemed to shrink at the doctor's lack of encouragement, and it pissed me off.

"Can you elaborate, Doctor?" My voice came out louder than intended.

He jerked his head in my direction.

"My, uh." I couldn't quite go with *Dad*. "Barry mentioned seeing Mom's leg move. Does that indicate positive change?"

"Random movement isn't unusual in a case like your mother's."

I moved closer to him. "What exactly is a case like my mother's?"

"I assumed you had the details. She suffered from an ischemic stroke, resulting from a blood clot. She appears to have struck her head when she fell, which could explain her condition. The longer she remains unconscious, the less optimistic we are about a recovery."

The color seeped from Barry's face. I prompted the doc. "You mean a full recovery, right?"

"Well, I'm, ah." He cleared his throat and looked directly at me. "Yes," he conceded. "A full recovery. We should consider a feeding tube, though."

Barry winced. "Your mother would hate that." His voice was barely above a whisper.

The doctor put his hand on my stepfather's shoulder. "It will keep her strong and comfortable." For the first time, he spoke less like a robot and more a flesh and blood man who had at least a passing acquaintance with compassion. "But we've got twenty-four hours before we make that call. Let's see how the CAT scan looks and go from there."

Stopping at the door, he said, "Nice meeting you, Miss Winters," and was out before I had a chance to remind him it was Tucker, not Winters.

"Did you hear that, sweetheart?"

For a second, I thought Barry was talking to me, but Mom was his sweetheart.

"You'll be better in twenty-four hours."

I questioned whether my stepfather was self-delusional or if he was misinterpreting the doctor for my mother's benefit.

"Why don't you go home and get some real sleep?"

"A shower would be good, and I ought to stop by the office to see if it's still standing. I'll be back before dinner."

He kissed Mom on the cheek before leaving. I noticed he had missed several belt loops, and his shirttail was untucked. Mom's absence was affecting more than his sleeping patterns.

Alone with my mother, I grew strangely self-conscious. If I started my one-sided conversation this early, I'd run out of material before lunch. I gave up on figuring out how to change the channel on the TV, where *Friends* was still playing, and picked up the newspaper Barry left on the windowsill between an enormous floral arrangement and a potted fern.

After a quick glance at the usual dreary headlines—healthcare troubles, a local politician caught groping an intern—I turned to the horoscope page and read Mom's forecast silently.

Your ruler Venus is in retrograde this month. Avoid hasty decisions. Take some time off before jumping into anything of a significant nature.

This piece of fluff bordered on the absurd, so I searched for something more interesting among the other signs of the zodiac. What difference would it make whether I gave her Libra or Capricorn or Taurus? Virgo had more going on.

"Life is an adventure, but only if you will it so. Today could be the first step in your most exciting journey so far."

"Did you hear that, Mom?" I was truly terrible at this normal conversation crap. "Something big is waiting for you. All you have to do is get out of this goddamn bed and start looking for it."

Except for the gentle rise and fall of her chest, she remained motionless. Outside the door, tray tables rumbled on their way to patients capable of having adventures.

It had been years since Mom and I compared horoscopes. Surely, she would no longer begrudge me a happy prediction, so I ran my finger down the list and landed on Cancer. It was annoyingly ambiguous, but I read it aloud anyway.

"Attract what you want by getting rid of what you don't need."

"So, what do you think that might mean?"

I walked to the window. Darkening clouds skittered across the sky, blocking the sun. It had begun to rain. Not the California kind that comes in gushing torrents, washing away entire hillsides and houses along with it, or falls in drips and drizzles, creating deadly slick spots on the highway. This was gentle but steady, and I had the overwhelming desire to walk in it, to let it wash over me and cleanse me of whatever it was I didn't need in my life.

Instead of running outside, I returned to my mother's side, thinking about what to discard. I'd done a great job of keeping my physical space free from clutter. The few times I'd allowed Russ to come to my apartment, he'd remarked on the absence of knick-knacks and frills, calling me a minimalist. I didn't bother explaining my choice of décor was based less on style and more on survival. It wasn't only that I'd grown up in a home with a just-been-ransacked decor. It was that I couldn't breathe in a place filled with mementos, solid reminders of this or that special occasion because for every joyful memory, there were darker ones hovering in the background.

A slight ripple beneath her eyelids startled me with the briefest of hope. Then I remembered what the doctor had said.

"Was that random movement, Mom?" Or could it be her own dark memories trying to escape? Did hurtful pieces from my past cause her pain, too, or had she rewritten them? Resentment flooded over me, and I was filled with the sudden need to punish her.

"Remember my tenth birthday? That big girls' day out you promised—mani-pedis, the mall, a fancy lunch?" I kept my eyes focused on her face, hoping for nonrandom movement. "Me neither because it didn't happen."

Not even a ripple. Frustrated, I pushed harder. "Instead of the two of us spending time together, Mr. Yard Artist scored three tickets to that all-day country music festival. I hated all that cowboy shit."

Still no reaction.

"How about when I was thirteen, and you decided we'd go to Panama City with that guy you met at the diner? You know the one I'm talking about. The weirdo you caught trying on my bikini top?" In fairness, she immediately booked us two tickets on the next Greyhound bus back to Georgia.

I detected a slight change in her breathing. Leaning closer, I saw that her lips were cracked and raw, like an arid riverbed. I opened the Vaseline on the bedside table and scooped a small amount onto my fingertip. But when I reached out to her, I couldn't follow through. This laying-on-of-hands while she was trapped inside herself was too intimate. I forced myself to continue.

After wiping the greasy residue off my fingers with a tissue, my anger vanished. How could I blame her for wanting to find someone who could give her a future filled with passion and excitement? To be able to view herself in some cosmic looking glass, not as the fairest in the land, but a person who knew she was loved. It wasn't her fault that her only mirror held no magic. It was shattered and shrouded in cigarette smoke.

CHAPTER 11

A Positive Shift

On the cool October morning after the meatloaf disaster, encouraged by a deceptively hopeful horoscope, Mom began the day, cheerful and optimistic.

"Listen to this," she chirped.

Tonight's full moon promises a positive shift in your love life. The unsure becomes certain. Be prepared for an unexpected romantic gesture from your significant other.

She tapped out a cigarette from her omnipresent pack of Virginia Slims. "Oh my God, oh my God! It's happening, baby. Tommy Lee is going to propose."

I continued to twirl my spoon in my now soggy bowl of off-brand rice cereal and suppressed both a shiver and a snarky remark. Something along the lines of *the only positive shift involving that guy would be a seismic one that flung him off a mountaintop.* Or how *his most romantic gesture had been during your last fight when he slammed his fist into the wall instead of your face.*

I stretched my lips in what I hoped passed as an encouraging smile before sticking the empty spoon in my mouth. Over the summer, I dieted obsessively and lost five pounds, putting me at what I considered a barely acceptable one hundred and twelve.

I made a murmuring sound that could have been interpreted as encouragement or indigestion. It didn't matter what I said. Since she met Tommy Lee, he became her sun. She basked in his heat when the sky was clear and trembled in dread when thunderclouds came between them. She existed in a terrifying orbit, closer and closer to destruction.

Mom leaned her head back and blew smoke rings, a gesture I concluded she copied from the glamor queens in old movies—the ones made when smoking was sexy. As the clouds cleared, she narrowed her eyes and stared at me as if she really seeing me. I wondered if she would notice both my cereal deception and my hollow cheeks, and if she did, whether I would be annoyed or relieved. But the moment passed, and I remained unseen.

"I can't remember his mentioning dinner," she said.

Of course not. He was too busy calling you a worthless bitch and dragging you out of the kitchen by your hair. Obviously, his outburst of violence had been followed by make-up sex. I pushed my bowl away.

"But that would spoil the surprise. I bet Francine will cover the end of my second shift." Francine Nielsen worked at the diner for over a year before Mom got her job there. One of the few female friends my mother had, she was a big woman. With her long, flowing platinum hair and jutting breasts, she reminded me of a Valkyrie from the Norse mythology. Odin's handmaiden, slaughtering men on the battlefield.

Mom stubbed out her cigarette and lit another before continuing with her fantasy. "That way, I can come home early and get fixed up in case we go somewhere fancy."

Yeah, he'll take you to Olive Garden instead of Burger King.

She balanced the cigarette on the soap dish/overflow ashtray, then began removing curlers and shoving them into the oversized pockets of her terrycloth robe.

"Honey, how about you stay at a friend's house?"

No reason to tell her I didn't have overnight friends. There are strict rules among young girls. The one dealing with overnights is simple: If you spend the night with a friend, you must reciprocate.

After a few sleepovers, I realized neither adult screaming matches with the occasional plate tossed for emphasis nor interludes of passion punctuated with disgusting displays of public affection passed as normal. So, I stopped accepting invitations, and they stopped coming.

That day, I had no worries about making myself scarce. Tommy Lee wouldn't recognize a grand romantic gesture if it bit him on the ass. And as a Sagittarian born under the sign of the archer, he bored easily and valued, above all else, his freedom. While Mom viewed these traits as challenges, to me they represented hope.

In that spirit of hopefulness, I ignored my mother's request and extended my day as I often did. I stayed after school to finish homework in the library, headed to the mall to work my shift at Cinnabon, then drove slowly around my block until I assessed the danger. If Tommy Lee's rusted-out red pickup sat next to Mom's faded gold Ford Fairlane, I waited for the lights to go out before entering the house. If there was no mud-speckled truck in the driveway, I parked on the curb, eased open the front door, and tiptoed to my room.

A little after ten, only the sad sedan was there. I shut off the engine and climbed out of the second-hand Volkswagen Bug she talked boyfriend-before-last into giving me.

I listened for telltale signs of defeat, soft sobbing accompanied by the forlorn strains of some female country music singer drifting from behind my mother's closed door, heard nothing.

The day-old cinnamon bun I had for dinner was long gone, so I crept into the kitchen to scavenge for something to hold me over until morning. In the refrigerator, a half-empty carton of Chinese noodles from sometime last week, or maybe the week before, sat next to two shriveled oranges. Plastic containers with suspicious contents were scattered in front of a bottle of milk, but I lacked the courage to open any of them. Instead, I closed the door and walked to the small pantry where I located a box of Crunchy Oat Clusters and took them to my room.

Before the latest love of her life arrived, I'd been a sound sleeper. Once I slept through fifteen minutes of our faulty smoke alarm bleating while Mom cursed and struggled to turn the damn thing off.

After Tommy Lee, slumber came sporadically. Frequently, I woke to the sputter of a truck engine, often to the pounding of his fists on the door. Those nights I listened to him swearing and emphasizing his frustration with a heavy-booted thump. I lay there waiting, never knowing if their reunion would be happy or deadly.

Sometimes, however, I jolted awake to dead quiet. Those times terrified me the most because I could never be sure what had jerked me into consciousness. Was it the welcome noises of Tommy Lee storming out into the night? Or the echoing crack of a pistol?

•   •   •

Rapid knocking on Mom's hospital door brought me back to the present—a time when, until recently, I had been free of my mother's long-gone boyfriend. A small, blonde nurse entered and began performing the usual checks on my mother.

She moved efficiently, without emotion, probably the only way for her to deal with her work. Before Mom's stroke, I'd been a lot like her. I never became emotionally invested in any of my creations. Whenever the firm attracted an especially difficult client, Andrea assigned the project to me. As the office manager and my friend, she appreciated my flexibility but worried my professional detachment extended too much into my personal life. I assured her it made me the perfect girlfriend—if only for a short time.

Thoughts of my boss reminded me of the astrological advice to attract things I wanted by getting rid of what I didn't. Russ was on top of the discard pile. But other than for my mother to get out of this stupid bed, what did I really want?

I thought of the note and realized the only thing I truly desired was to discover who sent it. This acknowledgment brought me back to the problem of uncovering who might have meant to threaten or at least frighten her. Still too early to call Charles, I walked to the window. My mother's reflection behind me reminded me of an over-the-hill Sleeping Beauty. So far, kisses had proved ineffective. I would try a more direct approach.

"So, about that note you had when Carmela found you in the garden? It reminds me about how you and I never, ever—"

Jesus. Why all this reflection, self and otherwise?

"Anyway. Remember how Tommy Lee disappeared a few months after the night he planned to propose?"

Great. I had reminded her of how awful she felt after finding out how wrong she'd been about his intentions.

Now that I thought about it, his absence failed to trigger the usual hysterics. In fact, she had been unusually stoic when Tommy Lee hadn't shown up for breakfast, pretending everything was normal. And it wasn't all that far from the norm. There had been lots of mornings when his seat at the table remained empty. But when dinner time came with no word from him, I expected her to start to unravel. Only she didn't. No sobbing or cursing. She simply sat there, lighting another Virginia Slim with the end of the one she had just finished, creating a silence thicker than the smoke surrounding her.

By the third day, I allowed myself to hope. We never discussed the elephant—or in his case, the jackass—no longer in the room. We resumed our routines with no word from or about Tommy Lee. Several times I almost brought him up but feared saying his name might break the spell and call him from whatever black hole he'd fallen into.

About a month after he left, I overhead her whispering on the phone. "No, no one's been here, and it's been over a week."

When she saw me, she stepped into the bathroom. Not long after that, she began staying later at work, and I assumed she needed the overtime after losing what little income Tommy Lee contributed.

Four months and no sign of him. I allowed myself the luxury of believing in the possibility we were free. There were nights when I slept without waking to question the peaceful silence. It was as if a neighbor had unexpectedly opened his curtains, revealing the dull comfort of a normal life, and I was suddenly part of it. No low rumbling curses threatening to erupt in terrifying explosions followed by the shrill crescendo of fear and pain. I was a member of what I imagined an average home might be. One where the parents were happily divorced and bound by a truce that mandated serenity.

I never completely believed we were part of that peaceful picture and began having recurring dreams of flying dishes with sharp jagged edges and self-propelled pickup trucks threatening to run me down. Waking from those nightmares, I sensed something lurking in the shadows of my mind, but I couldn't or wouldn't summon it. Even without a name, whatever it was had the power to destroy our newfound almost normal.

"You felt it, too, didn't you, Mom?" I resumed my attempt at conversation with my captive audience. "You were different. I expected you to be destroyed when he left us, but I hadn't been prepared for you to be . . ."

Be what? No, it was more like not being at all. My mother went missing, too. Physically, she continued to show up, but it was as if the lights were on, and nobody was home. She'd stop talking in the middle of a sentence and stare into empty space. Several times, I heard the sound of her footsteps pacing up and down the hallway.

"Only you didn't completely fall apart until that night in January." Once again, I had reminded her of one of the most terrible moments of her life. And one of the best of mine.

The doorbell woke me sometime after midnight. I sat bolt upright, sickened with the certainty he was back. On multiple occasions, he locked himself out of the house, waking us by hammering with his fists and shouting for my mother to "Get her fat ass out of bed and let me in."

My initial terror subsided as I realized the person this evening was entirely too patient and polite to be my mother's boyfriend. Mom's slippers slapped on the cheap linoleum. The house was cold, so I wrapped up in my ratty yellow robe before peeking out of my bedroom. I could see the back of Mom's head as she looked through the peephole and exhaled a soft, "Oh."

She began stripping the pink curlers from her hair and stuffing them in the pockets of her sweatpants. Running her hands through her unruly waves, she squared her shoulders and released the bolt lock, hesitating a second before opening the door.

Light from the porch silhouetted her slender frame. I tried to move quickly, but the air had thickened. By the time I slogged through it, two uniformed officers stood in front of me. One stepped forward, hat in hand, swaying from side to side.

I was close enough to catch a whiff of the heavy-sweet cologne my mother always wore.

The policeman closer to us said, "We have some bad news." The rest was lost in my mother's wailing scream that culminated with her crumbling onto the floor.

I sat down beside her, cradling her head. The men helped me ease her into a sitting position against the wall.

"Why don't you bring her some water?" the officers suggested.

When I returned, Mom sat on the sofa, staring into space.

I listened as the other one explained Tennessee state troopers had discovered Tommy Lee's partially burned-out truck in a deep ravine off the side of Lookout Mountain. They had not yet recovered the body, but it was unlikely anyone could have survived the crash.

Other than helping her back into bed after the police left, the only thing I remembered about that evening was barely recognizing my own reflection in the bathroom mirror.

Even now, watching her lying there attached to tubes, I can still picture that pale-faced girl and feel the pull of her grim smile.

"They never did find him, did they?" I twirled a strand of her scarlet hair around my finger, then watched it spring back, thinking how easily we had purged Tommy Lee from our lives. Since his body was never recovered, shouldn't we have experienced at least some apprehension he might return? It could have been because my stepfather had ridden into town on his white horse and erased our fears.

"And good old Barry came along," I continued. "And he rescued us from your despair." I squeezed her hand. "And we've been living happily ever after until—"

Catching my breath, I went completely still, unsure if her response was real or only wishful thinking. I exerted gentle pressure and watched as my mother's slender fingers curled over mine. I looked up in time to see her eyelids flutter, then open, revealing her silvery gray eyes—clear and focused.

CHAPTER 12

An Insignificant Other

Mom's high-pitched warbling filled the room. When she tried to speak, garbled sounds spewed out. By the time Barry arrived, the nurses were discouraging her from straining her voice. But when she saw him, her babbling escalated into a crescendo of strangled wails.

The desperation in her frantic cries frightened me, and I was torn between staying to hold her and running from the room. Barry solved the problem by pushing aside two nurses and an intern before sitting on the bed and pulling her into his arms. He stayed that way, whispering and smoothing her hair until her body stiffened, then relaxed into his.

Her doctor appeared and insisted we step outside, so she wouldn't be distracted when he examined her. The rush from her sudden awakening left me shaken, and I sank into a chair in the hallway. Barry sat beside me and took my hand while we waited for the verdict.

After about fifteen minutes, the doctor came out and told us his initial exam had shown her only consistent means of communication involved lifting one or two fingers in response to yes or no questions.

"My girl is back." Barry grinned. "She'll be up and about in no time."

He remained steadfast in his belief even after the doctor warned us it was likely going to be a very long journey to recovery, and he had no idea what it might involve. But my stepfather never faltered. For him, the only option was the complete return of the woman he loved.

Rather than follow the recommendation she go to a rehab center, he wanted to bring her home as soon as possible. He set up round-the-clock nursing care and hired the finest therapists available. Carmela rearranged her schedule to be with us four days a week.

Determined not to get spooked by the silence inside the big house, I flipped on the TV in the kitchen, took a diet soda from the refrigerator, and headed upstairs without turning off the television. Although the sound of my own footsteps didn't bother me as much, I hurried down the hall and into my room, locking the door behind me.

I slipped out of my jacket and removed the envelope, amazed at how such an innocuous-looking object possessed the power to upend so many lives. Then I realized it was not what was on it, but what was missing. I read the note multiple times but only glanced at the outside long enough to see Tommy Lee's initials in the left-hand corner. That shocked me so much, I didn't notice the lack of a stamp or postmark.

It was bad enough someone—possibly Tommy Lee—sent the nasty little message to scare the hell out of us. Now I was certain that same person had been outside our home—close enough to watch my mother come and go for who knows how long. He was probably still watching unless he shifted his vigil to the hospital.

I remembered Carmela's account of the man who showed up at our door the day of Mom's stroke. Instead of being at the wrong address, was he the engineer of both the note and its delivery?

The thought sickened me. I dropped the letter onto the desk and rushed to the bathroom where I leaned against the sink. At the mirror, I once again saw the image of the teenager who cowered in her room in that gloomy, smoke-filled house. I automatically reached for my liquid cover-up stick, planning to erase her the way I usually did.

But instead of employing yet another temporary fix in the ongoing battle to wipe away my past, I put the make-up down.

Banishing that frightened girl would take more than a coat of Creamy Café au Lait Beige. It would require digging up memories I spent years trying to forget. It would mean uncovering why Tommy Lee simply vanished from our lives and facing how I alienated my two best friends.

Thinking about friendship reminded me of Charles. Talking to him would help me sort out my feelings and formulate a plan for finding the jerk who had tried to destroy my mother. It was almost four—one in California. I leaned against the headboard with my phone in hand and tapped on his name. He answered on the second ring.

"Liz! I was just about to call. Please say you have good news."

I settled deeper into the mound of flowery pillows. "Actually, I do." I spent the next few minutes providing details of my mother's progress.

"That's fabulous."

"Yeah." I hesitated.

"You don't sound thrilled. Tell Uncle Charles all about it."

I laughed, then told him all about it. He was aware of my resentment toward my mother for making me an unwilling participant in her dysfunctional relationships. Although I omitted my broken arm and the creepy poker guys, he knew how devastating Tommy Lee's return would be. When I read the note to him and speculated about the role it might have played in her stroke, he understood my desperate need to discover who sent it and why.

"It has to be him." I explained how my narrative about his disappearance seemed to have shocked my mother into consciousness.

"I'm not so sure," he said. "Why would he show up after all this time?"

Charles had a point. Tommy Lee had been gone almost fourteen years. Why come back now?

I admitted there was no logical reason.

"There's no telling what was going on in your momma's mind. Stroke victims get disoriented so easily. And even if that asshole sent the note, he can't hurt her anymore. I say don't push your momma.

When she gets better, you two can straighten it out. I'm more worried about the other asshole in your life."

He had been warning me for months about what he called Russ's obsession with me. They met during one of my boss's infrequent visits to my apartment, and Charles instantly detested him—said he was a dangerous narcissist.

I told him about the text messages and phone calls.

"But don't worry. I've got it under control. If I'm lucky, some bright shiny object will come along, and he'll forget about me."

"Well, he does seem to have the attention span of a gnat. But I still think you should be careful."

I promised I would, and we said our goodbyes.

I spent the next hour answering emails. Most were simple—a little client handholding, a few production questions. One from Andrea, however, was both cryptic and disturbing.

Hope your mother's doing better. We're holding down the fort. Lots of drama here with the third Mrs. Young. Worried the boss is coming unhinged. Probably nothing you can't handle but proceed with caution.

The firm's efficient office manager wasn't prone to exaggeration, so her use of words like *drama* and *unhinged* was a bit alarming.

I was still thinking about the email when Barry arrived, needing help preparing for Mom's return. By the time we finished de-cluttering the bedroom, I was too exhausted to do more than have a sandwich with him and go to bed.

The next morning, Carmela and April joined us. Together, we came up with a schedule so she wouldn't be alone.

I texted an update to Russ, and he responded with thumbs-up and heart emojis before asking when I would be returning to LA and his arms. I sent a shrugging shoulder emoji, a bit distressed at how easy it had become to express my feelings in such a superficial way.

Mom arrived a little after lunchtime via ambulance. Once we had her safely ensconced, the initial elation at her return to consciousness dimmed, and we began waiting for another miracle or at least a convincing parlor trick. But, other than the occasional awkward bleat, she remained silent. Worse, she no longer responded to our questions with a yes or no.

I was reading an article about a wrinkle cream aloud to her when Russ called and considered ignoring him. Since neither of us were fascinated with the beauty product, I picked up.

"I hope I'm not disturbing you." His icy voice cast a chill over the bright room.

"Of course not. Just hanging with my mother."

"Can I assume she's better then?"

"I need to get this, Mom, but I'll be right back." Her face remained impassive. "I didn't want to say anything in front of her. No way to tell how much she understands, but we're hopeful."

"Hopeful," he echoed in a flat tone. "I'm so happy for you." He emphasized *you*. When I refused to take the bait, he continued.

"I thought you were going to call me with updates. Or to check in to see how I was doing. What the fuck, Liz?"

"Until yesterday, she was pretty much the same."

"Not with your mother, goddammit. But there have been plenty of changes here."

I perked up. Could this be the forced break-up I'd been anticipating? I hadn't expected it to be so easy. It wasn't.

"The business is going to hell," he went on without giving me time to speak. "My whole life is a fucking mess."

"Russ, I'm not sure what you're—"

"You leave me out here all alone while you run home to your family and don't even ask about me. I feel like shit, by the way."

Not exactly what I hoped for.

"I understand your mother needs you. And you think you have to be there."

"Well, I—"

"But nobody gives a damn what I need. Not my fucking wife. Not you. Not a single, solitary person. But hey, I'm a big boy, right? Don't worry about me. I'll make sure I'm okay."

He disconnected before I said another word.

I was used to him being peevish and petty, but this new Russ had an edge I didn't recognize. I went straight to the messages he sent.

The first of the five was clingy, but not alarming.

No news doesn't feel like good news. Please give me a call. I'm lost without you.

His second was an attempt at romance and was so saccharine it made the loose filling in my back-tooth throb.

Just drove by our special spot on the beach. The ocean isn't as blue when you're not by my side.

He gave sappy another shot.

I listened to your voicemail message to hear how beautiful you sound.

Disgusted at his attempts to guilt me into a response, I almost skipped the final two. *Nobody likes to be ignored. I hate it. Remember the Hastings account.*

Bert Hastings was one of the company's first clients. He owned a small fleet of food trucks that served lower income areas in Los Angeles. After designing a successful print ad touting his company as providing "home cooking anywhere," we pitched him on expanding to a radio and TV campaign. He not only dodged our calls but had the nerve to switch firms and take our ideas with him.

Russ overreacted to what was not an unusual occurrence in the advertising world. He called Hastings a traitor and vowed to exact revenge. I urged him to let it go and thought he'd taken my advice. A month later, health inspectors shut down the trucks, effectively putting our former client out of business. When I mentioned it to him, he denied any involvement but insisted on taking me out that evening to celebrate "his enemy's downfall."

Was he threatening to shut me down? The idea was ridiculous but disturbing enough to make me finish reading his text attack.

Seriously, Liz. Enough is enough. Is that what you're trying NOT to tell me? Not nice, baby.

I winced when I read "not nice." He used the same phrase in some of our fairly tame sex games. Games where I was the cop who cuffed him to the bed or the French maid with a very naughty feather duster. Pretty harmless stuff.

The last time we were together, however, he suggested we take it up a notch with blindfolds and ropes. When I declined his invitation to be hogtied and helpless, he got aggressive, and I ended up locking myself in the bathroom until he promised to be good. He kept his word and didn't attempt to tie me up again, but I could tell he wasn't happy about it. The way he whispered "not nice" in my ear while thrusting angrily on top of me cemented my intent to break things off as soon as possible.

Looking through the arched window in the hallway, I saw the lace-like pattern of leaves on the gigantic oak. Greens in every imaginable shade shimmered with golden sunlight. Dizzy with the contrast between this uncomplicated beauty and the ugliness of my relationship, I wanted to pitch my phone and pretend my time with him had been nothing more than a dream—the kind that is neither good nor bad, merely something that gets you through the night.

It occurred to me losing my job would be bad but might not be the worst part of a break-up with Russ Young.

CHAPTER 13

Riptides of the Past

The next morning, my mother's simple one or two finger trick returned as did movement in her left arm and leg.

The household flew into motion. Barry was deliriously happy, April was optimistic, and I allowed myself a bit of hope. Mom's therapist, Rudolph, the muscle-bound German, warned us that regaining complete hand control was one of the most difficult areas for stroke victims. He spent over an hour demonstrating techniques, and we all took turns bending and stretching her fingers on a rotating schedule.

He said her inability to speak was most likely acquired apraxia—a common problem involving difficulty in sequencing sounds to put thoughts together. The plan was to spend at least two hours a day working with her on remembering how to arrange syllables into words. He explained speech recovery could be spontaneous or sluggish and was extremely frustrating for the patient.

For a woman like her, someone who was verbal to a fault, I imagined the process would be excruciating. I decided to create an ongoing narrative to motivate her participation in the conversation. No more prattling on and on about beauty products. I would provide her with stimulating substance. And nothing stimulated her more than her favorite subject, astrology.

The daily horoscopes in the newspaper were insufficient, so I turned to the internet. I discovered neither print nor online predictions had relevance for someone recovering from a stroke.

According to a well-known pundit, the first six months of the year were filled with boundless joy for those born under the sign of Libra, represented by scales, since they crave perfect balance. The tilted smile on my bedridden Libra made it obvious she had not benefitted from this astrological bounty.

When I checked her romance report, I discovered Uranus was transiting the solar seventh house. I stopped reading to repeat Uranus out loud and giggle.

It was time to take her fate in my hands. I would create readings designed specifically for her. Rudolph had just finished his review of vowel sounds when I arrived in her room shortly after lunch. I picked up one of her many astrology books to use as a guide.

According to my source, those born under the sign of the balanced scales possess great charm. It's easy for them to establish deep, personal relationships and an unerring ability to read the motivation of others.

I was tempted to ask if that was what she had with Tommy Lee. But I already knew the answer. It was strong enough for her to keep him around even after he hurt us both. I imagined the extent of the damage he could have rained down if he hadn't disappeared. And what did that say about the strength of her personal relationship with me?

Now was possibly the only chance I'd have to ask questions still tormenting me from our early years together. I understood how unfair it was to bombard her with veiled accusations while she lay flat on her back, unable to escape. But her approach to motherhood hadn't been fair, either.

"I can't remember when you weren't involved in a toxic romance, can you?" I paused, politely giving her a chance to respond. She maintained her silence. "Is this what happened with you and my father? You won't talk about him, but that hasn't stopped me from wondering why he left when I was four and never came back. Did it have something to do with me? Did I sour things between the two of you? Is that why he split?"

Her eyes misted with tears, and I was struck with the good news that she comprehended what I was saying. Then I realized that was also the bad news.

"I'm sorry, Mom." I took her hand and automatically began tugging the thumb away from her index finger in one of Rudolph's prescribed moves. After a few seconds, I released it and pulled two tissues from the box on her bedside table. I wiped her eyes first, then my own.

"Let's check out what next month looks like for you." I thumbed through the pages, desperate to jazz up the mysteriously mundane. Carmela interrupted my search.

"Your mother has a visitor. She says they used to work together." Her tone indicated the intruder lacked credibility in our housekeeper's eyes. "Her name is Francine. Francine Nielsen."

There was a flurry of movement behind her, and a tall, big-boned woman with a mass of yellow curls perched on her head like a roosting hen inserted herself into the room. Even though I'd only seen her a few times, I had no trouble remembering her. Less a Norse warrior now and more a giant bird of prey, it was impossible to forget those protruding breasts. Once they could have been the prow of a ship; today they were more in the canvas awning category but still impressive.

Carmela reached toward Francine, and I was tempted to see what she would do if she caught her. My money would have been on our housekeeper, but the Viking woman might have done some damage, so I intervened.

"It's okay, Mela. We know Francine."

Her glare suggested she didn't view knowing a person and welcoming them as the same thing. "I will be close by," she said before staring at Francine with what I pictured as her version of her aunt's evil eye.

"Nothing worse than uppity help." Francine approached the bed.

"Carmela is family." I blocked her from getting closer.

"Sure, sure. I was just in a hurry to see how this old gal was doing."

Lucky for her, the "old gal" was too weak to get up and slap the smirk off the woman's wrinkled face. Nobody referred to my mother as *old* or a *gal* without facing the consequences.

"She's doing much better. But she tires easily, so I'm going to have to ask you to limit your stay."

"Of course, sugar." She brushed by, keeping her back to me. "Hey, there, sweetheart."

Dressed in a gauzy black top and skin-tight pants, Francine made up for her funereal choice in clothing with her heavy use of bronzer and blush. Bright blue eyeshadow gathered in colorful little furrows on eyelids overwhelmed by spidery fake lashes that enhanced her predatory look.

"Remember when we used to go dancing, don't you, Gin? Those were some good times, weren't they?"

My mother's hands became uneven fists.

"Are you okay?" I pushed Francine aside.

Mom's gaze shifted frantically from side to side. She flung her left arm up, then dropped it. A low gurgling sounded from deep in her throat.

"You need to go. Now." I grabbed Francine, expecting her to resist—secretly hoping she would, so I could smack her for upsetting my mother. But she allowed me to guide her away from the bed. When we reached the doorway, she jerked free.

"I didn't mean to get your momma in an uproar. She always was an excitable person."

She made her exit, and I followed. At the top of the stairs, she stopped abruptly.

"Oh, my goodness. I left my purse." She bolted down the hallway with me trailing her. When she reached Mom's door, she entered and shut it behind her. Fearing she might lock me out, I raced forward.

Luckily, the latch hadn't caught, and I stumbled in to find Francine leaning over my mother, whispering.

She straightened and turned to face me. "It must be in the car. I tell you, honey, I'd forget my head if it wasn't attached." She sashayed from the room, leaving a trail of musk and venom in her wake.

My mother's low-pitched wail froze me mid step. A cross between a growl and a scream, her cry gradually became more human as she struggled to spit something out. Over and over, she repeated what finally took a familiar shape. The 't' was weak, but it soon became apparent. My mother was shrieking *Tommy Lee.*

Carmela and the day nurse came running, Mela brandishing a spatula, the nurse, a sedative. I tried to comfort Mom by stroking her arm and repeating "Everything will be all right." I stayed by her side long after the medication kicked in, fearful that by saying his name aloud, she had summoned the man back into our lives.

•   •   •

Frustrated by my inability to protect my mother from Francine and whatever bile she spewed, I set out to discover as much as possible about the woman. I powered up my laptop and took it with me while I sat by Mom as she slept.

Carmela must have contacted Barry because he arrived a full two hours ahead of schedule and found me in the middle of a Google search for Francine Nielsen. I closed my computer when he entered the room.

"She's resting." I stood and motioned for him to come with me to the hallway.

"What the hell happened? Carmela said she got hysterical while some big blonde woman was here." He ran his fingers through his thinning hair.

"Francine Nielsen stopped by." I detected a tiny twitch in the corner of his eye. "She's an old friend of Mom's although she hasn't mentioned her in years." Of course, I hadn't been around enough to determine who was or wasn't one of my mother's friends. "Do you know anything about her?"

"Can't say I do." Another eye twitch. "How did she get your mom so riled up? Mela said Ginny was screaming her lungs out, but nobody could make out what she was saying."

I hesitated, then decided to tell him the truth. "I have something you need to see. Meet me in the theater."

Cool and preternaturally dark, the room was part of Barry's attempt to sell me and my stepsister on the house. He included it when Mom insisted on the big redesign, thinking we would be thrilled at the prospect of entertaining our friends in his state-of-the-art in-home cinema. The poor guy had no clue about what April and I did with various boyfriends on those over-sized reclining seats. With both of us gone, it was seldom used.

He flipped on the lights, and we each sat on plush leather recliners, trying to adjust them so we could talk without having our faces less than a few inches apart. Giving up on achieving optimum comfort, I hovered on the edge of my chair while he leaned halfway back.

"You need to see this. Carmela found it in the garden beside Mom."

He stared at the crinkled paper. After a few seconds, his hands began to shake, and his face lost its color.

"I don't understand." The acoustics of the room dramatically amplified his voice. He slumped in his seat.

After years of working in advertising, where the truth is set in elastic rather than stone, I had developed an excellent bullshit detector. And for the second time in less than an hour, beginning with his denial about knowing Francine, it was going off. Possibly, he didn't get exactly what the note meant, but he knew something. I decided against calling him on it. My stepfather wasn't a natural liar, and I suspected the pressure of extended fabrication would be more than he could handle. Sooner or later, he would break.

"Me, neither but it seems threatening." I fixed my gaze on the corner of his eye for the telltale movement. "I can't think of anyone who'd want to threaten her unless maybe it's Tommy Lee."

And there it was, both eyes twitched before he shielded them with his hands. Surely, he wasn't going to say he had never met my mother's ex-boyfriend. I had vivid recollections of the times she'd gone to work with a black eye or swollen lip and was certain my stepfather knew where they came from.

He didn't pretend ignorance, but his answer was more surprising than an attempt at dissembling would have been.

"It couldn't be him." He lowered the recliner.

Now, he was the one focusing on me, possibly to discover my tell. But what would I lie about? I really had no idea what the note meant.

"If not him, who else would want her to know they remembered that jerk? He might have met Francine once or twice, but I don't think they were close. It is strange she'd show up after all this time, though." I paused to give him a chance to respond, but he looked past me at the dark screen.

"He had a sister somewhere, but they never spoke. And he never mentioned parents or even friends, other than those disgusting guys who came over to play cards." I shivered at the memory of a fat, greasy face looming over me.

"Have you shown this to anyone else?"

I shook my head. "Shouldn't we take it to the police?"

"No!" His voice reverberated throughout the room. "I doubt it has anything to do with the stroke. And if it did, having people digging around in our lives could make things worse, much worse."

"Okay," I conceded. "But why did they send it? She hasn't even heard from Tommy Lee since . . ." Had we ever actually discussed the last time they'd spoken?

"Not since that no-good son-of-a-bitch disappeared, leaving you guys high and dry." There was something mechanical about the statement, but before I could question it, he stood and abruptly changed the subject. "You remember Carmela's nephew Sergio?"

The non sequitur was unsettling, but I did recall the name. His mother had died before the family came to the States, and Carmela had raised him. Barry gave him a job managing different locations. He was dark-skinned with slicked-back hair and a short, wiry build. stiff and shy whenever he was around me and Mom, but always polite.

"Didn't he work for you?"

"That's right. He recently started his own security business. Very discreet. I'll give this to him and see what he can come up with."

"Tell him to start with Francine," I urged.

He agreed and moved toward the door, signaling our meeting was over. I was torn between the need to know more and comfort at having someone else in charge.

"I'm going to sit with your mother for a while. Why don't you take a break? Get out of the house, do a little shopping." He reached in his back pocket, pulled out his wallet, and opened it in what I suspected was every father's go-to move for getting kids out of their hair—the proffered credit card.

"Thanks, but I'm good."

"Please," he urged. "Buy yourself something pretty."

"I can't think of a thing I need. I will take you up on that offer to get out, though." Since my arrival in Atlanta, I had been from the airport to the hospital and home with a quick stop for fast food. I was getting stir crazy. "I decided to go down to Canton Street and walk for a bit."

He kissed me on the cheek, and I surprised myself by putting an arm around his neck in an awkward half-hug.

"That's great, honey. Enjoy yourself. Everything's fine."

From the hallway, I heard him mutter under his breath. It sounded as if he said, "Or it will be when I'm finished."

•   •   •

The more I thought about Francine standing over Mom like some slutty angel of death, the angrier I became and not just with her. I was furious with myself for not yanking a knot in the bitch and frustrated with Barry's reaction. The way he dismissed the idea of getting the police involved had been surprisingly vehement for a man with his gentle disposition. Even more troubling, though, was how I reacted to that dismissal. Instead of experiencing discomfort at concealing the situation from the authorities, it was as if an unidentifiable weight had been lifted from my shoulders, and I reveled in the lightness of being.

Downtown Roswell was a short walk from the house, so I set out on foot. I drew my lightweight sweater closer, chilled despite the warm spring sun. At the end of the long drive, I stared at the beautiful home Barry had provided for my mother and me. I'd been too angry and lost at the time to appreciate it and still had the sense I didn't belong there. Had Mom felt the same way, or had she been so desperate to leave her past behind fitting in hadn't mattered to her?

Determined to clear my head, I began speed walking toward the downtown area. While I might not have taken to Barry's beautiful house, I fell in love with the city. As the seventh largest city in Georgia, it's maintained that charming, small-town atmosphere people expect from the South. Cheerful shops and restaurants line the narrow main street, exuding goodwill that's only a little less genuine than that of Southerners in general.

Not that we aren't sincere in our seemingly open friendliness. We just assume you understand manners and emotions don't always coincide.

My time in LA helped me realize that projecting warmth, real or not, creates possibilities. It makes people feel better. And that's what walking in Roswell did for me. Sure, the town was created by slave-owners who exploited Irish immigrants to run their cotton mill. And yes, the Union had forcibly relocated those workers in Northern prisons, and many of them never came home. But despite that dark history, passersby happily window shopped, greeting strangers with wide smiles and happy hellos.

I cheered at the prospect of mingling in that sunny world. As I strolled along surrounded by trees, blossoming in vibrant pinks and pristine whites, I could almost forget the terrified look on my mother's face when Francine walked from the room. But the sound of her strangled attempt to shout Tommy Lee's name was more difficult to vanquish.

The bold red awning protruded over a door in the same color and announced I had reached The Painted Monkey, an eclectic little place that offered treasures of all sorts. I stopped to peek at the paintings on display in the window—monkeys galore—and had to check it out.

A clean, floral scent filled the crowded shop and drew me to a table heavily laden with soaps and candles and lotions and creams. I unscrewed the top of a sample jar and sniffed. Lavender with a hint of vanilla, the same light fragrance as those Whitney had burned throughout our apartment. I closed my eyes and when I opened them, another customer stood beside me. I started to give her the requisite smile, but when I saw the slender, dark-haired woman's high cheekbones sprinkled lightly with freckles, my lips froze into a tight half-grin. A closer look reassured me this woman was not my former roommate.

"Excuse me," she said.

I stepped aside but kept staring as she departed. As I left the store, I would have sworn several of the painted monkeys lining the walls were laughing at me.

Outside, a cool breeze tousled my hair. I turned my face toward the sun, wondering what would have happened if the woman in the shop had been Whitney. Would I have bolted out the door or stood my ground and faced my past?

CHAPTER 14

Approaching Certainty

In college, I rewrote myself, editing out the ugly parts of my backstory. By the time I made it to California, the girl formerly known as Elizabeth Ann Tucker no longer existed. But without my past, I would never be completely whole. That could explain why I settled for the kind of half-ass relationship I had with Russ and others before him.

Still shaken from my non-encounter, I maneuvered through the crowded sidewalk, slowing down when the young woman pushing a stroller in front of me stopped to reinsert a pacifier into her toddler's mouth. A teenage couple sauntered by, arms wrapped around each other. An elderly man sat on a bench reading a newspaper. Surprisingly, I didn't have the urge to create better, more exciting scenarios for them. Instead, I envied the ease with which they seemed to be living the lives they had.

I longed for those pure moments of uncomplicated self-acceptance. But if I wanted that for myself, I had to accept the blame for drifting through life without setting my own course. I had to stop letting others—even well-intentioned ones like Barry—control my decisions. And I had to make amends to the people I'd hurt.

By the time I reached the end of the drive, I decided to start with Whitney.

"No, Buster, no!" A stout woman in jogging shorts ran toward me, chasing a black Lab. The dog ignored her and continued to bound forward, tail wagging.

"Good boy." I held out my hand and braced for impact. The big boy, his entire body wriggling now, reared on his hind legs. I raised my knee, gently bumping his chest, and sent him stumbling backward into the grasp of his owner.

"I'm so sorry." She clipped him on the leash. "He's been like this ever since he discovered my neighbor's pool. The big goof stands on the hill, hurls himself over the fence, and takes a running dive. Once in, it's almost impossible to get him out."

"No worries. I've always been a dog person." I recognized her as our next-door neighbor.

She reached into her pocket and removed a small plastic baggie. "Wait a second. You're Ginny's daughter."

She took a treat from the bag and held it in front of the animal's quivering nose before commanding him to sit. He plopped down, tail wagging, and accepted a biscuit.

"I was so sorry to hear about her stroke."

I updated her on my mother's condition before she gave in to her pooch's insistent tugging.

On the way up the steep driveway, I thought of Whitney. Then I saw a dark brown sedan parked by the garage. Instantly, I went to a worst-case scenario involving an emergency visit from the doctor. But that would have involved an ambulance, wouldn't it? Unless medics had come and gone already.

Get a grip, Liz. It's probably one of Mom's bridge ladies or a friend of the family. I shifted into a slow jog and threw open the door where Carmela stood, hands on her hips. Directly in front of her with his back to me, a man with salt and pepper hair loomed over her. He wore expensive denim jeans and a Hugo Boss polo, both purchased from the designer section of Bloomingdales. I knew because I'd been with him when he bought the outfit. It was Russ.

Not someone to suffer fools, Carmela appeared to have been in the process of ejecting this particular one when I came running. The fact he had gotten as far as into the foyer was a testament to his insistent charm.

"Miss Liz, this man is here to see you."

"Baby!" He turned and rushed toward me, grabbing me in a tight hug. I squeezed my hands between us and pressed them against his chest, but he didn't let me go. Instead, he whispered in my ear. "We need to talk. Now."

I pushed harder, and this time he released me from the fierce embrace but grabbed my hand and held it.

"It's okay, Carmela." I smiled, hoping to reassure her. "This is my boss." I yanked free. "Russ Young."

I took his arm and steered him down the hallway into the library, then shoved him inside and shut the door.

"You can't be here." I flinched when I saw his irises were all dark pupil, like some black-eyed demon from the sci-fi network. While this could have been the result of pot, his drug of choice, he was normally dull and drowsy after smoking. His overall twitchiness today suggested cocaine, something he rarely did around me because I hated it and him when he'd been snorting the stuff.

"Is Denise aware you're here?"

He responded to the mention of his wife's name as if struck by a jolt of electricity. "Of course not, baby." He reached for me, and I took an involuntary step back. "What's wrong? Aren't you glad to see me?"

A chill started at the base of my spine and shot upward, causing me to clench my jaw to keep my teeth from chattering. For a second, I was that helpless fifteen-year-old, standing in the kitchen with a man who saw me as a possession, to do whatever he wanted with.

But Russ wasn't Tommy Lee, and I was no longer that girl.

"No, I am not glad to see you. I have too much on my plate to deal with us."

Shock registered on his face, and I realized I never directly confronted him about anything having to do with our relationship.

"I didn't come here for you to deal with me." He spoke softly while clenching and unclenching his fists. Once again, I thought of Tommy Lee. "I came here to support you." Not as soft. "To be someone you could lean on." Louder now. "Because we love each other." By the end of the statement, he was almost shouting, daring me to contradict him.

It wasn't the time for a full-on showdown. I needed to calm him down and get him out of the house. Then I could work on a plan to convince him he wanted to break up with me. Something along the lines of what a terrible girlfriend I was, leaving him on his own—except for his wife—while I frolicked in coma-land with my mother. If I played it right, I might salvage my job although that no longer seemed quite as important.

"I mean it isn't fair for me to ask you to hang around when I'm so busy caring for Mom."

I put my hand on his arm, but he jerked away.

"If playing nursemaid for the woman you never even visited before all this shit happened is keeping you tied up, where were you when I got here? Are you sure someone else wasn't *taking up your time*?"

So, that was what this sudden interest in being here for me was all about. He thought I was messing around instead of spending every waking moment loaded with guilt about abandoning the woman who was now a shadow of herself.

"That's it." I opened the library door. "Get the hell out."

His mouth dropped open, reminding me of the big-mouthed bass mounted on the wall of Barry's den. "There's no reason to be upset. We can work this out."

"I said go."

"Okay, okay. But only if you meet me later at my hotel."

I sighed but agreed to dinner at the Ritz, then ushered him to the front door where Carmela and Barry were waiting.

"Mela told me you had a visitor." He looked at me, ignoring my soon-to-be-ex.

"This is my boss, Russ Young, but he can't stay. He has business downtown." I pushed him past my stepfather, who had not extended his hand—a gesture, or lack of one, that for him was tantamount to spitting on someone's shoes.

I walked him to his car where he leaned in to kiss me goodbye. I turned in time for his lips to graze my cheek and whispered, "You're supposed to be my boss, not my boyfriend." I nodded toward the front windows. Rustling drapery indicated someone had been checking on us. A surprising rush of warmth for my stepfather's protectiveness came over me.

The rental car moved down the driveway, providing a moment of relief. I walked back inside to an empty foyer. The expansive staircase in front of me seemed to stretch on forever as I dragged myself to my room.

Pillows were piled high on the cheerful rose-covered bed, but the floral pattern reminded me of my mother lying in the garden. The cause of her stroke had most likely been simmering inside her for a very long time. But for me, the person who sent the note played a big role in setting off the explosion and its aftermath, currently playing havoc with her brain.

I lay back on the bed, staring at the two-tier chandelier above me. Mom's decorator must have studied at Versailles. Light reflected off the dangling crystals as I replayed Barry's denial. And then I remembered. The night my mother thought Tommy Lee might propose, she asked Francine to cover her shift for her. Mom was already working for my stepfather, which meant he had to know the waitress. And even though I suspected he was lying, I went along with it, the way I'd done most of my life.

Well, no more. I had taken step one in getting rid of Russ. Tonight, I would finalize the process. And I would call Whitney to explain why I had run out on her in college. My last step would be to talk to Grant about how things ended between us. But first, I would take care of the big-breasted bitch who had frightened my mother.

I returned to Google where I found a Chicago Francine Nielsen's Pinterest page filled with a host of miniature goat videos, instructions on making a fish braid, and pictures of red high heels. Definitely not the woman from our past.

Linkedin offered another who taught preschoolers in Reno. Definitely not the right one. The woman who towered like a hungry vulture over me in Mom's room would have sent four-year-olds running in terror.

People Finder led me to an F. C. Nielsen in Kennesaw, a city north of Atlanta, not too far from Roswell. I searched for F. C. on Facebook and was rewarded with a snapshot of our morning visitor. Her cover photo featured her—straw-like hair piled on top of her head—on the back of a motorcycle with her arms wrapped around a chubby man in a helmet. She worked at Big Mike's Bar Bee Queen in Acworth and was "in a relationship," presumably with the fat guy on the bike.

Before getting ready for my meeting with Russ, I called the restaurant to see if I could find out Francine's work schedule. I almost gave up, but on about the eighth ring, a deep-voiced man who identified himself as Mike answered.

"This is Mike at Big Mike's."

I got all Southern sweet on him. "This is Callie at Callie's house. Can Francine come to the phone?"

"Francine, huh." He paused to tell someone in the background to "fire up the goddamn grill," then returned. "You a friend of hers?"

Something about his tone suggested I might not want to be, so I hedged. "I'm not sure you'd say a friend. More like an old acquaintance passing through town."

"Right. Well, ma'am, I've been wanting to speak to her myself—ever since she walked out in the middle of her shift last week. Left me high and dry with fifty dollars missing from the register. If I get my hands on her—"

I disconnected and immediately blocked the number. So, she quit her job without giving notice days before my mother received the note. This had to be more than a coincidence.

I decided to pick up barbeque for lunch tomorrow. While I wouldn't be able to track her down at the restaurant, I would find her coworkers who would be as pissed as Big Mike about being left shorthanded. And nobody can dish dirt like an angry waitress.

The newspaper lying on the dresser was turned to the horoscope page. Apparently, Carmela and Mom had continued to bond through their devotion to the belief in psychic phenomena. My mother wasn't completely sold on consulting spirits and casting curses or love spells, and Mela thought palm readers were shady, but they came together over astrology. Our housekeeper must have been the one to highlight both mine and my mother's.

I read Mom's first and bit back a bitter smile.

By butting into other people's lives, you run the risk of alienating them. Bite your tongue and listen.

Had Carmela seen the dark irony or had she taken it as a sign Mom would soon be her old self, forever offering the unsought opinion?

My forecast was applicable but possibly a bit late with the warning.

Be cautious following someone else's story. You may fall into a world you never imagined.

CHAPTER 15

The Art of Alienation

In the end, I abandoned the idea of reading any horoscope to my mother. I did pay heed to the vague warning in mine. Instead of relying strictly on my ability to handle Russ, I decided I needed insurance—a get-away plan if things got too weird. In LA I had an assortment of girlfriends who would have been happy to help, but in Atlanta, I was more limited.

I called April.

"Is everything okay?" Like me, she seemed to be going to worst-case scenario.

"Everything's fine, but I need a favor."

"From me?" She sounded surprised, or at least wary.

"Nothing huge. You remember I mentioned it was complicated between me and the guy I've been seeing? Well, he showed up at Mom's—"

"Daddy told me he's an ass."

"I'm having dinner with that ass tonight. I don't expect things to get ugly, but I need a back-up plan."

"Of course. When should I be there?"

Touched by her eagerness to come to my rescue, I explained she only needed to call me at 8:30 with a dire emergency, and she agreed.

Even if we ordered as late as 7:30, I should be halfway through dinner with no possibility of being coerced into Russ's room.

I showered, then fretted over what to wear. My typical break-up outfit consisted of black pants and a simple button-up white blouse. I wore little make-up and pulled my hair back into a tight ponytail. The idea was to look as plain as possible and provide no distraction while I wriggled out of the relationship. If I'd laid the groundwork properly—becoming uncharacteristically clingy or cold and distant, depending on what turned the guy completely off—my soon-to-be-former boyfriend would leave feeling as if he'd dodged a bullet.

Everything spiraled out of my control before I had a chance to help him see I wasn't right for him. And the intensity of his reaction to my physical and emotional distance was far beyond normal for a man like him. Russ Young insisted on being in charge. It was that challenge—to hold power over someone so handsome and powerful—that got me into this mess. I hadn't planned on the relationship lasting long enough for him to figure out who was calling the shots. No harm, no foul.

But something shifted. I didn't believe for a moment he was really in love with me. The extent of his self-adoration provided little room for that. He did seem to be obsessed with the idea of loving me. If I was going to get out of this situation unscathed, I would have to be careful.

So, I chose the black pants and topped it with a soft pink, scoop-necked sweater instead of the nun-like blouse. I wore a pearl necklace with matching earrings and enough make-up to suggest I still cared but wasn't trying to be seductive—mascara, yes; smoky eye, no. I left my shoulder-length hair loose.

Satisfied with the effect, I went to check on Mom.

Barry had returned to his office, leaving one of the nurses keeping watch. I sent her on a break and sat with my mother, silently tracing the paisley pattern on her comforter. As an adolescent, I never shared the kinds of secrets I imagined other girls did with their mothers. I told myself I didn't miss that kind of relationship.

For the first time, sitting beside her now when she wasn't able to offer advice or consolation or whatever it was mothers were supposed to do, I missed it. I would tell her about Russ and Whitney and Grant. And to say I was sorry for never coming to see her. But most of all, I wanted to ask her why Francine's visit had brought Tommy Lee to mind.

I vowed to drop the subject if it upset her. "I didn't know you and Francine kept in touch. She's a piece of work, isn't she?"

She touched my wrist, surprising me with the immediacy of the reaction. I lifted her hand and brushed my lips across it as if reading a braille account of my mother's life. Despite Mom's faith in fortune-telling, I never put much stock in the palm's role in determining future events. The map of ropy veins and wrinkling crisscrosses on her cool, dry ones made me believe examining them might provide an accurate glimpse into the past.

But it wouldn't give me what I really needed.

Since her reaction to hearing Francine's name hadn't triggered an outburst, I decided to push the issue into a more appealing area.

"She is not aging well. And who wears blue eye shadow?"

The right side of Mom's mouth twitched slightly, and she tapped her finger once on the covers.

I smiled back. "And could those pants have been any tighter? Totally inappropriate. I got the impression she wasn't just dropping by to check in. Plus, leaning over and whispering in your ear like that gave me the creeps."

Her eyes widened.

"Please, Mom. I want to help you, but I can't if you don't give me some idea what's going on."

One lone tear trickled down her cheek. I brushed it away and resisted the urge to end my interrogation. Because that's what it was starting to feel like. As if I were some bullying detective, grilling a bed-ridden stroke victim. But I wasn't trying to pin a crime on Mom. I only wanted to help her and possibly myself as well.

"I'm going to ask you a few questions, okay? If the answer is yes, all you have to do is blink twice. If it's no, just keep your eyes shut. Can you do that for me?"

I held my breath. After a few seconds, she blinked two times.

Debating over whether to start easy and work my way to the tough ones. I compromised with something less challenging.

"Do you remember the note Carmella brought you in the garden?"

Mom tapped her finger rapidly, and for a moment, I worried she wouldn't answer. Finally, she blinked once, then twice.

"Could Francine be involved with that?"

Quicker this time, two blinks.

I sat on the edge of the bed and brushed her hair back from her face before continuing. "Does it involve Tommy Lee?"

Tears streamed from both eyes now. She opened her mouth and blew out a series of "O, O, O's" before managing to complete one solid, "No!"

Fearful of another episode of incoherent hysteria, I folded over her and put my head on her chest. "It's okay, Mom. No more questions. You just rest."

We stayed in this awkward position for several moments before a sensation tickled my scalp. My mother gently twirled strands of my hair.

•   •   •

On the drive to the hotel, I imagined Barry beaming with pride and hope when Carmela told him about Mom's newest communication trick. His love for my mother had been evident in the gentle way he touched her shoulder when he entered a room or smiled at her when she wasn't looking. I accepted it as a part of his being. Now it was etched in the deepening lines at the corners of his eyes and the curve of his mouth. And evidenced every time he brushed his lips across her cheek or smoothed her hair back from her forehead. He didn't just love her; he cherished her.

I wondered if she could distinguish his touch or if everything was the same to her now. My fingertips on her palm, the nurse's efficient hand on her pulse, Francine's poisonous breath at her ear.

Shivering at the memory of the big-bosomed harpy, I concentrated on the traffic bottlenecking where two major highways converged. The dying light of the afternoon sun reflected against the buildings of Atlanta's skyline, reminding me of Los Angeles without the hazy backdrop of the San Gabriel Mountains. It had been less than a week since I received Barry's call, not long enough to give me time to get homesick for LA, but had it ever really been home?

I reached my exit and pulled up to valet parking. In the bright, open lobby of the Ritz, dazzling glass and marble were disorienting. I tilted my head back and closed my eyes against the resulting vertigo. When I opened them, Russ was bounding toward me.

He'd gone for Hollywood casual: black T-shirt with a loose-fitting blazer over dark jeans and gray-tone Converse tennis shoes with no socks. I wondered if he knew he was wearing his break-up outfit.

He wrapped his arms around me and nuzzled my neck. "God, you smell good."

I stepped back and looked into his pale blue eyes. Once his throaty compliment had sent sparks up my spine. When I didn't respond, he seemed to take my inability to speak as a sign I was overcome with desire. He kissed me and said, "Let's go upstairs."

I put my finger on his lips and smiled. "First, we have to talk. Besides, I'm starving."

He narrowed his eyes and clenched his jaw. His smooth mask of civility slipped, and he looked at me with the same fury he showed when he learned of Bert Hastings's betrayal. The expression dissolved so quickly I might have imagined it.

"Sure. Let's talk."

Apparently, he planned for the possibility I wouldn't be swept off my feet and into bed and reserved a table as a contingency plan. The maître d escorted us to a clam-shell booth. I scooted around to create space, but Russ ignored the hint and sat as close as possible.

Photo-laden walls and dark wood paneling made the room seem smaller than it was—cozy, I suppose. The heavy scent of cooked meat mixed with Russ's cologne kept me from taking a deep breath. I glanced at my watch, surprised to find it was only 7:15.

A waiter appeared, and I asked for a glass of Riesling, wishing I could have a strong shot of bourbon. Russ ordered a vodka martini. His eyes stayed on me as I kept mine glued to the menu. If April texted at exactly 8:30, I needed an entrée that would arrive around 8:00. That meant no rare meat. It also meant I had to drag out dinner.

"I've heard the food is good. Why don't we share some appetizers?"

He frowned, reminding me of his constant struggle to remake me into a thinner version of myself. In LA, nobody ate a full meal. On the few occasions we risked being seen out together, I'd always gone by In-N-Out Burger on my way home for an order of fries or a milkshake.

His disapproving stare thrust me into the role of a modern-day Scarlett O'Hara: By God, I would never be hungry again. I liked my curves and was sick of trying to fit into a Russ-approved size zero.

I glanced at our server, and he sprang toward our table. I decided to try the fried green tomatoes and black-eyed pea hummus. Russ shook his head when the waiter turned to him.

"How long has it been since you've eaten?" he asked as the man went to place our orders.

Ignoring the not-so-veiled implication I was turning into a sow, I shrugged. "I had a light lunch."

He gave up the role of diet warden and sipped his martini, before placing his hand over mine. At one time, I found the gesture sexy. Now it made me feel small somehow, insignificant.

Unless I got a better read on him, I wouldn't be able to reestablish the roles of our soon-to-be-over relationship.

"It's been hell without you, baby. I can't sleep. I can't eat. When are you coming home?"

I didn't bother pointing out I'd been away less than a week. Clearly, his penchant for ongoing drama created this alternate universe where we were a West Coast Romeo and Juliet, hopefully, minus all the poisoning and stabbing.

"The doctor thinks Mom is on the right track, but nobody knows how long it could take for a full recovery if that's even possible. I can't leave until we know more."

He motioned for another drink, then said, "Things are crazy at work. I may have to bring someone in to cover for you."

The production industry is competitive and often cutthroat. We both knew "bringing someone in" was code for replacing me. A month ago, his words would have caused my stomach to lurch. Today, they had no effect at all.

"If that's what you have to do, I understand."

"If that's what *I* have to do?" he hissed. "Don't put this on me. You're the one running out on me. Your stepfather has plenty of money. He can hire people to sit with your mother."

Of course, that's what Russ would do. Jesus. What had I seen in this jackass?

"You don't get it, do you? I want to be with her. I need to be with her."

"What about me?" He slapped his hands on the table at the exact moment the waiter arrived with my tomatoes and black-eyed peas. As the unfortunate young man attempted to set down the plates, Russ's elbow hit his arm, sending hummus flying.

"What the fuck," Russ shouted as the sticky mixture slopped onto his Hugo Boss blazer.

The horrified waiter snatched a napkin from a neighboring table. "I'm so sorry, sir," he said, frantically wiping pulverized peas from Russ's sleeves.

My boss knocked his hand away, stood, and shrugged out of his jacket. "Do you have any idea how much this cost?"

His face had turned an alarming shade of red.

I rose and tugged the coat from him. "I've got this," I said to the waiter. "Why don't you bring the check?"

"I'm not ready to go," Russ shouted. Then in a lower voice, through gritted teeth, "We came here to have a nice dinner, and, by God, that's what we're going to do. Sit down."

I sat, still holding the gooey jacket.

"Bring another order of that pea crap and my goddamn martini. And more wine for her."

The waiter scurried off, and I wanted to join him.

By now, everyone in the restaurant was watching us. It would have been the perfect time to tell him we were over and dump the remainder of the hummus on his head. But I sipped my wine and speared one of the fried green tomatoes.

"So, this is the oh, so gracious South." He drawled, in an attempt at a Southern accent.

A man in a dark suit approached our table, carrying a tray. He introduced himself as the manager.

"Please accept these compliments of the house and, of course, the appetizers are on us."

"Actually, they're on him," I quipped and was rewarded with a nervous laugh. Russ glowered at me over his martini. The tiny glob of smushed peas stuck to his earlobe did me in.

I fought against the rising tide of laughter, knowing if it started, I would be powerless to stop it. Then I saw our waiter, standing with his back against the wall as if preparing to face a firing squad. I realized there was nothing funny about a grown man pitching a hissy fit.

And just like that, it was over. If keeping my job meant aligning myself with this man-baby, it wasn't worth it.

"Thank you, but the accident was his fault. If he'd been paying attention instead of being an asshole, it wouldn't have happened."

Russ's mouth moved, but nothing came out.

"What the hell was that about?" He sputtered as the manager hurried away.

I smiled. "That was about time."

"As usual, you're not making any sense. Finish your goddamn drink, so we can get out of here." He drained his martini.

I swirled my wine, suddenly fascinated by the bubbles.

He flung his napkin on the table and said, "Let's go."

"I'm not finished with my tomatoes." I cut a crusty bite off one, ate it, then began slowly carving off another tiny piece.

"Are you fucking kidding me? Get your ass up and out of the booth before I do something we'll both regret."

My ears roared with the sound of a different voice threatening to teach me some manners, and I dug my fingers into his arm.

"I've already done something I regret, and it's you." I eased myself up and sauntered toward the exit, planning not to look back. Like Lot's poor wife, I couldn't resist it and immediately wished I hadn't seen the white-hot fury on his face. Fearful of becoming a pillar of salt, I took out a twenty-dollar bill and offered it to the waiter when I reached him.

He grinned and shook his head. "Totally worth it to see you dump that asshole."

CHAPTER 16

Unsure Becomes Certain

Inside the car, my phone vibrated. It was April texting, *"Terrible problem at home. Need you now."* She sent the message at exactly 8:29, sometime during my farewell shot at Russ.

I responded, *"On the way. Thanks."*

Still on an adrenaline high from my dramatic exit, I opened the windows. Pink sang on about starting a fight, and I cranked up the volume, joining in on the chorus. It wasn't until I reached the house that the magnitude of my actions hit me.

I reestablished control in the relationship, while dealing my career a fatal blow. I might be able to scrounge up some freelance work, but Russ had a reputation for being vindictive and wouldn't be above going after anyone who even considered hiring me.

I pulled Mom's car into the garage next to Barry's matching Mercedes. Voices drifted from upstairs. By the time I reached the landing, I determined Barry was talking to the night nurse. The woman turned the corner and walked toward me, smiling.

"It's been a good evening so far. Your father's with her now."

Instead of giving my standard correction—stepfather, not father—I smiled and nodded. Then I knocked softly on the bedroom door before easing it open. Barry sat on the blue-striped armchair reading the paper to her.

"You're home early. Is everything okay?"

"Everything's good, thanks." I perched on the edge of the bed and took Mom's hand. "What have you two been up to?"

"We've been talking up a storm. Isn't that right, honey?" He looked at my mother, and, after a few seconds, she blinked twice.

I kissed her forehead and walked into the hallway, trying to decide whether I should share what I learned about Francine.

Barry followed, the curves of his smile dissolving into deep creases. At sixty-one, he was almost ten years older but never looked it. That had changed. Except for the slight droop of her lips, my mother maintained her smooth-skinned beauty. My poor stepfather hadn't fared as well. His confident gait and strong stride were gone. His shoulders slumped when he walked, and he shuffled his feet. It was as if for spouses of stroke victims, time moved like dog years.

"How about a drink?" He closed the door behind him.

My adrenaline-fueled Russ-rush had dissipated, leaving me agitated. A drink sounded good.

Owning a combo diner-liquor store meant my stepfather possessed a very well-stocked bar. Normally, I stick with wine or beer, but when Barry was pouring, I took what he offered. And it was almost always bourbon. I eased down on the soft leather sofa and tipped my glass, bracing for the familiar burning sensation. When it came, it was followed by a hint of sweetness. We sat quietly for several seconds before he cleared his throat.

"I hate interfering in you girls' lives. And I'm just going to say this one thing and let it go. Okay?"

"I'm listening."

"I don't like how that Russ character treats you. Frankly, there's nothing likable about the man. I understand he's your boss, but something's not right." He paused to take a long swallow. "There. I said it. If it upsets you, I'm sorry, but sometimes men just get a vibe about other guys. And that guy sends off real bad vibes. I guess that's more than one thing. But you mean too much to me to keep quiet, especially now with your mother the way she is."

"I agree, which is why I broke up with him tonight."

"You did?" He grinned and held up his glass. "That's some excellent news. I say we drink to it."

I clicked my tumbler against his and took a healthy swig, pleased at myself for getting it down without having a coughing fit.

"I'm not sure how good it is since it probably means I'll be out of work, but it was the right move."

"If money's an issue, forget about it."

I started to protest, and he held up his hand. "I understand you want to be independent, but if you won't accept it as a gift, we'll call it a loan."

"That's sweet of you, but I'll be okay."

"Of course, you will. Still, it doesn't hurt to have someone in your corner." He smiled and patted me on the shoulder. "And you're welcome to stay with us as long as you want."

A few weeks ago, hell, a few days ago, the very thought of coming home for an extended length of time terrified me. It would be admitting I couldn't cut it on my own, or, even worse, facing the fact I hadn't moved away so much as I had run away.

"Thanks, Barry. I do appreciate your support."

He rose to pour himself another bourbon.

I waited for him to sit, then asked what I'd been wondering about for hours. "Was Sergio able to find anything about Francine?"

"Not yet, but he's still working on it." This lie was possibly more significant than whatever information Sergio might have uncovered.

"Think I'll head on up to bed." I kissed his cheek and walked to the doorway. "Thanks for, well, for everything."

On the way to my room, I saw Mom's door was ajar. I thought she was asleep at first, but she opened her eyes and gave me her half smile.

"Ssssit," she requested and tapped a finger on the space beside her.

"Shouldn't you be sleeping?"

She mumbled and twisted her lips. "Dead." The word came out strong.

"Who, Mom?" I asked. "Who's dead?"

Her rapid breathing slowed to a deep, steady rhythm, and she closed her eyes.

In my room, I undressed, dropped my clothes in a pile, and fell into bed. With the comforter pulled up to my neck, I stared at the ceiling. Whether from the lingering effect of Barry's bourbon or exhaustion from dealing with Russ, my mind felt as if it were encased in thick, white cotton.

Mom hadn't specifically named Tommy Lee as the deceased, but wasn't that the only thing that had ever really made sense? The burned-out truck, the absolute nature of his removal from our lives. The only logical conclusion would be that he hadn't survived the crash. There was, however, nothing logical about the fact they never found his body. And the way my mother said it—clear, cold, and certain—didn't sound as if it were based on conjecture.

I searched my memory for anything that would help me make sense of the situation.

Eventually, I fell into a dreamlike state, where pots and pans and plates flung themselves in a smoke-filled kitchen and the same driverless truck pursued me up alleys and down streets. Sometime before dawn, the nightmare took a turn into uncharted territory. The pickup was no longer empty. I was lodged in the driver's seat.

The tacky topless hula dancer Tommy Lee installed for luck mocked me from the dashboard as I tried to veer onto the shoulder of the road. No matter how hard I pumped the brakes or how desperately I tried to turn the steering wheel, I couldn't control the erratic vehicle. It sped closer and closer to a rocky embankment overlooking a steep drop. When it reached the edge, the truck miraculously stopped, teetering, cartoon-style.

Before I opened the door to leap out, a low growling laugh caused me to whip my head toward the passenger seat. Beside me, teeth pulled back in a skeletal grin, sat Tommy Lee.

I bolted up, gasping for breath, and looked at the clock. It was 4:10. After stumbling to the bathroom, I stood in front of the well-lit mirror and splashed water on my face.

"It's only a dream," I said to my reflection.

I returned to bed but was terrified I would fall back into my nightmare. Where had such a vivid recollection of riding in that disgusting truck come from? I made it a point to avoid even sitting in it. So why did clutching the oily steering wheel seem so real? And how had the cracked leather seat been so distinctly physical?

The memory tugging at me since I came back to the South pounded fiercely behind my eyes. When I shut them, I didn't see Tommy Lee leaning close to me inside a truck that reeked of stale beer and tobacco. I saw him hurtling over the hood of the vehicle, eyes wide with surprise. Then I saw myself behind the wheel, looking at my grim, determined face in the rearview mirror.

I swam up from deep, dark waters of sleep. Slivers of sunlight fell across the comforter. A flash of relief hit me as I registered that Tommy Lee would never return to hurt us again. With that realization, however, came the memory of who had rendered him powerless.

Despite the warmth of the thick blankets, I shivered as I faced the fact Tommy Lee hadn't simply disappeared. As I predicted, he never took my mother out for that romantic dinner to propose or even to make up for his brutal behavior. Instead, he returned sometime long after I snuck into the house.

What I dismissed as nothing more than a dream turned nightmare—or maybe a nightmare turned dream—had been real. Just as I rewrote the lives of random strangers on the plane, I revised the time Tommy Lee vanished. Or had I simply edited reality, casually omitting the part where Mom shook me awake in the middle of the night? I forgot her urgent whispers telling me to get dressed. And I completely deleted the part where Tommy Lee pulled up as we ran to the car.

Birds chirped outside my window and a dog barked in the distance, but the rumbling of that ghost engine eclipsed the sounds of morning. When I closed my eyes, I saw my mother in the headlights. I didn't know what she was screaming, but I could feel her hands pushing against the small of my back, shoving me toward the truck Tommy Lee had left idling in the drive, blocking our escape. I saw his bemused look turn dark as he walked to Mom.

I stopped when I reached the driver's side, hauled myself inside, and locked the door. Tommy Lee stood behind the sedan, slapping the hood and shouting. Then his body shot backward, and he landed near the bumper.

I sat in the truck, hands gripping the steering wheel, waiting for him to leap to his feet. But he didn't move. The engine grumbled beneath me as she opened the car door and pulled a canvas bag from the back. She raced to the truck and hurled it into the back. Before I could slide across to let her take the wheel, a scrabbling sound outside my door stopped me. Tommy Lee pressed his blood-streaked face against the window. He pounded the glass with his fist.

Mom leaped onto the passenger seat and began screaming. "Reverse! Put it in reverse."

Confused, I stared at the steering column which looked nothing like my Beetle's four-in-the-floor set-up. The pounding stopped. Seeing him stumbling toward us startled me into motion. I stepped on the clutch and slammed the gearshift into what I thought was reverse. But we lurched forward, and he flew over the hood into the windshield. Glass shattered, and he landed out of sight. The last thing I remembered was a sickening thud.

CHAPTER 17

Emotional Overload

Steam filled the shower and blurred my vision, the same way a forgetful fog obscured my memory of the night Tommy Lee died. The sound of the impact that sent his body flying over the hood was crystal clear. Bricks from the wall my subconscious constructed were crumbling but still concealed any view of what happened after he hit the ground.

Mom wasn't strong enough to dispose of her former lover by herself. I imagined Barry and Sergio had driven the truck to the mountain and pushed it into the ravine. But what had they done with the body?

How confused my mother must have been the next morning when she discovered I had no memory of the previous night. Did she face every new day, fearful the horrors that retreated to a dark spot in my troubled mind had found their way into the light? I can imagine her relief at not having to deal with a homicidal daughter, but was this emotion mixed with suppressed anger at me for taking away her one true love?

No wonder my mother disappeared into herself for all those months. But allowing me to remain peacefully unaware of my actions disappeared a part of me. All this time, I blamed my inability to form a real relationship on the way she behaved with the men in her life.

And while that might be true, it didn't compare with her inability to help me come to terms with our shared secret.

I needed to confront her about the night Tommy Lee vanished. But if my suspicion about the note triggering her stroke was remotely correct, what might happen if I stopped talking about wrinkle cream and horoscopes? What if I came out and told her I remembered what it sounded like when a 5,000-pound truck slams into a two-hundred-pound man?

Would she slip back into blissful nothingness and decide to stay there? Unlike me, her mind hadn't protected her by checking out on the reality of that night. She'd been living with what we'd done, completely aware of its enormity. Maybe knowledge of her complicity in the murder had exploded—with or without help from the note. Regardless, I knew I couldn't jeopardize her recovery by letting her in on my recent epiphany.

I'm not sure how long I stood in the shower, but when the hot water began to cool, I rinsed off and stepped out. Wrapped in one of the soft, thick guest towels, I dried my hair, then stood in front of the mirror, surprised I still recognized myself.

I noticed the paper lying on the little oval table outside my room. I picked it up and turned to the horoscope page. If my personal message from the galaxy said something like "Avoid pork at all costs," I'd rethink my plan.

The language of love can only be translated by the heart. Listen to yours today.

After last night with Russ, I didn't expect to need a romantic interpreter. I skimmed over the forecasts between mine and Mom's, hoping to find something worth sharing with her.

Your inner core is on emotional overload. Don't let others add to your stress.

Definitely more relevant than yesterday's. Trapped inside herself, all she had was that inner core, and with the way I'd been trying to question her, I contributed to the stress.

Barry was feeding her oatmeal with one of April's silver baby spoons.

"We're just finishing. She's doing great." He dabbed at her chin.

"I brought news of our futures."

"Perfect. I'll run the dishes downstairs. Carmela's planning a big breakfast for us." He kissed Mom lightly on the lips, and she gave a grimacing smile. "Head on down when you're ready."

I turned to her. "Let's start with yours."

I cheated and read only the first part about her inner core, then made up the rest.

Free yourself from the burden of unreleased stress by opening up to the world and conquering the things that frighten you the most.

The section about conquering fears was spontaneous, probably having more to do with me than with her. But what was I more afraid of? The person who sent the note or the girl who ran down Tommy Lee. When I looked up, I encountered her unblinking stare.

I cleared my throat. "That means you need to cut loose and get out of that bed. What do you think?"

She rolled her eyes. At the familiar gesture, I beamed.

"I admit it's not all that interesting. Mine's got possibilities, though."

This time when I finished reading the corny message about translating love with your heart, a single teardrop glistened on her cheek.

"Hey, there's nothing to cry about. I mean sooner or later I'm bound to find Mr. Right."

She reached for my hand and clasped it. I thought about how hard it must have been for her to look at me after Tommy Lee's death and wondered how different things might have been if she'd banished him from our lives before I killed him. Would we have settled in at Barry's and enjoyed some version of a normal mother-daughter? Was it too late for us now?

In the hope that it wasn't, I began telling her about my disastrous, doomed relationship with Russ. About how he was married and that I never loved him. It was supposed to be fun with nobody getting hurt, only everything had gone wrong. I blurted out that I hadn't really been in love since....

Grant's name caught in my throat.

"Wow," I breathed. "I don't know where all that came from. It's your fault for being such a damn good listener."

Her smile wasn't as crooked now.

Someone knocked at the door before easing it open. It was her speech therapist. I greeted him and kissed her. It was as if I dropped several pounds of angst. Then I realized exactly where it had landed. Seems like her original horoscope had been right when it warned of not letting others add to her already heavy load.

•   •   •

After stuffing myself with bacon-and-eggs-with-pancakes-on-the-side, I announced I had a craving for barbeque from Big Mike's in Acworth.

Mela's mouth dropped open. "You did not have enough?"

I laughed and assured her I was too stuffed to eat another bite but had heard about the barbeque joint from a co-worker who'd been shooting a movie in the area.

I paid close attention to my stepfather's expression when I mentioned the name of the restaurant, but he only smiled. That meant either Sergio wasn't as good an investigator as reputed, or he hadn't reported back to Barry yet. There was a third possibility: Sergio had told him, and Barry was getting smoother at deception.

As a teen, I took issue with many things about the man—his constant need to know where I was and who I was with, the way he smacked when he ate popcorn, his eternal good humor—but I always considered him to be truthful. I sneered at him for being such a Boy Scout. But I had been wrong. While his Honest Abe routine wasn't completely an act, he did an excellent job of keeping the truth buried. And now, he might be doing the same thing.

I excused myself and went to check my email to see if I'd received a formal "fuck you, you're fired" message from Russ. Nothing yet, so I got on the road to Acworth.

The drive after the morning rush was almost pleasant. A few stretches of the median sported bright patches of golden-yellow wildflowers, reminding me how much I missed having seasons. Steering wheel held in my right hand, I stuck my left arm out the window and let it soar with the wind.

Google maps said I had about thirty-eight-minutes to decide how to approach Francine's coworkers. Fearful Big Mike might recognize my voice or be a jumbo-sized jerk or both, I decided not to include him in my amateur investigation.

As the daughter of a waitress, I was comfortable talking to them. From easy-going and patient to sarcastic and sassy, the waitresses I knew had—for the most part—been survivors. Capable of dishing out more than the daily specials, they had a high tolerance for taking crap from surly customers. But when they'd had enough, God help the unlucky soul who stepped over the line.

They also tended to be loyal to each other. They might snipe about a colleague to another waitress, but they rarely let the general public in on the complaint. Unless, of course, one of them broke the cardinal rule: don't leave your coworkers hanging, especially not during peak hours. If Big Mike's account was accurate, Francine had left both her boss and fellow employees in the lurch without apology or explanation.

By the time I reached my exit, I came up with a story to help me strike up a conversation with one of the waitresses. I would say my mother was a friend of Francine and lost her home address. So, I promised to stop by the restaurant to get the information for Mom.

When I was about eleven, Mom's boyfriend of the month took us to the beach at Lake Acworth. Mom complained about the brown sand, and I refused to walk on the squishy mud. The trip was less than stellar.

I was impressed with the updated look of downtown. The city planners kept the old Americana-flat-topped brick buildings and iconic Coca-Cola sign. The newer boutiques and restaurants situated among the historic structures reflected the same style. Benches and green spaces were scattered throughout the area, creating the kind of hometown people wished they'd come from but didn't really want to live in.

Big Mike's was located on the other side of town next to a pawn shop. I parked in front and a bell tinkled as I entered. I was the only customer in the place.

A tall blonde anywhere in age from mid-fifties to late sixties stood behind the counter, fiddling with the register tape. "Be with you in a minute, hon." She tucked in a piece of hair that had escaped her starched up-do. "This darn thing is about to drive me nuts."

"No problem. I'm not in a hurry."

She popped her gum a few times before getting the paper back in the machine. "There." She looked at me for the first time, and I was struck by the size and shape of the mole above the right side of her mouth. In what I suspected was an attempt to turn lemons into lemonade, she had transformed an ordinary birthmark into an extraordinary heart-shaped creation, reminiscent of a French hooker from a World War I movie. I forced myself to look away from the startling design and into her faded brown eyes.

"How can I help you today?" she asked, smoothing the red apron she wore over a white uniform.

I read her nametag, then said, "Jeanine, I heard from a friend you all have the best barbeque around these parts, so I'm here to pick up a little bit of everything for my momma's birthday lunch."

"You came to the right place." She took my order for several pounds of ribs, pork, slaw, and beans. When I finished, she offered to throw in a pint of mac and cheese on the house, and I accepted, then ordered a coffee for while I waited.

From a small table near the door, I surveyed the room, hoping Jeanine wasn't covering the floor as well. A second woman, younger with short black hair brushed into spikes, came out of the kitchen to refill ketchup bottles.

When she reached me, I squinted at her badge. "Good morning, Coral."

Her scowl indicated she didn't agree with my assessment of the day, but she arranged her unnaturally dark lips in the semblance of a smile and returned the greeting. The contrast between the black shade of lipstick and her pale skin was unsettling. Before I initiated further conversation, Jeanine called her name. She smoothed her uniform, then turned and walked to the counter where she picked up a steaming mug of coffee and a miniature pitcher of cream.

"Can I get you anything else?"

"This is perfect. Do you know if Francine is working today? She's an old friend of my momma's."

She narrowed her heavily mascaraed eyes and put one hand on her hip. "An old friend, huh?" She kept her gaze focused on me, making it difficult to maintain what I hoped was an innocent expression.

"They went to school together about a hundred years ago and lost touch. Momma thought I might get Francine's address or phone number, so they could catch up."

She either bought my story or didn't care. "Francine worked here until last Monday when she disappeared without a goodbye or a kiss my ass. If you want my opinion, your mom's better off staying out of touch with her."

"She *disappeared*? Could something bad have happened to her?"

"Not something bad. *Somebody* bad. That no-account man of hers got out of prison. My guess is he moved in and told her to quit her job, so she could stay shacked up with him until he screws up again and gets sent back."

"Goodness. Momma didn't say anything about her having a husband in or out of prison."

"Not many people know about him. She didn't take his last name. We had some drinks after work, and she let it slip her old man was up for parole. Said she wasn't coming home until he made good on his promises. She didn't say what they were."

The welcome bell jingled, and a young woman, not much older than twenty-one or two, entered, carrying a fat baby and holding the hand of a little boy in a droopy pair of toddler jeans. He stopped just inside the doorway and began screaming something about Big Macs. She dragged the protesting kid to the counter.

Coral started for the kitchen.

"Last question, please. Did she say what kind of promises he made?"

Her eyes narrowed. "I need to check on your order."

I stood and took a card from my purse. "If you hear from her, would you give me a call?" She slipped it into her pocket, then joined Jeanine, who was dealing with the harried mother. Coral leaned close to her coworker. Whatever she said caused Jeanine to glare in my direction at the same time the baby spit up on both the counter and into the toddler's hair.

"Shit, shit, shit." The young mom used her shirt tail to wipe off the little boy, and he began echoing "shit, shit, shit."

"I'm so sorry."

Jeanine assured her it was no big deal.

In the midst of the meltdown, Coral dashed into the kitchen and returned with paper towels and disinfectant. She handed a wad to the mom and began wiping and spraying the counter.

Watching the frenetic scene, I tried to create a fantasy starring the poor mother the way I had done with the people on the plane. But there was too much real life in play to write her a fanciful backstory, and I was stuck with the picture of what the young woman's reality was. She would keep cranking out babies until she woke up one morning unable to remember who she was before she'd become a baby machine. Or maybe her home would be overflowing with children who loved her, and I would be the same gloomy cynic, only older and less cute.

A man with a low hanging belly barely covered with an apron in what appeared to be blood-spatter patterns arrived carrying two enormous brown paper bags. I didn't need to see a nametag to know my order was being delivered by Big Mike himself. Relieved when I realized the bloody design was only sauce, I smiled at him. He left without returning the gesture. I finished my coffee and gave Coral a ten-dollar tip.

Wishing I'd requested a box for the barbeque, I placed it on the floor behind the passenger seat, lodging it tightly to avoid spillage. Before pulling away, I checked the rearview mirror and noticed the black sedan easing toward my bumper. I waited to see if the driver would back up. When he didn't, I considered getting out to ask him to give me more room, but decided Mom's power steering was up to the task and wriggled my way out of the tight space.

On the expressway, I replayed my conversation with Coral. I wasn't shocked at the revelation Francine had married a convict. I did wonder why she had chosen not to use his last name. She seemed like the type of woman for whom snagging a husband was a cause for celebration. And she didn't strike me as being a feminist. The only explanation I could come up with suggested she knew he had committed a crime and expected he would eventually be thrown in jail.

I arrived home a little before noon. April's Lexis sat in the drive. I parked beside her and was walking around to get the food from the backseat when I noticed a car at the end of the driveway. A tickling sensation on the back of my neck made me pause to take a closer look, but when I did, the dark sedan sped away, too quickly for me to be sure it was the same one from the restaurant.

Great. Now I was rewriting my backstory, making what was most likely someone looking for an address into something suspicious.

Juggling the bags full of barbeque, I fumbled with the unfamiliar lock and inserted the key at the same time my stepfather opened the door.

"Boy, that smells good," he announced. He took the food from me and carried it to the kitchen, where April arranged place settings for four.

"Is Carmela joining us?" I asked.

"No, she had to run some errands," he answered, seconds before the doorbell rang.

"I'll get it." My stepsister bolted from the room. When she returned, our mystery guest accompanied her.

CHAPTER 18

Fear of the Unknown

After welcoming Grant Albright with a hasty "Good to see you," I excused myself to check on Mom and fled upstairs.

"What on earth could she be thinking?" I asked my mother as I brushed her matted hair. "Is she seriously trying to get the two of us together?" I stopped to work through a complicated tangle and remembered he had the same shy smile and ridiculously adorable dimples as when I first met him.

"Oh, my God!" I almost dropped the brush. Had I completely misread the situation? Was there something between Grant and April? Surely not. I mean, she was so not his type. Funny, once I'd been sure he wasn't my type, either. Then I focused on Mom.

I touched her shoulder. "This is important. Two blinks for yes. One for no. Got it?"

She blinked twice rapidly.

"Good. This is the question. Are you ready?"

One blink with a pronounced pause between it and the second followed. I interpreted her message to mean she was stroked out, not stupid.

"All right. Here it is." I took a deep breath. "Are April and Grant dating?"

She closed her eyes, then opened them. But it might not be that simple.

"Have they ever dated?"

She blinked, then held her eyes wide open before closing them and keeping them closed.

"What the hell does that mean? Seriously, I need to—"

April popped into the room. "Is everything okay? Food's on the table, and everyone's waiting."

"I'm fine. Mom loves barbeque, and I wanted to see if she wants us to stick some in the food processor for her."

My mother bobbed her head up and down.

"Wait a minute. You're nodding now?" Apparently, that whole blinking routine had been her idea of a little joke.

"Dad didn't tell you? After you left, her therapist got her communicating like a pro. He says her language skills should start to return soon. Can we get you something?"

Mom shook her head.

"Later, then. Come on, Sis. That barbeque isn't going to eat itself."

My mother smiled an almost perfect crescent and blinked one eye in what was definitely a wink.

I caught up with April before we reached the top of the stairs. "Is there any special reason you invited Grant to lunch?"

"Me? I didn't invite him. He and Daddy need to go over some financial stuff."

"Sure, but it would have been good if somebody told me ahead of time. What if we don't have enough food?" Sounding peevish even to myself, I stomped down the steps.

The men were talking and laughing as we entered the kitchen.

"You should have started without me," I protested, knowing full-well no Southerner would have done such a thing.

"Don't be silly, honey. Grant and I were going over some boring money stuff while we waited for our lovely ladies to join us. Isn't that right, buddy?"

"It is. Barry tells me your mom's doing much better. Says pretty soon she'll be back to her sassy self."

"She's getting there." With the blink, half blink wink routine when she could have nodded, I suspected she was a lot closer than we imagined.

April moved platters of meat to the table, and I added the sides.

"Wow," she said when we finished the arrangement with clearly enough food to feed a football team. "I'm afraid we should have gotten more."

"Good God, ladies. If we eat all this, they'll have to bring in the paramedics." Barry cleared his throat. "I'd like to say a blessing if it's all right with everybody."

Everybody was a tactful reference to the brief period during my senior year in college when I'd become pretentiously agnostic. My position was primarily a reaction to Mom—who had never expressed any religious views—taking a sudden interest in achieving salvation through the Presbyterian church Barry had attended for years.

At the time, I expressed my aversion to meaningless rituals, and my stepfather deferred to my request to skip the blessing. I'd long since returned to a healthy belief that there was a God whom I was disappointing on a regular basis but neglected to let Barry in on my return to—if not the center—at least, the outskirts of the flock.

I nodded.

"Bless us, Lord, and these Thy gifts we are about to receive from Thy bounty." His voice broke on bounty, and we waited for the traditional sign-off.

"And thank you, Lord, for bringing our little family together to watch the miracle of your healing love on dear Ginny and for letting our good friend join us. In Christ's name we pray. Amen."

April and Barry echoed *amen*.

Grant took a bite. "This is amazing. I don't think I've ever been to Big Mike's. How'd you hear about it?"

I repeated my lie about learning of Mike's reputation from a colleague and stole a glance at Barry, whose only reaction was to take a gulp of sweet tea.

Grant wiped his lips and grinned at me. "It's almost as good as Wild Willie's."

His reference to one of our favorite college spots freshman year brought back memories of late nights with him and Whitney. After a night of stuffing ourselves with sliced pork and beer, we ended up in our dorm room. Usually, my roommate would out drink or out smoke us both and drift into unconsciousness, leaving us talking until dawn. Sometimes the three of us would fall asleep on the floor piled up like puppies.

I noticed the conversation had stopped and realized they were waiting for me to speak. "I'm sorry. I drifted off for a minute."

"That's okay." Barry reached over and patted my hand. "You've got a lot on your mind."

More than you know. I smiled as I traced an eight in my mac and cheese.

When it became apparent I had nothing to add, April stepped in. "Speaking of having a lot on your mind, I must be losing mine." She stood and walked to the counter. "I forgot to give you this message." She tore a note from the to-do-list notepad and returned to the table. "It's from Whitney Harris."

I stared at the little pink square. In the aftermath of remembering I was a killer, my plans to get in touch with my former roommate were forgotten.

"I always liked Whitney," April said as she dropped a scoop of slaw on her plate.

Unlike me, Whitney found my stepsister amusing and treated her like a pet, teasing and praising her in equal amounts. I gave Grant a sideways glance, but he seemed unaffected by the mention of our old friend's name.

"Do you ever talk to her?"

"Not in a long time," I answered without looking up. I turned to Grant and asked, "What about you?"

The doorbell rang before he could respond.

"I'll get it," I said and hurried from the room.

Standing at the window, I could see a pink and green florist truck. When I opened the door, a young man in a green shirt and khaki pants greeted me.

"I have a delivery for a Miss Liz Tucker." He held an arrangement of over a dozen white lilies with miniature white roses sprinkled throughout.

"That's me." I signed the form he presented, and he made sure I could handle the oversized bouquet before leaving.

I set the flowers on the oval table by the door and removed the card.

All is forgiven. Love, R.

Wrapping my arms around myself, I shivered. I expected repercussions from last night, but this was too weird.

April came to my side. "Whoa. Somebody's popular. Are these from the guy you needed rescuing from?"

Barry and Grant's arrival spared me the trouble of summarizing the disastrous evening.

"Beautiful bouquet," Grant said. "Which one of you has the admirer?"

April picked up the lilies and held them out to Barry. "They're for Ginny, from her Sunday school class."

Sunday school class?

"Well, that is mighty sweet." Barry examined the flowers. "Kind of fancy for a church group. I would have thought they'd go the potted plant route."

"You boys sit back down. Liz and I'll take them to her room."

I followed my stepsister up the stairs wondering why she'd made up the cover story and even more curious about how she knew I'd want to keep Grant in the dark about Russ.

"We can stick them on your bedside table," she said when we reached the landing.

"No, I think Mom should have them. I'd hate for her class to get their feelings hurt."

She handed the heavy vase to me, and I peeked into the room. Mom was sleeping, so I put the flowers on the window seat and eased out to the hallway where April was waiting.

"Thanks for keeping Russ a secret."

"No problem. When you read the card, you turned a little green. Plus, there's no reason to shut Grant down before he has a chance to get started. Right?"

I almost told her we had only been friends—but she was halfway down the stairs. I followed her to the kitchen, wondering if she knew more about my past with Grant than I suspected or if she just enjoyed playing matchmaker.

When we returned, the men were in the middle of a discussion about stock options.

"Sorry, girls," Barry said. "No more shop talk. How about some of the pie Carmela made for Liz?"

April removed the fluffy chocolate cream concoction, my favorite, from the refrigerator. She stood at the counter, slicing it into generous pieces while the guys compared golf scores. The topic was as alien to me as conversations Whitney and Grant used to have about skiing trips or escapades from their days in different private schools. I experienced an unwelcome return of that old feeling of being on the outside looking in.

Until Mom met Barry, the only club I ever heard about was the Fox Tail Lounge, Tommy Lee's favorite place to go after he and Mom had a big fight. The closest I'd been to skiing was sliding down the hill on a garbage can lid after one of Atlanta's rare snowstorms. And I spent so much time in high school picking and choosing the right kind of boyfriend, I had little to contribute to the escapade department—at least, nothing I wanted to share.

"Why does Mela only make stuff like this when you come home?" April asked as she passed out plates.

"'Cause she likes me better."

"Daddy," April whined. "Make her stop."

Barry looked flustered, then relieved when we started laughing.

I spooned a bite of the thick custard into my mouth. "God, this is good," I sighed. "But if I keep eating like this, I won't be able to fit into any of my clothes when I go back to LA." I licked chocolate off my spoon.

"I don't think you have to worry," Grant said.

A warm sensation crept from my chest upward. I took a sip of tea and used my napkin to fan my neck.

"I hear they're making a bunch of movies and stuff in Atlanta now," Barry said. "I bet you wouldn't have trouble finding work. If you ever wanted to stay here, that is."

This wasn't the first time my stepfather broached the subject of my returning to the area. But it was the first time he didn't irritate me by bringing it up.

"My firm represents at least two production companies, and the president of one of them is a friend. Just saying." April swirled her spoon through whipped pie topping.

"I sense a campaign to bring Liz Tucker home. And I'd like to go on record as supporting it." Grant laughed softly.

"I appreciate the sentiments, but I'm not quite finished with life on the West Coast." Of course, it could be done with me if Russ blackballed me in the industry and threw in a little character assassination for fun. Surprisingly, this prospect failed to cool the warm glow washing over me.

It wasn't news Barry and Mom would be happier if I lived closer, but I never suspected April might like seeing more of me. And it didn't hurt to know Grant approved of the idea.

We finished the pie, and April insisted on cleaning up. Barry excused himself to ask Mom if she was hungry.

"I hate to go, but I have some work to do at the office," Grant said.

I hated it, too. "It was really good to see you."

At the door, it was as if we had slipped back in time. Only instead of the few hours I would lose on the way to California, I had lost years filled with possibilities.

"I know there's probably some rule about having two meals in the same day with an old friend you haven't seen in forever, and I realize we just finished stuffing ourselves, but I don't care. I want more time with you, and tomorrow isn't soon enough. Will you go to dinner with me, say seven o'clock, so we can do more catching up?"

I searched for a witty reply about breaking rules or exhausting my caloric allowance for the day. But when he added, "Please?" and smiled, I gave up on being clever.

"That sounds good," I said. And without any hesitation at all, in front of God and everybody, I kissed him on the lips.

He ambled down the drive, and I recognized the silver hatchback as a Prius. Quite a few people in LA kept a Prius for a second car when they needed to impress someone by looking environmentally correct. But Grant never worried about the impression he made. In college, I thought he was naïve not to consider what others thought of him. I no longer believed that.

After he drove away, I noticed some flyers stuck to the mailbox and went to check the mail. It was stuffed with a big stack of magazines and letters. As I closed the box, an engine started on the other side of the street. A dark car bolted from the curb. The driver threw it in reverse, backed into the neighbor's drive, and left, leaving a trail of thick black smoke behind.

The vehicle moved too quickly for me to be positive it was the one that had blocked me in at Big Mike's. There were thousands of others in the vicinity. Still, the coincidence was unnerving.

The note from the flowers crackled in my pocket as I jogged to the porch. Safely inside, I slammed the door shut, then locked it. I felt the heat generated from the fury on Russ's face the previous evening. Would the kiss between me and Grant be the spark to ignite that rage into a deadly explosion?

CHAPTER 19

Just Observe

After Grant left, I couldn't shake the feeling Russ might be stalking me. I considered emailing my boss, apologizing for the way things ended between us, then realized I wasn't even a little bit sorry and didn't want to pretend I was. Play-acting got me into this situation in the first place—getting off on the fantasy I could control a man like him when he always held all the cards.

Besides, if I sent him anything remotely nice, he'd take it as a sign of encouragement. I had to discuss whether he thought we could work together at least long enough to finish my last project. Now might be too soon, though, especially if he was the one in the car outside the house.

Frustrated with my inability to settle things with Russ, I returned to the much more disturbing problem of the note. Obviously, Tommy Lee hadn't sent it, and if Francine wrote it, did that mean she knew he was dead? More importantly, did she suspect I'd been the one who killed him?

Regardless, Francine's involvement held the key to it all. I reviewed her page but found nothing useful.

I spent so much time trying to forget everything about Mom's former boyfriend, I overlooked the most obvious of all possibilities. He had another love interest. From what I learned and observed about

Francine, it wasn't difficult to imagine she and Tommy Lee had been carrying on.

There was also the issue of Francine's husband. According to Coral, he reappeared after spending time in prison. If she hadn't been involved with Tommy Lee, what did the note's obscure reference to something not forgotten mean?

I thought about the night the police showed up to tell us about the burned-out truck. I attributed Mom's hysterical reaction to the realization he must be dead instead of a combination of fear and relief when she discovered the cops weren't there to arrest me.

It had been easier than expected to purge him from our past, especially since—except for a few calls to the police asking for information she hoped they didn't have—Mom never spoke of his absence. After her initial collapse, she became oddly composed. And I had been so afraid that speaking his name might beckon his return, I never asked about him.

After all these years, he still had the power to bring out the terrified girl trembling inside me. A chill passed over me as I touched the keys, and I draped a sweater around my shoulders before hitting enter.

I found fourteen exact matches. I scanned the pages, rejecting Tommy Lees in their eighties and thirties. Then I came across two articles on a missing persons page.

Written on November 15th, approximately a week after our late-night visit from the police. It was brief and revealed nothing I didn't already know. A truck registered to Tommy Lee Fagan had been found in a ravine off Lookout Mountain. No bodies were recovered from the wreckage. It ended with a description of the supposed owner of the vehicle.

The subject, age 37, has brown hair and eyes, and is approximately 5 feet, ten inches tall, and around 190 pounds. He has a scar over his right eye.

I reread the passage several times, unable to reconcile it with the hulking bully who left a trail of broken bones and spirits. Rubbing my arm, I moved on to the next article and almost dismissed it when his name didn't show up in the first few paragraphs.

The subject of this story was a man named Glen Larson, who had been arrested while in possession of an unspecified amount of cocaine. I had trouble making the connection. Tommy Lee was a trainer at the local gym. He probably used steroids, but I doubted that half-wit who shared our home had the organizational skills or ambition for high-level crime. The conclusion of the article suggested I might be wrong.

Police suspect Larson is part of a drug ring operating out of Cherokee County and are interested in questioning several of his known associates, including Tommy Lee Fagan, who is currently listed as a missing person.

Authorities warned both men could be armed and dangerous.

Dated only two months after his truck was discovered, it implied there was not only a tie between the men but also a connection with the two events. Furthermore, it pointed to the possibility Tommy Lee and Larson worked together in multiple criminal endeavors.

I Googled "arrest records" and located a search engine site. After entering Larson's name, his mug shot popped up on the screen. I caught my breath and pushed my chair away from the image.

A faint odor of garlic and stale beer wafted over me. Suddenly, I was back in my room, hiding under the covers from Tommy Lee's buddy, good old Glen-Gus.

I don't know how long I sat there staring into Glen's piggy little eyes before I made myself click on the link promising details of his record. He had been convicted of drug trafficking and sentenced to fifteen years in a state facility south of Atlanta. The last update included the information a parole hearing had been scheduled around the same time Coral said Francine's husband came back into her life.

The bright floral room with its plush pillows and thick beige carpet provided a jarring contrast to the cramped little space where I huddled in the dark, waiting for Tommy Lee's friend to burst through the door.

But he didn't, and after that night—a few weeks before Mom's boyfriend disappeared—I never saw him again. Until now.

The lush, green lawn outside my window underscored the fact I no longer resided in a world where young girls lived in fear. Today, I lived in fear of the ghosts of my past.

If Glen was out on parole, did he think his partner ran out, leaving him literally holding the bag? Did he expect Mom to have answers for him? I had my own questions, though. And who better to ask than his wife?

I Googled *recently granted paroles,* then typed Glen's name into the public access records. Seconds later, the information I needed appeared. The board released Glen Larson on parole two weeks ago. The same time Francine deserted her post at Big Mike's.

This was no coincidence. He had to be her shady husband, which meant the appearance at Mom's bedside was connected to the note. I closed my eyes and saw my mother's former friend leaning over her, whispering poison into her ear.

My impulse was to confront her, but it was after 4:30, only two and a half hours before what I was beginning to see as my ill-advised dinner with Grant. I'd already showered, but my online encounter with degenerates from my youth coated me in an invisible layer of filth.

The guest bathtub was a gigantic whirlpool affair installed after I left home. After pulling my hair into a high ponytail, I poured in a healthy amount of bubble bath, undressed, and eased into the warm water.

Normally, the pulsating jets soothed my nerves. But when I closed my eyes, images of a body catapulting over the hood of a truck shook me. What kind of person forgets her role in a man's death? Even worse, what did it say about me that now that I knew what I'd done, I felt nothing more than a vague sense of unease?

Truthfully, I harbored far more guilt and pain about hurting Grant and Whitney than I did about ending Tommy Lee's life.

•   •   •

Until the end of my junior year, I never let myself think about Grant as anything but a good friend. And if Whitney hadn't left us alone that summer, I would have kept those feelings buried.

"Please, please, please," she begged. "I'll go crazy among the socially in-bred natives without you. I promise it will be better than last time."

Last time was Christmas our freshman year when she tricked me into a week-long stint at their beach house on Sea Island, where we alternated between listening to her parents bicker and sneaking liquor into the room we shared.

"It was great," I lied. "But if I'm going to graduate in December, I have to knock out my PE credit."

That part was true. Both Grant and I somehow neglected to meet the required hour of physical education. The idea of spending two hours a week engaged in mandated gym class reminded me too much of high school PE with a bunch of girls judging each other before smashing volleyballs down each other's throats. When I complained to Grant, he said he'd take something with me, but we had trouble agreeing on the course. I wanted to sign up for Walking for Fitness. He wanted Introduction to Bowling. We compromised with Beginning Badminton.

"I don't see why you have to graduate early in the first place and leave me alone here our last semester senior year just so you can gallivant around in Los Angeles," Whitney complained.

"I'll be working, not gallivanting. Besides, you and Grant will be fine. You won't even notice I'm gone."

"Me and Grant?" She raised her eyebrows. "Right."

From that first night at the fraternity house when I came across them on the dance floor, I'd been confused about the nature of their relationship. I was certain there was a connection between them. But they never became an official couple.

Whitney went to the beach with her parents and left Grant and me behind. We partnered up on the badminton court where, much to his dismay, I continued to giggle whenever someone said *shuttlecock*.

Since neither of us worked—Grant was taking a break before starting his own internship, and Barry insisted I shouldn't have to worry about anything but school—we had lots of free time. After a rigorous hour on the indoor court, we usually headed to his place to hang out by the pool, something the three of us had done. Only now, it was just the two of us.

In past summers, Whitney and I would change in his room while he loaded up the cooler with beer and soda. We both wore skimpy suits, but I was a bit more self-conscious than Whitney, who seemed to enjoy the leers and sideways glances of boys by the pool. I was never uncomfortable with Grant.

But this summer was different. I became keenly aware of the vast expanse of flesh exposed by my new bikini the first day Grant and I were alone at his apartment. And if his flushed face and stammering speech were any indication, he shared my discomfort.

"Wow." He smiled and rose slowly from the sofa. "You, uh, I mean, wow."

Suddenly, the room became too small, too warm. I dug a cover-up from my bag and slipped it on, then bolted for the door. By the time we reached the pool deck, I'd gotten over my initial shyness, but he remained quiet.

Instead of sitting beside me, he dropped his towel and went straight to the diving board. With his reflection shimmering in the rippling water, he was a sudden stranger to me—narrow waist, taut hips—and I reminded myself it was only Grant. Only he wasn't the same boy I dismissed as too sweet and naïve the day Whitney and I met him.

Hidden by my sunglasses, my eyes lingered on him as he bounced, then sprang into the air, sleek and powerful. He hit the water and began gliding underneath the surface. I held my breath until he emerged, swam to the side, then hoisted himself out of the pool and sat on the edge, legs dangling. He froze for several minutes, reminiscent of a young Greek water god, before running toward me. I fought the impulse to leap up and reach out for him. He bent over me and shook himself like a Labrador puppy. The spell was broken. He returned to being my old familiar Grant. But I had seen behind the curtain, and not only would I not be able to unsee the man he'd become, I didn't want to.

CHAPTER 20

A Curveball

The water cooled and most of the bubbles fizzled into soapy islands around my knees. I pressed down on the fancy drain release, smiling at how different it was from the ragged rubber plug on a rusted chain in the house Mom and I shared before Barry.

When I stepped out of the tub, the white wooden hamper jammed against the door startled me. Without thinking, I must have moved it there. It had taken years for me to be secure enough with a lock that I didn't feel the need to barricade myself in my bathroom. A few days in my mother's house and my neurotic habits had returned.

Only it hadn't been neurotic when Tommy Lee and his friends were hanging around.

I wrapped myself in a towel and shoved the obstacle to the side, leaving the door locked. With my hair pulled up and away from my freshly scrubbed face, I became the helpless teenager I once was. I yanked out the elastic band and shook my head. I could still see the shadow of that girl, but it was easy to banish her. I applied concealer, blush, and mascara, and my former self faded. I slipped into a pair of dressy jeans and a sweater that accentuated my curves without excess spillage, then walked to Mom's room.

Dressed in a lacy pink gown with a matching robe—her peignoir set, she would say, in a terrible French accent—she was half sitting up watching the home shopping channel with the sound off.

"You are beautiful." Someone, definitely not my stepdad, had applied her make-up in the tasteful, understated fashion she adopted since becoming Mrs. Barry Winters. Before her life as a wealthy almost-society matron, she favored a more dramatic style—winged eyeliner with blue shadow and bright red lipstick. Now her eyes were more natural and her blush more subtle. I wondered if, like me, she was disguising her former self. Or was it something else? No longer forced to deal with violent, unpredictable men, had she evolved into the person she was meant to be?

Then I remembered her terror as Francine stood over her. A shot of anger blasted through me and not just at the woman who had somehow threatened my mother. I was furious at the realization of how easy it was to revert to the person you insisted you had left behind.

"Sit," Mom said in a remarkably clear voice and patted the bed.

"Oh, my God. You're talking."

She nodded and struggled to respond. "A little." Not as clear now.

"That's amazing." I touched the lace on her shoulder. "You're amazing."

She shook her head.

"Yes, you are."

She shrugged and smiled. Fearful she would be able to tell I was different now that I had seen blood on my hands, I avoided direct eye contact. I blurted out the only information I knew would distract her.

"I've got a date tonight with Grant."

"I lllike him," she sputtered.

"Me, too, but I'm not sure how things will turn out. We have a lot of history. And I just broke up with Russ. The one who sent the flowers, so that's kind of complicated."

Now that she was regaining speech, I found myself less willing to share the details of my life with her. It wasn't that she had ever been judgmental. In fact, she had rarely been critical of my behavior since she married Barry. And not much before either. Absence of criticism, however, had never been the same as approval, and, in my mother's case, it seemed more a lack of interest.

But I had issues to discuss with her, and they were more important than my disastrous love life. I might not be able to confront her about that horrible night but hopefully pressing her about Francine's visit wouldn't be too stressful.

"I don't want to upset you, but I'm worried about, you know—the note."

She picked at a loose thread on her blanket.

"If you have any idea who sent it, please tell me."

Her eyes widened and, for a second, I was afraid she would cry. Despite her agitation, I didn't let it go.

"Could it be Francine then?"

She motioned for me to lean forward and grabbed hold of my arm. "Stay away from her."

Before I asked why I should avoid the Viking bitch, Carmela came in with a glass of iced tea and pastries. "Miss Liz, I should have brought more cookies."

"No, please," I laughed and patted my stomach. "I've done nothing but eat since I got here. Besides, I'm completely stuffed from the best chocolate pie in the world."

Blushing, she set the plate on the bedside table. "I am so glad you like it. You must eat more. Both you and Mrs. Winters are too skinny."

Carmela thought everyone was too thin, but I enjoyed the compliment. She helped Mom sit up, placed a breakfast tray across her lap, and wrapped my mother's fingers around the glass of orange juice before guiding it close enough for her to sip from the straw.

Mom's dependence on Carmela reminded me that despite her improved speech and comprehension, she had a long way to go. Although I never admitted it to myself, I hadn't planned on an extended stay. I used the possibility as an excuse to keep Russ at a distance, but I expected to check in to make sure she was okay, then go back to my California life.

Her unpredictable recovery made it more likely she might need me for much longer. Surprisingly, that didn't bother me. Without Russ and probably a job, I had no idea what would be waiting for me in LA.

And even if Mom hopped up and started dancing, there was the issue of the note and its implied threat.

Carmela settled on the chair, relaying a story about a disagreement between the neighbors, something about a barking dog jumping into their pool.

"But Buster is a good doggie. It does not hurt to have a watchdog nearby. And people around here hardly ever swim."

The argument concerned the exuberant black Lab and some noise ordinance. Our housekeeper never had much confidence in the elaborate alarm system Barry installed. It annoyed her to have some ghost voice telling her between beeps that she had left a door open. And she had no faith that the police would arrive within minutes as promised by the company. That was why—she explained to me when I found a baseball bat in the pantry—she kept her own brand of protection on site.

"I'm going to leave you ladies to solve the neighborhood crisis." I brushed a kiss across Mom's cheek. She waved her hand and smiled; Carmela nodded and continued her story.

My restless night left me sluggish, so I headed to the kitchen. Barry's voice echoed into the hallway from where he and April were at the table.

"Lizzie." He stood. "Come join us. You sit and let me get some caffeine for you."

"He can't be still." She grinned at her father as he sat a steaming cup in front of me.

We spent the next ten minutes or so celebrating Mom's continuing improvement. Then he announced he was going to pay her a quick visit before heading to the office.

"After seeing your reaction to the flowers, I'm guessing last night didn't go so well," April said as soon as he was out of earshot. "Did the text work?"

"It was perfect." There was no reason to tell her I was on my way home before I received her message. If Russ was sending flower threats, it might be a good idea to alert her that the situation had escalated.

"Things didn't go well at all." I gave her an abbreviated version of the disastrous evening, including the hummus explosion.

"Wish I'd been there," she sighed.

"I wish I hadn't. Not that it wasn't fun, but making an enemy of Russ was a stupid move." I told her about the note.

"Do you have it?"

"I think it's still in my pocket. Why?"

"Well, it might help if you decide to file a wrongful termination suit."

Impressed by my stepsister's cool response, I realized she had a point. California's laws offer more protection from vengeful employers than most states.

"Filing against Russ would be more damaging to my career than being fired by him."

"The mention of litigation would be enough with an ass like him. I bet he has a herd of angry ex-lovers, and some of them are bound to be ex-employees with grudges. Plus, going to court would give his wife plenty of ammunition against him."

"Wow. Remind me not to piss you off."

She shrugged. "It never hurts to have options. How did you get involved with that creep?" Then immediately held up her hand. "Stop. I didn't mean to say that. I've been in relationships that make yours seem like a fairytale. Possibly a Grimm one, but still."

I realized my stepsister and I had more in common than I imagined.

"On a brighter note, you and Grant got pretty friendly. Can I assume you're going to see him again?"

"Exactly when did you observe this so-called friendliness?"

"When you walked him to the car. I don't know why you're so determined not to like that man. I'd jump on him in a heartbeat if he wasn't so hung up on you."

I wanted to be annoyed with her, but the idea she thought Grant was hung up on me made it difficult to feel anything but warm.

"Do you really think he's hung up on me?" Damn. I'd turned into a love-struck middle school girl.

"Please. Daddy's seen more of him since you came home than he has in the last year. What gives with you guys?"

"It's a long story. Maybe I'll tell you when we have more time, but now I'm running late for my date."

"I knew it," she crowed. "Go get ready. I've got an appointment anyway, but some day you're going to tell me what's been keeping you two apart."

Other than the soft-soled shuffle of Mom's nurse's shoes on the hard wood floor, the house was quiet. April's question echoed in my mind. What was holding me back? I found out from Mom less than a year after I left that Grant and Whitney weren't a couple. I wasn't even sure they had ever really been together, but what else could have explained the way they acted when she returned that summer?

Then I lay on the bed, thinking about how things changed when the break ended. The two of them whispering as I walked from the room. Whitney spending more and more time away from the apartment and when she was home, talking for hours on the phone with a friend she never named. And Grant pretending he didn't notice anything different about her when I mentioned her strange behavior.

Whatever had been going on between them cast a pall over us whenever we were together and created a chill between me and Grant. But that night before my graduation, we fell into the comfortable cadence of those weeks without Whitney.

The three of us planned our own separate celebration—a quiet dinner at Grant's apartment—on the eve of our commencement.

Whitney and I had errands to run, so we drove separately. When I arrived, I knocked and entered. He was on the phone.

"It has to be tonight?" He waved and mouthed. "It's Whitney." He went to the bedroom and shut the door.

They'd been dismissing me since fall semester began. I tried to ignore it, not be hurt by the way they kept shutting me out. But that night it pissed me off—enough that I stood in the hallway outside his room, straining to listen to the one-sided conversation.

"Jeez, Whitney. I don't get it. Why can't you wait?" There was a long pause. "Okay. okay. I'll tell her."

The door opened, and I scurried to the kitchen, where I flung myself onto a chair and pretended to be absorbed in the newspaper.

"Whit's not going to make it." He avoided my eyes while removing two beers from the refrigerator. "Her econ group called an emergency meeting about a project they're working on."

One of the many things I liked about him was his total ineptitude at prevarication. As a well-practiced liar myself, I'm a competent judge of other people's aptitude for deception. And this particular attempt to mislead me was especially weak. No way would my roommate allow academics to interfere with fun. Calling him out on the lie, however, would just be plain mean. He'd struggle with manufactured details before breaking into a cold sweat. He might even admit the story was a fabrication, but he would never betray Whitney's trust. Unshakeable loyalty was another of his admirable qualities.

That day, I found the trait infuriating. The same fury I experienced when my mother chose one of her boyfriends over me. Sharing smiles over secrets she never disclosed. Telling me I was too young to understand when I demanded to know why she let Tommy Lee back into our lives no matter how he hurt and humiliated her.

At the table Grant poured beer into icy mugs, and I devolved into the sad, powerless girl I had tried to leave behind. The two people I loved in an uncomplicated, joyful way I'd never known before had betrayed me, but I didn't have to remain a victim.

They hurt me. I would crush them by using the only weapon that never failed.

I lured him onto the sofa under the pretense of watching *Star Wars*. About ten minutes into the movie, I leaned my head on his shoulder, letting my left breast touch his arm. His breath quickened as I moved closer. I rested my hand on his knee.

We sat motionless for a few seconds before I turned my face to his. He kept his eyes on the television screen as I traced the outline of his jaw with the tip of my finger, stopping at the smooth spot above his mouth.

A gentle warmth spread over me, gathering momentum as it traveled from the tips of my fingers to my chest. My breathing became shallow, and I struggled with an unexpected urgency. I wanted to distance myself, stay in control, but when he kissed me, the heat from his body rushed over me.

We made it from the sofa to the bed, leaving a trail of clothing along the way. My ability to apply an emotional filter deserted me and I felt it all—vibrating desire, desperate throbbing, and a rushing tide crashing over and through me.

The next morning, I awoke to the insistent patter of rain against the window. Alone with the sheets and blankets tangled around me, I panicked, unsure where I was. Then the events of the previous evening flooded over me. I should have been ashamed or at least embarrassed, but I wasn't. I was exactly where I should be. My only regret was that Grant was no longer beside me.

I unraveled the bedclothes, stood and wrapped a sheet around me before starting for the bathroom. On the way, I heard him talking in the living room. I couldn't make out what he was saying, but something about his tone drew me to the hallway.

"Are you kidding me, Whitney?"

Surprised at the level of irritation in his voice, I took a few steps closer.

"Pregnant? Seriously?"

My heart pounded.

"Okay, okay." He sounded more resigned than annoyed. And frighteningly calm.

"No!" Not so calm now. "Don't come here." He paused. "I'm tied up right, but I'll meet you as soon as I can."

I didn't wait to hear where they were meeting, but I was sure it wouldn't be at our apartment. I backed my way into the bedroom, eased the door shut, and leaned against it. How could I have been so stupid? I let myself believe Grant and I had something, that even if he and Whitney had been more than friends, it must have been over. Because he wasn't the kind of person who would cheat on someone he cared about. But I'd been played, and it was exactly what I deserved.

CHAPTER 21

Listen to Your Heart

My memory of the rest of the morning is hazy. Gathering my clothes from the floor, dressing in the bathroom, making excuses for why I had to leave right away.

When I got to my apartment, Whitney wasn't there. Most of my things were ready for shipping to California where I would start my internship the next week. The graduation didn't begin until 5:00, leaving me time to finish packing before meeting Mom and Barry. They would be thrilled when I told them I would go home with them immediately after the ceremony instead of waiting a few days as I'd planned before discovering my best friends would soon become parents.

• • •

The doorbell woke me at exactly 7:00. I rolled from the bed and stumbled to the door, smoothing my hair on the way. From below, I heard Mom's attendant talking with Grant and hesitated. It wasn't too late to tell him I couldn't go out with him. I could use my mother as an excuse or blame it on a headache.

Truthfully, facing my past with him did make me queasy. I never said anything to either about the pregnancy. And since there had been no baby, I assumed Whitney decided against motherhood. Had she and Grant agonized over the decision not to keep their child, or had it been the only logical choice for them? Would it have made a difference if I'd stayed around to support them?

Tonight, I wouldn't take the easy way out.

I hesitated at the last step, suddenly shy at the sight of him. He'd brushed his curly hair back from his face, but a few tendrils escaped, giving him the same boyish look I remembered from the night we spent together. I closed my eyes for a second, and when I opened them, that boy had disappeared, leaving behind a very grown-up version of him. I struggled with an appropriate greeting.

"Hey," was all I managed to come up with.

The heavy sweet smell of hyacinth in the cool air washed over me as we passed by colorful flowerpots positioned along the walkway. When we reached the car, he opened my door for me, and I experienced a sensation of déjà vu. It had been some time since a man or boy exhibited that simple gesture of chivalry. Grant, however, had always been a door-opener.

"Sounds like your mother's doing better. Pretty soon she'll be ripping through packages from the home shopping network."

I smiled at his reference to her proclivity for responding to random special offers on TV. But my smile faded at the memory of the last dreadful fight she and Tommy Lee had over what he called her reckless spending. He'd smashed her commemorative *Gone with the Wind* plate against the kitchen cabinet, even though she bought it with her own money.

I stared out the window, wondering if I would ever find a way to banish the bitter memories that wormed into whatever sweetness I encountered.

Grant remained quiet until we were out of Mom's subdivision, then said, "Hope you still like seafood."

"Love it, except for—"

"Mussels," he finished for me. "You hate mussels."

There was something strangely intimate about the way he recalled that detail about me. It made me want to reach across the armrest to touch him. But I didn't.

"They're so gross, chewy and slimy at the same time."

"Well, they don't serve them where we're going."

In less than ten minutes we pulled into the parking lot of The Big Ketch, a laid-back seafood joint in downtown Roswell. Described as "beachy-chic," the building looked like a sprawling ranch-style home with a front patio.

We passed some little boys tossing bean bags in the general direction of a wooden corn hole slot. One overshot the mark, and his bag careened off the head of a toddler wandering on the lawn. The glancing blow knocked the kid off his feet. Luckily, he landed on his well-padded bottom. His mother ran to scoop him up as the mother of the thrower yelled for him to return to the table. Two men, presumably the fathers of the children involved, began shouting at each other.

"I told you it wasn't fancy. But the entertainment's free."

I would have stayed to watch the outcome of the fracas, but he ushered me inside to a room that reminded me of seafood places on the Gulf where Grant, Whitney, and I spent spring breaks.

Ocean kitsch décor lined the walls leading to an open dining area on one side and a bar with cozier seating on the other. The hostess greeted him by name and steered us to a table farthest from the young guitarist playing Jimmy Buffet.

"They make a mean margarita." The music was just loud enough that he had to scoot his chair closer for me to hear him. I inhaled a hint of spice and musk from the aftershave he'd worn since we met— the same warm scent that lingered on his pillowcase and sheets.

"Why not?" I responded although I could think of several reasons drinking tequila with this man might not be such a good idea.

He requested a special brand, assuring me it would be nothing like the stuff we had in college. I didn't bother telling him I had no recollection of the quality or even the taste of the fiery liquid we gulped down in shot glasses to officially end the evening. The drinks arrived at the same time the musician began his rendition of "Margaritaville," and we laughed at the timing. I sipped mine carefully, enjoying the initial iciness followed by the gentle burn as it traveled down my throat.

With his chair beside me, I had to turn slightly to look directly at him. I noticed the shadow cast by his long, dark lashes and wondered how something could be so different and familiar at the same time.

We took the waitress's suggestion and started with an order of boiled shrimp. Tables around us filled with people laughing and talking over the poor guy singing his heart out about broken shoes and hearts. It seemed as if we were the only ones who noticed when he announced his break.

"I forgot how noisy it gets in here." Louder than necessary because of the absence of music, his voice startled me.

"I think it's great." Sitting near enough to feel the heat from his body in the middle of all sorts of couples in various stages of their own relationships. The man with the receding hairline holding hands with his silver-haired companion. The barely twenty-one-duo, sporting what appeared to be matching tattoos. Even the couple with a toddler fighting to escape his highchair shared an intimacy that seemed stronger because of—not despite—the fact they sat in a crowded room.

I had an overwhelming need to take his hand. Before I acted on the impulse, the waitress arrived. I never considered peeling cold crustacean in the least bit sexy, but watching Grant's long slender fingers as they removed shells and dipped shrimp in hot sauce caused me to rethink my position.

"What are you waiting for?"

I took one from the bowl and followed his lead. "Oh my, God. These are incredible."

While working on the appetizer, we discussed entrees. I went with crab cakes, and he selected the lobster roll.

"Another round?" The waitress pointed to our empty glasses.

Already lightly buzzed, I should have passed but didn't. A rowdy group at the foot of the bandstand cleared out, drastically reducing the noise level. And for the first time that evening, I got that awkward first-date vibe—the one where you're driven to fill the conversational void with nighttime talk-show questions. *Do you find joy in your work as a mortician?* Or *are you a dog or cat person?* Or Mom's favorite: *What's your sign?*

I already had the answer to that astrological question. Grant was an Aquarius, a water creature the same as me. Only his designated him as generous to a fault and happiest when helping others. According to the stars, we're not in the least bit compatible. While Aquarians are open and straight forward, crabby Cancers move sideways, skirting obstacles and slowing their own progress.

I needn't have worried about small talk. In accordance with the characteristics of his sign, he immediately got to the point.

"So, Liz, I've never understood what happened back in school. You know, after," he lowered his voice. "After that night. Did I do something? Things were good between us, right? No. More than good, great."

I turned away from him, but he repositioned my chair, making it impossible to avoid his gaze. He brushed his fingers across my cheek before pleading, "Please, Liz. I think you owe us both an explanation."

Us both? I bristled inside. *Why would I owe him and Whitney anything?* Then I realized he didn't mean Whitney. He meant me. I never faced up to my own reasons for running away. Why I'd been so desperate to take back the best night of my life.

"You know why," I insisted.

"The only thing I'm certain about is that I've wanted to be with you since that day I saw you scarfing down chicken nuggets. And, that summer, you wanted to be with me."

Wanted to be with me since the day we'd met?

"How could you have wanted to be with me when you were in love with Whitney?"

"Whitney?"

Our waitress and another server arrived and passed out steaming plates of seafood, hush puppies, and cheese grits. When asked if we had everything we needed. I lied and told her we did.

After they left, I began cutting my crab cakes into bite-size pieces, keeping my eyes fixed on the plate.

"Why would you think I loved Whitney as more than a friend?"

I swirled my fork through my grits. He put his hand over mine and gently pried the utensil from my grasp.

"Please, Liz. Answer me."

"Because that's the only thing that made sense. You and Whitney. The two of you belonged together. You came from normal families that never had to worry about paying the light bill or being good enough. You joined country clubs. And you knew stuff—like which fork to use and where Nantucket is." *And you were going to have a baby.*

But too many years had passed to say that. I took a long sip of margarita, set down the glass, and pushed the lime around with my straw.

"Normal families? Are you kidding? Whitney's parents couldn't—can't—stand each other. My mother means well, but if it's not bridge or tennis, she's clueless. And my dad hasn't been completely sober since I don't know when. And nobody gives a damn where Nantucket is."

"Come on, Grant." I cleared my throat to keep my voice from breaking. "I saw how you looked at her on the dance floor that night. The two of you were meant to be together."

"On the dance floor?"

"At the Kappa house, the night we met. I came to take her home, and you guys were all over each other."

"That's because she was too drunk to stand up. I wanted to be with you. But you were busy getting swept off your feet by Chad. And after him, you started dating that football player. And after that—"

"Okay, okay."

"And then, we had our last summer together. You weren't with anyone, and Whitney was out of the way." He took my hand. "And then she came back, and you got distant again until that night before graduation. You can't tell me that meant nothing to you."

I closed my eyes and traveled back to the evening we sat in his kitchen after Whitney stood us up. Furious with them for keeping secrets, I wanted to get even for all the times they reminded me I'd never fit in their world.

What had begun as a petty attempt at revenge ended with the knowledge Grant meant more to me than I realized. I had fallen in love with him.

I blushed at the memory and sat quietly, realizing once again I had reached a crossroads in my life. Honesty was always an option, but it had rarely been my first choice. And I wasn't even sure what the truth looked like. When I initiated sex, I had no specific plan. I acted on a childish impulse. But what should have been an angry coupling softened into something entirely different. Unlike my previous conquests, Grant had been my best friend. I respected him. And he understood me in ways no one had. So, no, I couldn't tell him it was nothing. But after overhearing his conversation with Whitney the following morning, I had known it was a mistake.

"Of course, it meant something. But I thought you guys had your own thing, and I came between you."

And there was still the question of the pregnancy. I didn't want to bring up such a sensitive topic. I needed to talk about how they had acted since the beginning of fall semester.

"And if you weren't together, what was all the whispering when I left the room and phone calls late at night? And what about that time I found her crying on your shoulder right before Thanksgiving break? Something had to be going on."

"There was, but you have to trust me. It was all Whitney, and I promised not to say anything to anyone."

Was it possible Grant hadn't been the baby's father? I searched my mind for an alternate candidate for the role of baby-daddy and came up with nothing. "Surely, the statute of limitations on keeping a secret has run out."

"Just call her. It will mean a lot to her." Once again, his loyalty to Whitney spoiled what we might have.

"So, the two of you keep in touch?"

"Every now and then. The subject of how much we miss you always comes up." He reached across the table and took my hand. "Promise me you'll talk to her, okay?"

I remembered the pink sticky note with her number on it and agreed to call her the next day. We tried to revive the earlier easiness of being together. But the food was cold and the drinks, watery. He looked almost relieved when I suggested boxing up left-overs and calling it a night.

Waiting for the valet to bring the car, I noticed the lively children on the front patio had been replaced by tables of young couples drinking beer and laughing. Something about the easy way they interacted with one another gave me that lonely-in-a-crowd feeling. I took a step closer to Grant, once again fighting the urge to take his hand.

A less than comfortable silence hung thick in the air as we drove. As soon as we pulled into the driveway, I grabbed my doggy box, opened my own door, and hopped from the car. I hoped to avoid any awkward good night kiss scenario. But he overtook me and accompanied me to the top of the steps.

"Well, this evening didn't turn out exactly the way I planned." He stepped in front of me, slipped his arm to my waist, and pulled me close.

I tilted my head, and he held my chin, then kissed me softly. His lips became more demanding. I dropped my leftovers and pressed my body against his. We stood together, locked in an increasingly desperate embrace until, breathless, I had to pull away.

"I should go in." I fumbled in my purse for the keys.

"Right. I'll call you tomorrow. You almost lost your crab cakes." He picked up the box and added, "Don't forget about talking to Whitney."

Inside, I closed the door and leaned against it. The realization of how I'd gotten it so terribly wrong brought with it a dizzying uneasiness. Even if Grant and I didn't qualify as cheaters, I deserted my best friend at the worst possible time. I would follow his advice and talk to my former roommate.

I took a few steps toward the kitchen when I heard a soft knocking. Half hoping he'd returned to continue what we'd started under the front porch lights, I threw open the door.

But it wasn't Grant. It was Russ, and it wasn't passion in his eyes. It was fury.

CHAPTER 22

Goodbye to What You Don't Need

"Aren't you going to ask me in?" He pushed me aside and strode over the threshold.

I'd seen my boss angry before—at co-workers, competitors, something his wife had done—but this Russ was different.

"Let's please do this another time? It's late, and I'm tired."

"I bet you are from all your extra-curricular activities. Exactly when would be a good time? What about in a high-end restaurant where everyone watches you humiliate me? Wait, we already did that."

He grabbed my arm and yanked me toward the living room. I considered calling out for Barry but bringing him into such a volatile situation would only escalate it. Plus, Russ outweighed my stepfather by at least fifty pounds. I allowed myself to be led to my mother's Bergere chair where he commanded me to sit. I obeyed, and he settled onto the matching ottoman, moving it as close to me as possible.

"When you left me sitting there with everyone staring, I was devastated. The woman I loved would never treat me like that. After all I'd done. Flying to this god-forsaken town to be with you when you needed me the most. Making you my queen. Giving you a chance to make it in the most important advertising market in the country."

He placed his hand on my thigh, then paused to let the magnitude of his devotion sink in. Most of what he was saying was typical Russ-style bullshit—exaggeration intended to induce guilt.

"Later, I decided your bad behavior was tied to your mother's stroke and being stuck in this nothing little town. And I forgave you."

Another break in the narrative—this one most likely for dramatic effect.

"Imagine my surprise when I discovered it wasn't some sense of daughterly devotion causing you to lash out. Oh, no." He squeezed my knee hard.

"You're hurting me." I tried to pull loose, but he gripped harder.

"*I'm* hurting *you*? That's really something, coming from a little slut like you."

Maybe it was the increased pressure or the insult or the combination that unleased an ugliness in me. I channeled the tiny but powerful instructor from the self-defense course I took after moving to the coast and thrust the heel of my hand directly into the end of his nose. I repeated the motion two additional times. He howled, and I bolted.

He lurched from the ottoman and followed me into the foyer, blood streaming from between his fingers. "I think you broke it," he whimpered.

"Oh, for God's sake." I retrieved my purse from the table by the door and dug out a sizeable wad of tissues. "Don't be such a baby." I kept a healthy distance from him.

"Goddamn it, Liz," he sputtered as the bleeding continued to flow.

"I seriously doubt it's broken, but you know where to go if it needs fixing." Russ pretended he'd been born with that perfect Romanesque nose, but I'd seen pictures of him in high school, and he had quite the schnoz. His wife wasn't the only one familiar with the power of plastics.

"I can't believe you'd act this way. All I ever wanted was to make you happy."

"Surely, you can see we were a mistake from the beginning."

"It was a mistake all right, but it's all yours. You're finished in LA. When I'm done, everyone will know what a cheating, lying bitch you are."

Driven by a bolt of white-hot rage. I took a step toward him. "I wouldn't do that if I were you. Not if you don't want a wrongful termination suit coupled with sexual harassment. Head to LA and keep your mouth shut. Say I've taken an extended leave of absence. And when I'm ready, I will have whatever job I want."

"You're going to sue me?" He snorted, sending little red flecks flying. "Are you kidding? I'll have you arrested for assault."

"Go ahead. I'd love to see how that plays out with your wife."

"Everything okay down there?" Barry called out.

"Everything's fine," I replied. "Russ was just saying goodbye." I held the door open for him. "Isn't that right, Russ?" I said loud enough for Barry to hear, then lowered my voice. "If my stepfather sees you like this, he will call the police. And I doubt if they'll believe you when you tell them how a little bitch like me beat you to a bloody pulp.

"This isn't the end of it."

I slammed the door in his face and turned off the light. From the window, I watched as he stumbled down the drive. His car must have been parked on the street, too far away and too dark for me to determine if it was the same sedan I'd seen earlier.

After activating the alarm, I noticed my left-over box next to my purse. When I picked up the grease-stained cardboard container, my stomach growled. I carried the crab cakes to the kitchen and warmed them in the microwave.

I took a beer from the refrigerator and drank half of it while watching my seafood spin around and round. When I closed my eyes, I spun with it. I opened them and caught my reflection in the window. How had the girl in the glass remained the same when my world had flipped. Not only was my view of the past drastically skewed, I had derailed my present and future.

I sat at the table, ate crabmeat, then washed it down with beer and cleaned up my mess. Upstairs, except for the nightlight outside Mom's door, darkness greeted me.

Instead of being sleepy from all the alcohol, I was buzzed and logged in to read my email. I responded to a few questions from the man editing video footage, then opened one from Charles with the subject line *Shake it off.*

Sending a little distraction your way.

When I clicked on the link in the text, a lively cockatiel ruffled his feathers and beak-synced to a popular Taylor Swift song.

Still giggling over the bird "shaking it," I realized it was only a few minutes past eight in California. I grabbed my phone and called Charles to express my appreciation for what had been a very welcome distraction. Even more so was the sound of his voice.

"Truman and I were just talking about you." In the background, the Frenchie whined.

"Saying good things, I hope."

"Well, he's a bit dismayed you haven't been around to scratch his belly, but I assured him you'd be returning to sunny California as soon as your mother was back in fighting shape." He cleared his throat before asking, "Please tell me she's doing better."

I filled him in on her progress. When we exhausted the topic, he asked me about Russ. I lingered over the details of our fateful dinner, painting a vivid picture of how he looked wearing blackeyed-pea hummus. After giving Charles a few minutes to savor that moment, I described our latest encounter. When I got to the part about bloodying his nose, I had to stop to give him time to regain his composure.

"Oh, my dear God," he gasped between gales of laughter. "You have brightened an old man's day."

"What old man?" I countered.

"Again, brightening my day. But what about your other problem—the note?"

"I'm ninety-nine percent sure it's Francine." I explained her connection to Glen and his relationship with Tommy Lee.

"So, you don't think it was him? Tommy Lee, I mean."

"No. You were right. He's not in the picture."

I wanted to give him the whole story but couldn't. It might feel good to unburden myself to an impartial friend, but it wouldn't be fair to involve him in my criminal past. Plus, nothing brings the mood down faster than a murder confession.

He knew enough about the Grant and Whitney saga to be thrilled about my date, so I provided an abbreviated version of our evening.

"My goodness, girl. You lead such an exciting life."

"Not so much exciting as exhausting. Now tell me all about you and Truman. Anything new in the love department? Any hot poodles for our handsome boy?"

"I'm afraid neither of us has been very lucky. At least, my little neutered buddy has an excuse."

"Don't worry. You're too good a catch to sit on the shelf too long."

He gave me a quick inventory of the mail I'd received and promised to send a package with anything that looked official or pressing.

After a few minutes discussing the sorry state of politics in the country, he switched topics.

"I'm not even going to ask when you might be coming home, but we sure do miss you."

"I miss you guys, too. And I should know something more definite in a week or so."

"Lizzie, it's okay if you decide you're already there. Home, I mean."

The sound of his voice made me nostalgic for my life in LA, but I couldn't deny it felt good to be among people who had known and cared about me long before I moved.

I switched on the TV and flipped through the channels in search of mindless distraction. I passed on the local news and a rerun of a 1970s sit-com, then landed on an old gangster movie. It was the iconic scene at the breakfast table where the mobster smashes a grapefruit in his girlfriend's face, then leaves her alone and crying.

I shut my eyes, and it wasn't the humiliated actress I saw. Not my mother either. It was me.

In my blind determination not to let myself get pulled into a real relationship, I went from one good-time guy to another. I assumed Russ was as shallow and easily manipulated as he seemed. And to a point, he was. But I underestimated how dangerous he could be when his ego was at stake. And I ended up with grapefruit on my face.

But worse than the humiliation of listening to him berate, condemn, and threaten me was the acknowledgement I had done the one thing I wanted to avoid at all costs. I had become my mother.

CHAPTER 23

Fear of the Unknown

After spending most of the night tossing and turning, I fell into a thick, heavy sleep before dawn. My phantom truck barreled in and out of my disjointed dreams with different people behind the wheel—me, Mom, April, Barry, even Francine. In the last configuration, Tommy Lee grinned at me from the driver's seat. When he morphed into a snarling Russ, blood streaming from his nose, I sat straight up in bed.

The bedside clock read 6:43, earlier than I needed to rise, but no way would I risk dropping back into my horrific nightmare. I crawled out from under my tangled covers and headed to the shower.

I threw on light-weight sweatpants and a t-shirt, then opened my laptop and responded to several client emails, operating on the assumption I still had a job. Skimming through messages that could wait until later, I noticed one from Andrea.

Got a strange email from Russ yesterday. Something about putting feelers out for a production person. I'm guessing things aren't going so well between the two of you. Whatever it is, he'll get over it. Besides, I have no intention of breaking in someone new. Take care of your Mom and yourself.

When I went to check on her, the bedroom door was ajar, and Barry was speaking in what, for him, passed as a whisper.

"Don't worry, honey. We can always count on Sergio."

Barry's words set off a chain reaction in my brain. Flashes of my mother dashing around the truck. Or was I the one frantically racing to some unknown destination? Then a car beside the vehicle with a tall, slender man rushing to Mom's side. The memory became distorted, sometimes playing in slow motion. Other times fast forwarding too quickly to make out the images. The only part of the drama that remained crystal clear was my stepfather's utterance: *Sergio will take care of it.*

I entered without knocking, hoping to pick up something from their body language. He sat on the edge of the bed, cradling her in his arms.

"Is everything okay?"

He stiffened but continued to hold her until she patted his shoulder. He eased her onto the mound of pillows.

"Fine." She spoke much more clearer than the previous day. "Friends are coming…" She trailed off.

"Friends may stop by for a visit." Barry finished for her. "Shouldn't have said anything, but your mom hates surprises."

"I remember."

My mother and I shared a distaste for the unexpected, even when it was a happy distraction. I assumed she didn't care for them because they rarely turned out well for her. The men in her life thought tickets to the fights were enough to make a girl's heart race. My preference for the expected—or as Russ put it, my "total lake of spontaneity"—came as a direct result of being raised by a woman who changed her moods as frequently as her shoes.

"So, who are you expecting?" I asked, looking at him.

"Some people from work."

"Is Sergio one of them?"

He gave me a blank look. Mom stepped in. "No. Too busy." Even with her difficulty speaking, she was the better liar.

"Too bad. I always liked him. I ought to stop by his office to say hello."

She patted my arm, then looked at Barry. "Gggood news." It hurt me to see how hard it was for her to piece thoughts and words together.

"Good news?" He seemed stressed, probably from the strain of keeping up with my mother's lightning-fast deception.

She pointed behind me, and he smacked himself on the forehead. "How could I forget? This isn't just any old wheelchair. It's an Ezy Lite Cruiser Deluxe Slim." He unfolded the chair. "Check out the joystick. Five positions, but the manual says you need a light touch or you'll shoot out like a rocket. I told her she can't drive this baby the same way as she does the Mercedes." He gave her a stern look, then grinned at me.

On a normal day, it was difficult for me to muster a smile at his reference to Mom's lead foot, a running joke at our house. She had at least four speeding tickets in recent years, and that wasn't counting those she talked herself out of. To me there was nothing funny about the idea she might end up dead on the side of the road. The image of her trapped in the chair was more frightening.

"Rudolph says she'll start walking on her own any day now. In the meantime, she should get out of bed more. We'll set it up in the sunroom."

It was hard to imagine Mom immobilized in her favorite room. She had enclosed part of the upper deck during her big remodeling project, glassing in the open space and transforming it into a light, airy room, one of the few places she could smoke in peace. Despite giving up nicotine, she still loved the spot.

"I was about to bring your mother some breakfast. Carmela's not coming in until later, but I make a mean omelet," Barry offered.

"Caffeine, please?" Last night's unwelcome epiphany about the way my interaction with Russ mirrored Mom's relationship with Tommy Lee had been more than emotionally unsettling. It left me with vague nausea and no appetite.

"Coffee and oatmeal on the way."

"So, ttell me…." She looked to her right, searching for the words. After a brief hesitation, she said, "date" and sighed deeply.

"It was good." *Until I got all weird when I found out Grant had been into me all along, and I'd gotten it all wrong when I thought he and my best friend were starting a family together.*

I had learned a long time ago how dangerous it could be sharing information with a mother who, when provoked, had no qualms using my words against me. When I offered no additional details, her smile faded, and I braced for one of her cross-examinations, the kind designed to trick me into revealing emotions I wanted to keep private.

She only said, "Happy for you."

I felt a familiar pang of regret at not being able to trust her with my secrets. Now I recognized how much I had underestimated the woman. Yes, she betrayed little confidences by throwing them back at me when it suited her.

Like when I shared my devastation with her over not making the dance team my freshman year, and she brought it up at dinner in front of her current love interest when they'd been discussing their plans to go out dancing.

Or when, after I came to her in tears over the onset of my first period, she coquettishly announced to Tommy Lee at the breakfast table that he was living with two real women now.

But when the secret had the power to destroy us, the woman knew how to keep her mouth shut.

I was anxious to talk to her about my visit with Coral but didn't want to be interrupted by Barry. Besides, if I wanted to get any useful information out of Mom, I needed to catch her off guard. I noticed a magazine at the foot of her bed and picked it up.

"Let's see what's going on in the outside world." I thumbed through the ads and articles until I hit one of the more risqué selections. "Check this out. *What to Do When You're Bored in the Bedroom.*" I showed her the picture of a half-naked model lying beside her sleeping partner.

Mom rolled her eyes.

"How about 'Must-have Colors for the Summer'?"

She sighed and shook her head.

Barry came in with the breakfast tray before I got to the two-page spread of Madonna rocking it with a much younger man wearing a dazed expression.

In addition to our orders of coffee and toast, he included a plate of pastries alongside strawberries, blackberries, and blueberries.

"Can't have my girls skimping on the most important meal of the day." He set the plates on her tray and kissed her cheek. "I'll be back around lunchtime."

She held the spoon in an awkward grip to eat her oatmeal. I grabbed a cinnamon bun, and we sat in a silence that was companionable if not entirely comfortable. Nothing new, as there had always been a heaviness in the air between us.

"How'd you like the barbeque yesterday?" I resisted the urge to spit on my finger and wipe a glob of goo off her face.

"Better than this mush." She picked at the edge of her napkin, working the cloth until she could grip it with all her fingers. After missing her target, she swiped the clean side of her mouth before getting to the dirty cheek.

"I drove all the way to Acworth to get it." Her left eye twitched, but involuntary tics were par for the course in stroke recovery.

"I picked Big Mike's because I found out it was where Francine worked."

Her right arm jerked, slopping coffee onto the tray. I knew I was pushing hard—maybe too hard. But my fear of whoever had sent that note was greater than apprehension about slowing her progress.

She steadied herself and put the cup down. "Dddon't," she began. "Nnnot good."

Her speech regression frightened me, but I pressed on.

"It's okay. She doesn't work there anymore. She quit. Without," I paused, then finished with a flourish, "giving notice."

As distraught as she was over the mere mention of Francine, she still reacted with an audible gasp at my revelation the woman had walked out on her fellow wait staff.

"What a...a..."

"Bitch?" I offered, and she nodded. "That's pretty much what the gang at Big Mike's thinks, too. Not a surprise. What is weird, though, is the timing. She disappeared from her job about the same time as your fall."

She pushed the tray away and leaned back with her eyes closed.

I had become the interrogator. The role wasn't as satisfying as I expected.

"And you had the stroke the same day the Tommy Lee note came."

She winced.

"Please, Mom. Tell what's going on. Do you remember Glen Larson?"

Her eyelids fluttered, and she gripped the edge of the blanket.

"He was one of the guys who played poker at the house," I urged. I recapped my discovery about his conviction on drug charges and the mention of Tommy Lee in the article. She asked for water.

I guided the glass to her lips.

I repeated Coral's remark about Francine being married to a convict. Whether it was a result of the stroke or years of practice, her expression remained unreadable.

"Isn't it too much of a coincidence that Glen was a crook and your old friend was married to one? Do you remember if he and Francine ever dated? Was she part of the drug scheme? And now that Glen's out of prison, they've come back to ..."

To what? What could we possibly have that they would want? But I was thinking like that girl in the crappy little rental house. We weren't poor anymore.

"Money. Are they trying to extort cash from you?" But why would Mom give them money? Unless they found out what happened to Tommy Lee. But that wasn't possible. Not if Barry and Sergio had cleaned up our mess. The more I thought I knew, the less I understood.

"Not extort." She spoke slowly, hitting each syllable hard.

"But Francine is involved, isn't she?"

She twisted the end of her sheet with shaking hands. Her well-constructed mask of neutrality slipped, as lines on her forehead deepened. The only sound in the room was the whir of the overhead fan. I sensed that for the first time, my mother might be ready for honesty.

But the voice that penetrated the dense quiet wasn't hers. It belonged to April.

"What devious plan am I interrupting?"

CHAPTER 24

No Holding Back

Startled by my stepsister's question, I deflected. "I thought you were coming by this evening,"

"I am, but don't have to be in the office until later. So, what's going on in mother/daughter land?"

"Nothing important. Barry bought doughnuts."

"Yes!" She walked to the pastries and selected a cream-filled mini-doughnut. Popping it into her mouth, she chewed with her eyes closed before swallowing. "Best ever."

She took another, perched on the windowsill, and thumbed through a magazine. "What person in her right mind would wear that?" She held up a picture of a model in a striped jumpsuit. "She looks like an escapee from fashion prison."

Mom snickered, and I experienced a pang of jealousy. I was the one who cheered her up when her life derailed. Usually it was man trouble, but also work problems, overdue bills, an imagined slight from a friend. As a kid, I resented picking up the pieces and her spirits. Now that my stepsister had usurped the role of plucky sidekick, I missed it.

Rudolph ended my petty pity party by bursting through the half-open door to announce it was time for his girl to get those muscles working.

"We can take a hint, right Sis."

I promised to come back later, wondering if my promise sounded more like a threat.

"Nice of you to visit," I said as we went down the stairs.

"Will you please stop saying that?"

Shocked by her intensity, I followed her into the kitchen. She reached into the cabinet for a cup and began pouring from the pot. She ignored me when I held out mine for a refill. I waited until she sat on a stool by the counter before getting my own.

"I didn't mean to irritate you."

"I'm not irritated, damn it." She stirred the cream so violently I expected cracked crockery to start flying. "It's just...she's *your* mother and always has been. But I care about her, too." She dropped her head into her hands.

Holy shit. April was crying. I couldn't remember the last time I'd seen my stepsister with genuine tears streaming down her cheeks. I stood helplessly for a second before walking to put my arm around her.

"Of course she matters to you," I said, awkwardly patting her on the back. "And she loves you."

"Really?"

I stared into her wide blue eyes and was forced to acknowledge this might be the real April. Instead of the conniving creature I'd written her to be—a sneaky shapeshifter determined to one-up me and everyone around her—she'd been an insecure little girl, anchorless without a mother to help her define herself.

"Absolutely." I held her close. Not noticing when Carmela entered the room.

"Dios Mío!" she cried out. She encircled us in her arms and frantically rocked back and forth. Fearing she might overturn April's stool, I broke away first.

"No, Mela." I turned her face toward me. "It's not about Mom."

My stepsister joined me in reassuring our now sobbing housekeeper. "Ginny's fine. Liz and were—"

"Bonding, the way sisters do." I smiled at April, who wiped her eyes.

Only after repeated reassurances were we able to assuage Carmela. When she finally pulled herself together, she made us promise never to frighten her like that again.

"Yikes," April exclaimed. "I've got to get going or I'll be late." She gathered her purse and sweater, then turned to me. "Walk me to the door?"

She stopped on the porch and put her hand on my shoulder. "Daddy told me about that awful Francine person. He's worried she's bad news. I wish you'd let him and Sergio handle her, but I know how you get."

"How I get?" I bristled.

"No reason to go all pissy on me. It's a good thing how determined you can be. But please don't take off on your own. Let us help. Or if you decide to set off by yourself, at least tell me where you are. Okay?"

I considered denying my plans to keep looking for information on Francine. April's concern seemed as genuine as her distress about Mom. But I wouldn't allow my newly found affection for her to cloud my judgment.

It was after eight when I returned to my room. Since there was no *you're fired* email from Russ, I still had a job. Except the prospect of returning to it didn't thrill me.

After putting out a few fires, I continued researching Francine and Glen but not before giving into impulse and checking my daily horoscope. I rationalized the waste of time by telling myself a little glimpse of the future might be helpful in my search for clues about the waitress and her mystery-husband.

A curve ball is on the horizon. Don't let fear of the unknown hold you back. Take control.

A baseball analogy? Really? What a crock. And it wasn't so much about being afraid of the unknown that threatened to paralyze me. It was fear of the known.

Frustrated at how little control I had over the Francine and Glen situation, I replayed my conversation with Grant. Why was he so insistent I contact Whitney? Would she turn out to be the curve ball? What the hell was a curve ball anyway?

"Baseball is such a stupid game."

I saw the pink note with Whitney's number lying on the dresser. It was time to stop stalling and grab control of the only thing I could. I picked up the phone.

"Well, shit on a cracker if it's not Liz Tucker," Whitney exclaimed as soon as she heard my voice.

Whatever anxiety I had over contacting my old roommate dissolved into laughter at the familiar greeting.

"I wasn't sure you'd call."

Rather than confess I almost hadn't, I told her how much I appreciated her checking in on Mom.

"April says she's holding her own," Whitney said.

"She's doing better, speaking clearly, feeding herself. Her therapists expect her to get out of bed soon. I'm optimistic."

"You're hopeful? Then she should be up and running marathons in no time."

I smiled. Obviously, she hadn't forgotten that in college I wasn't exactly a ray of sunshine. Not even a *glass half-empty girl*, I was more a *what difference does it make, I'll probably knock it over anyway* type.

"Well, hopeful might be too strong, but she is better."

I listened for some flicker of anger or coldness in her voice—some emotional hold-over from the way I left things between us. But Whitney had never been the typical Southern girl, glossing over hostility with false cordiality. If she was mad at me, I would have known it.

"I can't imagine your mother not making a full recovery."

Whitney and Mom had met on several occasions and had hit it off, so much so I'd been a little annoyed at how easily they got along. I had recounted Mom's craziness enough for her to have a good idea how chaotic my early years were and expected her to share my anger and frustration. But I hadn't revealed the source of my bitterness—my mother's string of boyfriends in general and Tommy Lee in particular. There were some things too dangerous to tell anyone, not even your best friend.

"I hope you're right." Mom lying helpless attached to machines rubbed my nose in the inevitability of her mortality and lessened some of the resentment I carried. Most importantly, it made me realize I wasn't ready to let her go.

"Aren't I always?"

I certainly thought so during our college days, up until I overheard Grant reacting to the news of her pregnancy.

"If you're not too busy, maybe we could get together and catch up."

I had doubts about her agreeing to a face-to-face. For years, I carried the weight of what I considered my betrayal of Whitney. Casting myself in the role of vengeful seductress, I hadn't shifted any of the responsibility to Grant. After last night's conversation, I was confident that whatever had gone on between him and Whitney had been over when he and I got together and that he'd been as shocked as I was at the announcement of a baby onboard.

None of that mitigated my desertion of my best friend at what had to be one of the worst times in her life.

But she didn't hesitate. "I have a two o'clock appointment, but I'm completely free until then. If I come over, say, around ten, we can visit. I'd love to peek in on your mom and then take you to lunch."

I repeated the details, stalling for time to process the speed with which our reunion plans were proceeding. It was 8:30, which meant I had only an hour and a half to prepare for the meeting I never planned on having.

"Uh oh," she said. "When you start parroting back stuff to me, you're working on a way to get out of something."

I had forgotten how well she understood me. Even Russ hadn't picked up on my tell, and I was always trying to get out of something with him. But then he didn't have a clue when it came to my feelings for him or much of anything related to emotions.

"I was figuring how long it would take me to make myself presentable. Ten is perfect."

What should one wear to a luncheon with the friend you left in the lurch? Definitely not sweatpants. After rifling through the coordinated outfits in the closet, I selected a pair of navy pants and a pink-striped blouse.

I hadn't had a peaceful night's sleep since Mom's stroke, and it showed. I thought of Whitney with her flawless skin stretched over those high cheekbones and decided to up my makeup game. I used two coats of mascara, highlighter and blush, then finished with tinted lip gloss.

I stared at myself in the mirror and practiced what I hoped were natural-looking smiles. I smiled for real when it hit me I'd spent more time perfecting my look for Whitney than I had for Grant.

The opening notes to "Who Are You?" blasted from my cellphone. I rarely pick up calls from unknown sources but was afraid it might be a client calling from a number outside my contact list, so I answered.

Greeted by the faintly metallic click that usually signifies a switch to an automated message, I had my finger poised to disconnect when the sound of my own name stopped me.

"Liz." A deep, distorted growl erupted from the other end of the line. "Tell that bitch mother of yours she's running out of time. I want what's mine, and I want it now. Unless she wants the world to find out what happened to Tommy Lee, she better give it to me."

My hands shook as I eased myself onto the edge of the bed. Despite everything I knew to be true about his death, hearing his name spoken by this disembodied voice terrified me. And if the caller really was aware of Tommy Lee's fate, what did that mean for our family?

Then there was the issue of what that awful person said about wanting what was his. Money was the obvious answer, but as far as I remembered, my mother's boyfriend was always broke. It could be drugs. The cops caught Glen with cocaine. Was there more illegal contraband somewhere? If so, why did he assume my mother would have it?

I considered going to the police. But what would I say?

"Somebody is threatening us because they're sure we have something that belonged to Tommy Lee, but it can't be him because..."

"We got this note telling us they haven't forgotten something, but we have no idea what they mean because..."

I had to warn Barry danger was coming.

CHAPTER 25

Strategic Remembering

I left Barry three messages on his voicemail, each more detailed and more frantic. I avoided mentioning Tommy Lee's name but offered specifics regarding the caller's demands. After hanging up from the last one, my brain began to tingle. An elusive piece of information slinked through my mind. I had missed something important about the phone call.

I asked Carmela not to open the door for anyone but Whitney. I expected some level of resistance or at least persistent questioning, but she only looked at me and nodded her head. It struck me as strange how easily she accepted the warning.

Then I recalled she came from a country torn apart by violence from drug cartels and its own government. A place where extreme caution often made the difference between life and death. The agility with which she reverted to that state of vigilance reminded how hard leaving the past behind could be.

I locked the door and armed the alarm. At a little after nine, I took deep, cleansing yoga breaths to calm myself for the arrival of my former best friend. I tried to anticipate our initial contact. Would it be one of those awkward reunion events filled with quick hugs and judgment? Or would we return to the easiness of our past before I ran away?

The sound of the garage opening jerked me out of my reverie, and I rushed to the kitchen. Carmela beat me to the door where she greeted my stepfather and another man. Although he had a little less dark hair and a bit more girth, I recognized him as Sergio.

She wrapped her arms around her nephew "It's been too long since our last visit. Everyone, sit. I will fix something to eat."

Barry stopped her. "Thank you, Mela, but we're good. Please, Liz, can you join us?"

I realized he hadn't needed my warning to recognize the danger surrounding our family. I marveled at how he treated our situation as a get-together for a little chat instead of planning strategy against some unknown opposing force—unless that force wasn't unknown to Barry.

"So, Liz," he began. "Can you tell us more about the phone call?"

"The voice was all garbled, like when you use one of those distorter apps. The caller insisted we had something that belonged to him, and he wanted it back. He called Mom a bitch and said she was running out of time." My throat tightened. "And that he still remembered …" The name came out as a whisper: "Tommy Lee."

I kept my eyes fixed on Barry as I repeated the message, holding onto the edge of the table to stop my hands from shaking. Saying it out loud made it too real, but I had to focus on his reaction to the mention of the man who had terrorized my mother and me.

Barry gripped his mug hard enough to whiten his knuckles, the expression on his face unreadable. He turned to Sergio.

"Liz and I need to discuss a few things in private. You go on like we talked about earlier."

He slipped away with no goodbyes, and Barry led me to the den.

With each step, I became less certain about sharing my recovered memories. What if he hadn't been the one who helped Mom get rid of the body? What if landing on the windshield didn't kill Tommy Lee? The echo of that sickening thud after he disappeared from sight sounded in my ears, making it difficult to imagine he had survived.

Barry closed the door behind us and motioned for me to sit on the sofa. He sat across from me.

"I made some promises to your mom a long time ago. Promises about what I should never talk about."

"You don't have to worry. I remember what happened to him—to Tommy Lee." I paused and watched Barry's eyes widen. "At least what I did to him."

"What you did?"

I hoped he wouldn't make me recount the memory of ramming into Mom's boyfriend with his own truck. I might still be shaky about the events immediately after the collision, but I would never forget the sickening sensation of his body being crushed underneath the tires.

"I don't understand, honey."

"There's no reason to pretend anymore. I'm the one who killed him."

His mouth dropped open and his face paled to a light shade of gray. "You? Dear God, Liz. Never say that."

"But it's the truth, isn't it?" Was it possible I uncovered a false memory? Maybe I hadn't committed murder. Before I enjoyed even a few seconds of relief, it hit me. If I hadn't killed him, could he still be alive? I couldn't decide what would be worse.

"Nothing is as simple as it seems, especially not the truth." He stood and put his hand on my shoulder. "For now, I'm going to ask you to trust me. Serge and Luis will keep an eye on things until we figure out who that crazy caller is and what he really wants from your mom."

I considered revealing my discovery about Francine and Glen but hesitated. If I uncovered their involvement, surely Sergio had, too. Barry asked me to trust him, but he didn't trust me enough to share details about Tommy Lee's disappearance and its connection to the threats against Mom. So why should I spill my guts? I wanted nothing more than to turn everything over to somebody else and never deal with it again. Of course, I'd been doing that for over eleven years and how had that turned out for me?

Before I had a chance to reconsider filling Barry in, the doorbell rang, and we both jumped at the sound.

"Stay here," he commanded and walked out of the room.

The clock on the mantle read exactly ten. Whitney had always been punctual. I scurried to catch up with him.

He stepped up to the camera to verify Whitney's identity, then opened the door and moved to the side. The floor beneath me seemed to shift, the way it does when you walk onto shore after a day of sailing. If I believed in time travel, this was what it would feel like. Her hair was still dark, but instead of letting it cascade down her back, she wore it in a sleek bob that barely grazed her shoulders. Her cheekbones were as sharp and her lips as full. Other than a few faint lines at the corners of her wide-set hazel eyes, she was the same beautiful girl who swept into the dorm room and changed my life.

Rather than rushing toward me like the old Whitney would have done, she stopped just inside the foyer and stared. Fearful she regretted coming, I held my breath for a moment. Then she exclaimed, "Oh, my God. You're exactly the same."

"You stole my line."

Barry grinned at us. "You both are kids to me."

Dressed in a black pencil-skirt with a beige silk blouse, my friend was as lovely as she'd been in college but had a different aura. Still sleek and sophisticated, she seemed softer somehow.

"I'm so happy to see you, Mr. Winters." He ignored her extended arm and moved in for the hug.

"It's been too long. And please, it's Barry."

"It has been too long, *Barry*. I'd love to say hello to Mrs. Winters. If she's up to it, of course."

He shook his head slowly. "I'm afraid Ginny had a rough morning. She's sleeping, but I'll check on her later for you. For now, why don't you girls go to the living room?"

After he walked away, I led my friend to what Mom liked to call the parlor and ushered her to the sofa. Sudden shyness changed me into my twelve-year-old self.

Whitney sat and patted the spot next to her. "Sit with me and tell me how your mom's doing."

Sharing the details of my mother's recovery gave me the buffer I needed to ease back into the intimacy of our lost friendship. I had just completed the summary of Mom's accomplishments when Carmela bustled in pushing the fancy beverage cart usually reserved for bridge club.

Whitney jumped to her feet and called out, "Mela! Don't tell Mr. Winters, but I missed you most of all."

I had forgotten how much she enjoyed watching her kneading dough or chopping vegetables. I had experienced the bone-chilling cold of family dinner at her house and suspected our housekeeper's warm acceptance was the real reason my friend loved hanging out with her. Carmela held onto her for a few seconds, then began setting up coffee and pastries.

"If Miss Liz had told me sooner about your visit, I would have made empanadas." She shot me a disapproving glance before adding, "She did not tell me."

"It was last minute," Whitney explained. "I'll make sure you have plenty of notice next time."

Mela gave a dismissive *humph* before continuing to pour coffee. But when Whitney began asking questions about her family and her salsa dancing, she overcame her irritation. They both forgot about me completely, probably a good thing as I'd fixated on Whitney's comment about "next time." Was there the possibility we might pick up where we'd left off before I slept with Grant?

"Miss Liz," Carmela said, louder than normal.

"Sorry, I was daydreaming."

"Mela asked if we needed anything else," Whitney intervened. The way she rescued me from Professor Kowalski's interrogation. "I told her we're fine."

"Yes, this is perfect."

She smiled and excused herself, leaving us to catch up.

After a few seconds of silence, she cleared her throat. "I'm so glad you called. I planned to stop by to see your mom as soon as I heard about the stroke, but it's been so long since I'd seen any of you, I…" Her voice trailed off.

"I've wanted to talk to you so many times," I began. "But the way I left things, I had no idea how to begin."

She drew her eyebrows together and stared at me. "What do you mean?" She seemed genuinely confused. "What exactly did Grant tell you?"

"Nothing, and he still won't. But I overheard the call the morning of graduation."

"What call?"

"The one where you asked him to come over because you were so upset?"

"Wait a minute." Something akin to comprehension spread across her face, and I expected her puzzlement to turn to anger. Instead, she grinned. "You were with him?"

Not the question I wanted to answer so soon, but her happy reaction disarmed me. "Yes."

"I knew it!" Her grin widened as she pumped her fist. "He was practically walking on air when I saw him. I flat-out asked if he'd finally gotten you into his bed, but he never kisses and tells." Her expression dimmed. "I was bummed when you didn't tell me about it. I guess I understood, though. I hadn't done a lot of sharing myself."

Not shared? If sleeping with the same man wasn't sharing, what was?

"I can see why you were upset with me, but I could never understand what happened with you and Grant. He was devastated when you left. We both were."

"I'm so sorry. I just didn't know what else to do. But I should have never deserted you when you were, uh, you were in trouble." Tears welled at the thought of Whitney dealing with an unwanted pregnancy and Grant's surprising callousness.

She shook her head. "Hey, don't cry." She reached into her purse, took out a tissue, and handed it to me. "It wasn't that bad."

"Not bad?" I echoed, dabbing at my eyes. "How can you say that? I disappeared when you needed me the most."

"Well, I was pretty torn up. But I had Grant although he wasn't too sympathetic, considering the circumstances."

"Not sympathetic? How could he not be when you were pregnant with his baby?"

Whitney gasped and began choking. I patted her on the back and gave her my napkin. After several seconds of coughing and spewing coffee from her nostrils, she regained control.

"Pregnant? Where did you get the ..." She stopped to wipe her nose. "You overheard my conversation with Grant that morning and thought I was carrying his baby."

"I'm so sorry. I should have stayed. I would have supported whatever decision you made. But after what happened, I couldn't face you."

"Oh, my God." She tucked her hair behind her ears. "I wasn't pregnant. And if I had been, he wouldn't have been the father."

"But if you weren't..."

"It was Angela Kowolski who got knocked up."

As I repeated the name, recognition slowly began to dawn. "Are you talking about Professor call-me-Tony Kowolski?" I struggled to unravel the connection between Whitney's conversation with Grant and the professor's expectant wife. "Why would you be upset about—"

And then it all came rushing back. I dropped out of the honors program, but Whitney remained, keeping the same advisor all four years of school. Her sophomore year, she became his student assistant. I made it no secret I considered him a big phony and repeated the numerous rumors about his inappropriate contact with naïve female students. I also pontificated on many occasions about my contempt for extramarital affairs and those who allowed themselves to be degraded by cheating men. Cosmic irony.

"You and Tony?"

She nodded. "Grant swore he hadn't told you, so I assumed you figured it out on your own and were disgusted with me because I'd become a silly woman with no self-respect. The kind we both hated."

"I could never hate you." But it would have been easy to have silently judged her. I supposed I wasn't the only one to morph into something I never expected.

"Well, I detested myself. I was so fucking stupid. He completely suckered me into believing I was the most important thing in his life. In his eyes, I became more than a pretty girl from a good family. He praised my intelligence and my potential to be a great writer. He insisted he and his wife had gradually become more like roommates than lovers. I fell for all of it—his impending divorce and our upcoming wedding."

"Oh, Whitney." Russ came to mind, and the similarity of our situations made me squirm. Of course, I hadn't been some lovesick schoolgirl.

"What an idiot. The asshole didn't even have the nerve to tell me she was pregnant. He left the picture of the sonogram up on his office computer."

"I wish you'd told me."

"Me, too. Grant's a great guy, but he sucks as a confidante. He kept begging me to clue you in, but I hated to disappoint you."

"I wouldn't have been disappointed." And it was true. I learned early on that low expectations were the only safe ones. I would have been dangerously angry at Tony Kowolski but never at Whitney.

"Me and Grant hooking up? That's hilarious. I loved him like everyone else did. He was, still is, one of the nicest guys I know. But nice guys didn't do it for me. Besides, he only had eyes for you."

Regret threatened to choke me. For so long I'd punished myself for being the cause of a terrible rift between my two friends. I turned my back on a man who might have really loved me and wasted my time with men like Russ. Or maybe somewhere deep in my subconscious, near that dark place where I hid Tommy Lee, I feared what would happen if Grant discovered the real me.

"He still is crazy about you."

"Well, he showed some interest at dinner last night."

"You've already seen him?" She clapped her hands. "I knew it. I want details, and I want them now."

I gave her the abbreviated version of our date, omitting the part about me thinking he loved her. Before she demanded more information, someone tapped at the door.

"Sorry to interrupt you girls." Barry stepped into the room. "But I need to borrow Liz for a quick second."

Puzzled, I joined him in the hall.

"If you wouldn't mind, honey, could you and your friend have lunch here? Carmela's whipping up some chicken salad, and we've got so many casseroles we'll never eat them all."

Now that I had recovered from the initial shock from the phone call, I wondered if Barry's reaction had been extreme. I started to say we'd be perfectly fine venturing into downtown Roswell but saw no reason to cause him any more distress.

Whitney okayed the change of plans. "It will be easier to talk. And Carmela is the absolute best cook in the world." She drew one long leg underneath her. "Let's talk about your exciting LA life."

I confessed neither my life nor my job held much glamour or fulfillment. Until I said the words out loud, I hadn't realized how dissatisfied I'd become. I didn't mention Russ.

"Now your turn. You must have a pretty cushy position if you're able to work in lunch on the spur of the minute."

"I wouldn't call it cushy, but I do have a lot of independence. I started a non-profit that partners lower income girls with women in different careers. The idea is to help them see possibilities beyond their circumstances." She waved her fork in the air. "Well, don't I sound like a pompous ass? I just left a fund-raising meeting, and I'm still in that mode."

"You don't sound like a pompous ass at all." Honestly, she'd never sounded less ass-like. Her enthusiasm filled me with a strange longing. "Weren't you all set to go into the corporate world?" She and I had spent hours debating which career offered the most in prestige and profit.

"I was and I did. The summer after graduation, I stayed at the beach house. Then Daddy got me a job at one of his friend's real estate companies. I didn't suck at it. Actually made quite a bit of money. But I hated it. There was no time to, well…well to do more important things. With what I earned combined with what I inherited from Granny, I set up the foundation."

"Is that herbal Granny?"

"Yep, good old pot-smoking Granny. She kicked cancer and lived to be ninety-two. Said staying stoned kept her alive and kicking."

We were still laughing when Carmela announced lunch was ready. On the way to the kitchen, we passed the ornate geometric mirror Mom's decorator selected. It captured our smiling faces across multiple surfaces, and, in at least one of them, I saw the reflection of our eighteen-year-old selves.

CHAPTER 26

Conquering Fears

A light drizzle fell as we said our goodbyes.

"God, I've missed you. Please tell your mother I wish her well." She hugged me tight.

Her remark reminded me Mom had slept throughout our visit. Not a good omen for her recovery.

"I will definitely be back—soon if it's okay with you, that is."

"Absolutely."

She pulled me close once more before running to her car. The farther down the drive she went, the darker the sky became and the less hopeful I felt. As she disappeared around the corner, rain started coming down in torrents.

Reminiscing about happier times with Whitney energized me. I took comfort from being with someone who understood me. But so much of my past had to stay secret.

She probably guessed my lack of interest in permanent relationships had something to do with Mom's proclivity for romance with the wrong guys. I had no words to explain the helplessness of being with a mother who transformed herself into whatever her boyfriend wanted her to be. I never shared how devastating it was being the last one picked on a team of three. She strayed from the pattern when Tommy Lee broke my arm, but I didn't discuss that with anyone. If I opened up to Whitney about how disappointed I'd been to discover he hadn't died that day in our kitchen, I suspected she would have immediately started looking for another roommate.

Rumbling sounded in the distance, signaling an approaching storm. Restless and irritable, I had to get out of the house. The idea of allowing Barry to continue dictating plans for handling the situation became unbearable. He obviously wasn't being completely honest with me. If he refused to tell me the truth, and Mom wouldn't, it was up to me to sort it all out.

First on the list would be to identify the creepy caller.

The call! That's where the tickling sensation in my brain came from. How did he get my number? The only person with both it and a connection to Francine was Coral, the dark-haired waitress I gave my card. She seemed genuinely miffed at her colleague for quitting on such short notice, but relationships between waitresses can be complicated. If she suspected I was snooping around where I didn't belong, it wasn't much of a stretch to think she would have alerted her friend, who most likely would have relayed the information to her husband Glen.

I was caught in a grown-up game of gossip—the one we used to play in elementary school where you make up something to whisper to the person to your right and so on until it comes back to the originator of the chain. Only this version ended in the threat of violence.

From the foyer came muffled voices and the sound of Carmela's laughter. I slipped upstairs to my room and sat on the bed deciding how to reach Coral. Confronting her face to face would yield the best results, but that meant finding out her work schedule. And if she wasn't at the restaurant, I would have to get her address.

I searched rental homes in Acworth and jotted down the information for the house with the lowest monthly payment. Next, I looked up law firms in the Atlanta area and selected Dunn and Dunn. I took a breath and punched in the restaurant number.

Since he proved himself immune to my charm, I was relieved when he didn't answer.

"Big Mike's, Jeanine speakin'"

"Good afternoon, Jeanine." In an attempt to sound businesslike and anonymous, I made sure not to drop a single syllable. "My name is Sarah Baker, with Dunn and Dunn's estate division. I'm trying to get in touch with one of your employees, a Ms. Coral Wright. Can you help me?"

"You mean Coral Bailey?"

"Bailey?" I rustled a magazine, pretending to check my records. "I'm sorry. You're absolutely correct."

"She's not working today."

"I really don't like to bother her at home. But this is a time sensitive issue and, well, I hate to admit it." I lowered my voice. "But I screwed up. Her file got in the wrong stack, and I didn't realize no one notified her about the money."

"Money?"

"Oh, boy. I shouldn't have said anything about that. Please don't mention it to anyone else. I'll just stop by her place this afternoon. Let's see." I made more paper shuffling noises. "Here it is: 122 Valley View Drive. Thanks so much—"

"Wait a minute. Coral lives on Davis Road, not Valley View."

"Davis Road? Oh my God. I'm still looking at the wrong file. You may have saved my job. One more thing. Would you mind giving me her current number in case she's not home?"

Jeanine paused, and I feared I'd lost her, but Big Mike yelled something in the background, and she shouted back, "Hold your horses." Then she rattled off some digits and told me she had to go.

I was still thanking her when she hung up.

Pleased with my clever deception, I returned to Google, where I found Coral Bailey's exact address and put the location in my phone. It was on the far side of the city, near Lake Acworth, but if I left soon, I could be there a little after two.

It was too quiet in the upstairs hallway. I should have pressed Barry about what he meant about Mom's bad morning. Had she become dangerously stressed as a reaction to me badgering her for details about our past? Or was she simply exhausted from carrying so many heavy secrets?

Regardless, no way would I leave without looking in on her. I didn't, however, plan to include Barry. He wouldn't want me to go alone and might insist I take Luis or Sergio with me. Someone tagging along could be messy. So, I tread lightly to her room and eased in, where she lay with her eyes closed. Her breathing was slow, but steady. Rather than risk waking her, I tiptoed to my room, grabbed my raincoat, and taped a note, explaining I was running errands, to her door.

I avoided the kitchen, going out the front and around to the outside garage. Luckily, our bodyguards had parked off to the side which meant I could get into Mom's car with the remote, giving me time to drive away before they reacted.

I had an attack of guilt, backing onto the street and even more so ignoring my stepfather's call as I drove through the increasingly heavy downpour toward the expressway. Once I reached the interstate, I shed most of my misgivings about my mission and began planning what to say to Coral.

All I had to do was convince her to tell me how to get in touch with Francine, but it wouldn't hurt to try to find out if she knew anything about Glen. I decided to be as direct and truthful as possible, telling her that contact with the couple upset my mother, and I wanted to speak with them personally to settle their dispute. It occurred to me I might not be lucky enough to catch her at home, but I could use the same pitch over the phone, hoping that would work as well as a face-to-face encounter.

The rain brought a thick fog with it. I drove through deep water, momentarily unable to see much of anything. As it cleared, Barry's statement about the truth never being as simple as we expected came to mind, and I wondered if he'd been right. Or if he was purposely misleading me with another lie. After all, what could be simpler than the fact I'd run over a man with his own truck?

An eighteen-wheeler in front of me slammed on its brakes, and I pumped mine cautiously, slowing to a crawl. A muffled boom resonated overhead, and a flash of lightning crackled on the horizon. In the echo of the thunder, I recalled another sound—the soft thud as I finally got it right and put Tommy Lee's rusted truck into reverse.

Something more troubling rippled through the undercurrents of my mind. Before I brought it to the surface, the map lady warned my exit was fast approaching, and I shifted all my concentration to the labyrinth-like directions to Coral's address.

By the time I reached Davis Road, the rain eased into a respectable shower. The lights inside the small house indicated someone was there. I slowed down, intending to park in front of the squat ranch-style home. When I saw there were two cars in the driveway, I decided to circle the block. As I passed, I took in a beat-up red compact of an unknown make and suspected it belonged to Coral. The second car was a dark sedan, similar to the one at my mailbox. But hadn't that been Russ stalking me?

"Get a grip, Liz." I said the words out loud to myself. "How many dark sedans do you think there are?"

Still, if Coral had company, it would be difficult to talk to her. So, I parked several houses down. While I waited, I concocted different scenarios explaining the presence of the second car. It belonged to an FBI agent she worked with to break up a gambling ring Big Mike ran from the restaurant. I was making up a backstory with an illicit affair between Coral and a local judge when a tall woman bolted from the house, her stringy blonde hair flying behind her.

Even through the raindrops on my windshield, there was no doubt it was Francine. I hit the start button and cracked my window a few inches, simultaneously slumping down in the seat. I doubted she would have known who I was from this distance but didn't want to chance it.

She leaped into the sedan and raced the engine before screeching toward the road. Coral stepped onto the porch and shouted in

Francine's direction, then disappeared into the house. Without thinking, I put the Mercedes in gear and followed.

Everything about tailing cars, I learned from on-screen detectives. I knew not to get too close, preferably keeping at least one other car between you and the person you're following. Since we were the only ones on the road, this wasn't an option, but I kept a sensible distance between us.

Other standard procedure involved wearing sunglasses and a ball cap, but the rain was too heavy for the first, and I didn't own the second.

From the way Francine drove, she wouldn't have noticed if I'd been dangling from her bumper. Whatever she learned at Coral's sent her hurtling toward her target, too fast to look in her rearview mirror. A woman with her attitude probably couldn't imagine someone might have the nerve to pursue her. In her world, she was the predator, and people like me and Mom were the prey.

On the expressway the thrill of power, similar to the one I had about vanquishing Rush, came over me. I kept pace with the woman who terrorized my family, cranked up the classic rock station, and sang along with an old AC/DC tune, not caring that I mangled the lyrics.

Once she exited the freeway, following her became trickier. But I soon learned it didn't matter. I knew her destination. She was headed toward Roswell and my mother.

CHAPTER 27

Unreleased Stress

Francine parked around the corner from Buster's house.

The rain dissolved into a dense mist. I hoped it would coat her windshield with the same filmy filter as it did mine, making it easy to drive by her without being identified. I took the chance and turned past the house, taking the same route she had a few minutes before.

Halfway down the block, beside an enormous row of hedges, sat her car. From my vantage point at the end of the street, I had no idea who might be in it. I slowed to a creep. Almost directly behind her, I sped up just enough to glide by, looking to my left as I passed. It was empty.

Lights from an approaching truck and the accompanying blast of a horn jolted me out of my confusion. I jerked the wheel to the right, scraping the tires on the curb, but missing the brick mailbox. I inhaled and exhaled slowly before driving back around to assess the situation.

Nowhere in sight, Francine had abandoned the car. I rounded the corner and stopped farther down the street. A mud-streaked burgundy van sat on the other side of the road. None of the neighbors would be caught dead in a vehicle like it. And area service people entered from the back of the stately houses.

That reminded me of Carmela's lost delivery man who came to the door the day Mom received the note with no postage mark. What if he hadn't been some random guy? What if he was Glen Larson?

If so, it followed he was here now, casing the house. That possibility included the likelihood he and Francine planned to meet there.

Even with additional security, I was apprehensive about the effect a surprise visit from the Larsons might have on my mother. I pictured Glen's face coming toward me and the mixture of fear and repulsion that sent me running. After all this time, the image still disgusted me. But my terror had been replaced by something unidentifiable.

I opened the car door and stepped into the mist. With my hood up against the drizzle, I strode down the sidewalk. Midway, it dawned on me that the emotion driving me was anger. Not the kind of white-hot fury as when I confronted Russ. Not that at all. More icy, so cold it numbed me. My emotions froze to a point where I didn't recognize myself. And this stranger frightened me more than anything.

A thick paste of dirt and oil coated the windows, making it almost impossible to see inside. I started to pound on the glass but caught myself and tapped lightly with my knuckles. No response. I rapped a little harder and still nothing. I slipped my fingers under the handle and pulled, only to find it locked.

The dust on the side had been disturbed by a rectangular outline, the type a magnetic sign might leave. That's when I saw the space between the glass and the frame. Less than two inches, I couldn't maneuver my hand in far enough to unlock the door.

I stepped onto the slightly raised curb and leaned forward, still no clear view. When my foot slipped, I grabbed the edge of the window to steady myself. It gave way, and I stumbled against the filthy van. I regained my balance and tugged harder. Although it remained fixed, I could see stained yellow foam erupting from gashes in the upholstery.

A bare-breasted hula girl danced on the dashboard. Her beady eyes stared at me as if we were old friends. I squeezed mine shut, and for a few awful seconds found myself lodged behind the wheel as Tommy Lee barreled helplessly over a cliff. I bit my lip and faced the figurine.

"Stop looking at me like that." In that moment the brown-skinned beauty became the same gyrating dancer whose owner I ground under the tires of his truck. But that wasn't possible. The fire would have melted the plastic figure into an unrecognizable blob. This realization didn't make me feel any better since this one had to belong to good old Glen. The buddies shared a taste for tacky.

Dropcloths were draped on the floor in the back. Suddenly, every crime drama with a kidnapping victim flashed in front of me.

A gust of wind blew my hood off, exposing me to the pelting rain slushing down my neck. I covered myself and looked at the house. From the street, I couldn't see behind the garage where Luis and Sergio had parked but was comforted by their presence.

I pictured Glen smirking as he stood at our door pretending to be lost. Neither Barry nor Carmela would be fooled again, but it would be stupid to underestimate the Larsons. They might not be the brightest bulbs, but they appeared to be highly motivated. He was willing to risk a return to prison to get whatever he believed Mom had. And his wife's hostility toward my mother scared me even more than her partner's greed.

I waded through puddles behind my neighbors' backyard to hide my approach. Rivulets of muddy water trickled down the sloping terrain, creating a slippery obstacle course. Several times I almost lost my footing but made it to the wrought-iron fence separating the two yards. The underwater glow from the pool highlighted the impact of the downpour as it rippled and swirled on the surface.

Beyond the water our glassed-in porch jutted above the stone patio. Its state-of-the-art privacy shades rolled down to protect against intense sunlight. From my vantage point, I detected a glimmer of light that spilled onto the lawn. I stayed low when I passed under the kitchen windows.

Directly under the sunroom, I stood and listened. A murmur of indistinguishable voices floated over me. A harsh bleat of laughter, followed by a thud that sent me stumbling backward into something soft but solid. I gasped as strong arms held me.

"It's me."

I turned at the sound of Carmela's whisper. She put her finger to her lips and motioned for me to follow her into Barry's enormous playroom. It stretched the length of the house, filled with grown-up toys—a pool table, an arcade machine, a jukebox, and a fully stocked bar.

With the lights out, I had difficulty navigating the crowded room and stayed close behind her. She moved quickly and stopped at the bottom of the steps.

She led me up the flight of stairs and into the garage. Within seconds, we were standing in front of Barry's black Mercedes SUV.

"What's going on?" I tried to keep my growing panic at bay.

"It happened so fast." She ran her fingers through her short, thick curls. "Your mother and Mr. Barry were sitting in the sunroom when the doorbell rang. I was in the laundry room, so he called out to say he would answer it. I should not have left him alone. He was halfway down the hall before I caught up. I stopped when I heard shouting. That horrible woman, the one who upset Miss Ginny, screamed at him. I started to run upstairs. Then there was a crash as if someone fell against the table that holds those little glass shoes she loves so much. Dios Mío, I'm afraid it was your father." She put her hands over her eyes.

I coaxed her to continue.

"A man spoke softly before sounds of more scuffling. I left my cell phone in the laundry room, so I ran toward the kitchen to use the house line. But the struggle stopped, and footsteps sounded in the hallway. I feared they might be looking for me, so I hid here."

"What about Sergio and Luis? Where are they?"

"It must have been—how do you say it? A diversion? Yes, a diversion. Mr. Barry received a phone call telling him there was a fire at his office. He sent my nephew and his boys to check it out. He said he would take care of his..." She swallowed hard, then resumed. "His girls." She slumped against the wall.

"Only two of them?"

"I cannot be sure."

I reached into my back pocket for my phone, but it wasn't there.

"Dammit!" In my furious determination to root Glen out of the van, I left it in the car. "Let's think this through. Could you make out anything they said? Something the woman mentioned before the crash?"

"I'm sorry, but the rest is a blur." Her lips quivered.

"No worries. It probably doesn't matter any—"

"Wait! She demanded Mr. Barry take them to your mother."

I collapsed on the bottom step. So, Francine specifically asked to see Mom. Did that mean she didn't think my stepfather had the answers, or was she planning to use my mother's condition as leverage to get whatever she and her crooked husband thought we had?

Barry would never willingly escort them to the sunporch. And he wouldn't stop resisting. Not unless Francine and her companion used extreme force. The logical conclusion was that my mother and stepfather were being held against their will, quite likely at gunpoint.

Even if they made it out physically unscathed, what did those thugs want? If they started spilling their guts, they might stir up interest in Tommy Lee.

"We need to get to the sunroom and distract them," I said to Carmela. But when I looked up, she no longer stood there.

"Mela," I called softly. "Where are you?"

"I am over here."

I heard a hinge creak and walked to the other side of the stairs, where I found our housekeeper on her knees in front of an old cedar box.

"Last year, when the big storm came through, my apartment flooded. I had to get my things out in a hurry. Your mother told me I could store them here." She continued her frantic rummaging. "I have taken most of it to my place, but this one—my chest of hopes, I think you call it—seems safer here." She dug deeper, then leaned back on her knees and held up a dark gray and black pistol.

"My God, Mela, in your hope chest?" What kind of hopes did my sweet housekeeper harbor?

She removed a leather apparatus attached to a band. "It's a Glock 19," she announced with a smile. "But it has a sensitive trigger. So, it is dangerous to carry without this holster. I have been meaning to take it back to my apartment, but my shotgun is better—not so difficult to hit what you are aiming for."

I waved it away. "I've never even held a gun. I'd probably end up shooting myself. You keep it. Besides, we can't just walk in and start blasting."

"Of course not. That's why you put it in the holster and cover it with your sweater. When the time is right, you do what is necessary."

I imagined myself fumbling with the deadly weapon while Glen laughed and shot me. "I don't think so. Once I'm there, I'll convince them Mom and Barry don't have what they want. Then maybe they'll take whatever cash we have on hand and steal stuff to sell."

I knew how absurd it sounded as soon as I said it. The man had been stewing in prison for over ten years, thinking Tommy Lee was somewhere enjoying the benefits due a successful drug dealer. He wasn't about to accept Mom's word that she had no idea where her former boyfriend had run away to or that he'd deserted her without leaving a share of the profits.

No. Glen would insist on payback in the form of both money and revenge, a package deal. Even if we came up with enough cash to satisfy him, he would still want to find his old partner. And if we convinced him his old buddy was dead, he might feel cheated out of the chance for vengeance and take his anger out on us.

"It is too dangerous," Carmela said. "You must let me do it." She began wrapping the band of the holster around her waist. "Do not worry, I never miss."

"If someone gets shot, we'll have to call the police, and you know you can't be holding the gun."

No one in the family ever discussed our housekeeper's legal status, but I sensed a wariness on her part whenever anyone mentioned the authorities. Even if I were wrong in my suspicion about her legality, it wouldn't be a good idea for her to be involved in a shooting. Mom would never forgive me if Carmela got deported to Colombia.

"People like that won't just take what you have and leave."

She spoke with the certainty of someone who had firsthand experience with people like that. I touched her shoulder.

"You're right. I'll need a backup plan." By now, my eyes had adjusted enough to the darkened basement to make out the outline of the shelf under the window.

I walked to it and surveyed its contents. A fat plastic container of bleach sat on the bottom, too bulky to serve as a concealed weapon. Next to it was a can of disinfectant, also too big for a sneak attack, and a box of mothballs too small to do more than annoy our intruders. I almost gave up until I noticed a cannister labeled Wasp Away. Holding it up to the shaft of light from the window, I read the claim it was ultra-strength, deep-woods insect repellant. Touted as safe enough for children, the label warned against getting the product in the eyes. Not as good as the pepper spray at the bottom of my purse locked in Mom's car but better than nothing. I removed it from the shelf and held it up for Carmela's approval.

"This is perfect."

She mumbled something about bullets. I smiled and stuck the bottle in my pocket inside my sweatshirt.

"Here's the plan. I'll walk in through the front door and pretend I don't know they're there. Like I'm looking for Mom and Barry and just stumbled in on all of them in the sunroom. Then you run to the neighbor's and call Sergio. He and Luis can take it from there."

She glanced down at the gun holstered at her waist. "What will you say to them?"

"Don't worry about that. You forget what an excellent bullshit slinger I've always been." Of course, that was when I wrote misleading ads or found a way to end a relationship or made up an excuse for not coming home for Christmas. Our stakes were much higher.

She didn't seem sold on the idea but agreed to walk with me toward the front of the house. When we reached the grassy area between our fence and Buster's house, she stopped.

"I have a bad feeling about this. Dios Mío!" she whispered and crossed herself. "There!" She pointed to the sky. "See it? The clouds are covering the moon. That is a warning that terrible things await."

"Let's make sure we're not the ones on the wrong side of the moon. It's going to be the Larsons' turn."

I gave her a gentle shove and sprinted to the house.

CHAPTER 28

Stress Released

"Goddammit, Glen! How will we to get him to talk now?"

From outside the sunroom door, I recognized Francine's angry voice and panic threatened to paralyze me. Barry was in trouble, and whatever rendered him silent had to be very bad. I resisted the urge to charge into the room, fearful of both what I might find and what I might cause.

I needed a new plan, one that didn't call for me being trapped with Bonnie and Clyde. Separating them might even the odds a bit. And while bringing insect repellant to a gunfight hardly qualified as a brilliant maneuver, it should sow chaos and possibly allow me to get the jump.

Get the jump? The words echoed in my brain, reminding me I was an advertising producer from the suburbs, not a hardened street cop. Now, however, wasn't the time to quibble over vocabulary.

I moved down the hallway to the bottom of the stairs and called out, "Barry? Mom? Are you guys up there?" Then I clomped up the steps, calling out, "Anybody there?"

At the top of the stairway, I stopped, held my breath, and waited. Except for Buster's faraway barking, there was silence. I hoped the vigilant labrador signaled Carmela's arrival at the home of his owners and help would soon be on the way. I was putting a great deal of faith in Sergio's ability to overcome Francine and Glen. And even more in a goofy dog whose biggest accomplishment had been perfecting the breaststroke.

I walked down the hallway, measuring each step to keep myself from running. Outside Mom's room, I knocked loudly, then paused to gauge any reaction from downstairs. Muffled footsteps startled me, and I ducked into the bathroom.

Sweat beaded on my forehead. My breath came in ragged bursts that reverberated off the rose and blue striped wallpaper. I considered stepping into the tub and drawing the shower curtain but feared my assailant watched the same thrillers I did. So, I flattened myself against the wall, hoping the door would conceal me if someone opened it.

From outside the bathroom, hinges creaked. I debated bolting and making a run for it, but that would mean losing the element of surprise. My only advantage was that whoever was after me assumed I was unaware of the danger of the situation. And I had to keep it that way.

The heavy clump of boots thundered nearby, and I regretted not paying more attention to the sequence for Carmela's sign of the cross. It probably wouldn't have the same effect offered up by a non-Catholic with no idea what it meant. And since I couldn't conjure up any helpful Protestant gestures, I closed my eyes and reached for the toilet handle.

The sound of rushing water filled the room, but I wasn't positive it could be heard from the outside, so I turned on both taps as far as they would go. Then I returned to my previous spot and pressed my ear to the wall.

At first, there was nothing, but in a few seconds, the footsteps continued, closer and closer. I slipped the bug spray from my pocket and removed the top. With it sticking out in front of me, I positioned my foot near the bottom of the door in case my pursuer decided to enter.

Worried the person on the other side would question the continuing outpouring of water from the faucets, I wondered if I should turn them off and risk getting caught in the open. Luckily, the theory that most criminals aren't all that bright proved true, and my criminal eased the barrel a few inches through the opening.

I threw all my weight against the door, slamming into the gun and trapping the gunman's arm from the elbow down. Screams of pain filled the air as the weapon dropped to the floor. I kicked it behind the toilet and stepped in front of a very angry Glen Larson. He cradled his arm, seeming to forget about me for the moment.

I jumped out and sprayed him directly in the eyes. He sputtered, then began howling.

"I'll kill you, you bitch."

While he rubbed at his face, I stuck the spray back in my pocket and retrieved the gun, hoping its trigger had the right amount of sensitivity—not so much that it would explode when I picked it up, but enough to blast Glen into eternity without me having to fumble for the safety. This was especially important as I had no idea where to find the safety.

"Water," he sputtered. "I need to rinse this shit out, or I'll go blind." He took half a step forward.

"Don't come any closer. I've got your gun, and it's pointed directly at your fat face."

My plan of separating them had gone much better than expected. Unfortunately, I hadn't had the time or foresight to move beyond it. That left me stuck in a small bathroom with a large, very unhappy ex-con.

He squinted at me, and I became that helpless teenager pinned to the wall. I steadied myself and gripped the gun tighter. Screw that. I was in charge.

"Okay, okay," he said. "Just please let me rinse my eyes. They really hurt."

I studied the man in front of me. From the looks of it, prison hadn't done much for Glen. He was no stereotypical ex-con with bulging muscles and crude tattoos. He was a lump of unrisen dough. Only one thin piece of hair remained, and he combed it over, creating a greasy streak across the top of his head. Instead of garlic and beer, he smelled like a wild animal trapped in a trash can.

"Stop being such a baby." I poked his belly with the gun, and he stiffened. "Just do what I tell you. Now turn around."

I nudged him into the master bedroom, letting him get a safe distance in front of me before following. A rush of adrenaline shot through me, and I almost understood why people loved their weapons. The power of being at the right end of a gun was invigorating.

"In the closet."

"But my eyes," he whined.

"Do you want me to spray you again?" I held the canister up with my left hand. "Because I will."

He cringed, then scrambled inside.

"Take off your clothes and throw them out here." Apparently, not only was the power behind a firearm energizing, it was also inspirational because there was no other source for my idea to have Glen strip down to his birthday suit. Perhaps I had unconsciously applied the principle of imagining an audience nude to ease the fear of public speaking to my current situation.

"Take off what?" he sputtered. "The hell I will."

I stepped into the closet and misted the area in front of him with repellant. He jumped back.

"Okay, okay." He grabbed the end of his shirt and wriggled it up and over his head. It stuck for a moment before he shrugged it off. Tufts of gray hair sprouted across his sagging chest. His face faded from fire-engine red to not-quite-ripe tomato, and I worried he might be lively enough to challenge me.

"Everything," I commanded.

"I always suspected you were a kinky girl." He leered as he undid his pants, let them fall to the floor, and stood there in yellowing tidy-whiteys. "Anything you like?"

"Not much to see under that big old belly. Stop stalling and drop your panties. Then toss everything out here."

He hesitated and this time I waved the gun. "Is this one of those you barely have to squeeze?" I moved my finger closer to the trigger, hoping I sounded as if I'd had experience with a variety of triggers.

He tugged his underwear down over thick thighs and knobby knees, scooped up his pants and covered himself for a second before tossing it all out.

"That's good. Now get all the way to the back and sit down."

As soon as he turned, I stepped forward, slammed the door, and locked it, thankful for my mother's paranoia about someone stealing her clothes. Still holding the gun, I sat on the bed, planning my next move. Removing Glen from the equation had been easier than I'd expected. He was fat and slow.

Francine was another story. She would definitely be armed. And if I came in carrying a weapon, I had no doubt she'd shoot. Unlike Carmela, I had no place to hide it. My purse was in the car and all of Mom's were in the closet. Maybe not all of them. A quick survey of the room revealed a small leather handbag dangling from a chair. I dumped the contents on the bed and shoved the muzzle in, but the grip stuck out the back. I needed something to drape over it.

After rummaging through several dresser drawers, I hit the jackpot—scarves of all colors and sizes. I chose one that matched my sweatshirt, in case Francine was fashion savvy, and tied it to the strap. If I held the bag under the shoulder farthest from her, I'd be okay. Unless I shot myself.

Glen pounded on the closet door. I ignored his demands to be released and left the room. He kept up the racket, but it was fainter now. Hopefully, it would be impossible to detect from the sunroom.

I had no idea how much time passed since I snagged my captive but was certain it was enough for his wife to get anxious. Worried about what she might do if her anxiety turned into panic, I decided to distract her as fast as possible. I began by calling Barry's name while clomping down the steps. I continued yelling for both Mom and my stepdad until I reached the sunroom. The shades on both doors were drawn, but a sliver of light shone from within.

"Are you guys in there?" I took a deep breath and pulled the door open. The only thing keeping the room from total darkness was the glow from a small table lamp.

Mom sat in her wheelchair with Francine standing directly behind her, a pistol to my mother's head.

"We've been waiting for you. Come on in and have a seat."

I feigned surprise. "What are you doing…wait. Oh my God. Why are you holding a gun?" I stepped back, touching the butt of my own to make sure it was still there and out of view.

"I said sit down," she snarled and waved her weapon at the sofa.

When I took a closer look at my mother, I didn't have to pretend to be terrified. She was pale with pupils so big her eyes were almost black. I feared she'd gone into shock.

I moved toward her. "Are you okay?"

"Stay right where you are." She jabbed the back of Mom's chair with her weapon, which caused it to roll a few inches in my direction. "And put your ass down on that couch unless you want to end up like your step daddy."

She pointed to the corner of the room where my stepfather sprawled on the recliner. His head hung down on his chest, and a jagged slash covered the side of his face. Blood poured from it.

"Barry," I called out, eliciting a low moan from his direction. "What did you do to him?"

"Like you, he had trouble following instructions, so Glen gave him a little love tap. Of course, that jackass hit him too hard—the man's an idiot—and since your mother's still too addled to talk, we were waiting for him to come to. You're here now, so we won't have to. Give us what we want, and we'll be on our way. If that moron ever gets back, that is."

I looked at my mother, trying to determine if she'd lost the power to speak or was keeping quiet on purpose.

Before I decided, Francine interrupted my thoughts. She kept her eyes on me as she stuck her head out the door, hollering Glen's name.

"Goddammit! Where the hell is he? Wait a minute. Why didn't he see you?"

"How should I know?" I spoke with much more confidence than I felt. "Could be he's checking outside, and that's why the neighbor's dog is going crazy."

The barking from earlier reached new crescendos. I hoped it meant help was arriving. Both Barry and Mom seemed to be getting weaker by the second.

Francine fidgeted with a strand of hair. Her agitation worried me.

"Why wait for Glen?" I used my soothing-the-bear-tone, the one that worked on Russ—until it hadn't. "Tell me what you want, and I'll do my best to help you."

"*I'll do my best to help you,*" she mimicked in a high-pitched, childlike voice. "Don't get cute with me, pulling that innocent little girl shit with me. I know exactly what you and that bitch did." My stomach flipped. Was there something else about that night I didn't remember?

"I'm not trying to be cute. I have no clue what you're talking about." I reached out in supplication.

She narrowed her eyes and stared at me. "Whatever. I want to know where you hid the money."

"Money?" This was not what I'd been expecting. My genuine confusion seemed to surprise her, too. And for a second, an expression that could have been doubt passed across her face. Unfortunately, as soon as it was gone, anger replaced it.

"I'm running out of patience. You know exactly what I mean. The two hundred thousand dollars from the coke. Glen stuck it in a canvas bag at our apartment. They were going to split it up after he unloaded the last of the drugs. Only my dumbass husband got arrested. Both Tommy Lee and the cash disappeared that same night. There's no way he vanished into thin air without help. And your sweet little momma would expect to get her share."

A fleeting image of my mother tossing a bag into Tommy Lee's truck came to me. I remembered how she returned to her car to retrieve it while I sat behind the wheel. Until that moment, I hadn't wondered what might be valuable enough to risk both of our lives for. Now I understood.

"Are you kidding me? Do you honestly think my mother would have let Tommy Lee live with us if she'd known he was dealing? And if we had a boatload of money, why would we have lived in that crummy house?" The lies slipped out effortlessly.

Of course, it hadn't been too long after that Mom married Barry, and we moved in with him. Sometime afterward, he started expanding his business.

"Maybe you didn't get any of it," Francine conceded. "But nobody disappears like that without help, and your mother would have done anything for that son of a bitch. Glen and I lost ten years together, and that bastard is going to pay for it."

I wanted to tell her she was wrong—that my mother had chosen me over the son of a bitch when it mattered most. But had it been me or the money she protected? And if I hadn't run him over that night, would she have eventually taken him back?

"I'd love to see him get what's coming to him. After he disappeared, Mom was a basket case. Plus, the miserable piece of shit cleared out our bank account. We were dead broke." I was on a roll now, hoping to buy time before help arrived. "We haven't heard from him since. My guess is he got mixed up in another drug ring and somebody shot him."

She scowled without lowering the gun. "Well, if what you're saying is true, we're done here. Glen's going to be pretty pissed off, though. The way he sees it, he's owed $100,000 plus ten years' interest, which we figure puts it at $200,000." She grinned. "And if that asshole

Tommy Lee didn't leave it behind, you can cover the debt. That's chump change for your high rolling step daddy. He probably has at least $50,000 in his safe. If need be, we'll hang out until tomorrow, while he visits the bank. Afterward, we'll skedaddle and let you pick up doing whatever you rich folks do. For now, let's all sit tight until he gets back."

I wasn't foolish enough to accept that we would be allowed to return to our lives. With us alive, it was only a matter of time before the police picked them up.

She looked at her watch and then at me with an expression that sent a chill up my back. "Dammit! That fool's been gone way too long. Something's happened to him."

"I bet he got scared and ran off without you."

She glared at me through narrowed eyes. "Or you did something to him."

"What could I possibly have done? The basement stairs have needed replacing forever. He's probably lying down there with a broken leg or worse. Want me to check for you?"

Suddenly, Buster's faraway barking was no longer far away. It sounded as if he was standing directly below us.

"Shit! What's that damn dog doing?"

"Oh my God! The neighbor's killer Doberman Hannibal Lecter has escaped again. He'll tear Glen to pieces."

She lowered the gun and started for the window. I leaped off the couch and detected a slight blur of movement from the corner of my eye. Mom held her legs straight out in front of her. The way the wheelchair jolted, the joystick must have been wide open. Francine tripped, steading herself against the windowsill. My mother repositioned the chair and came directly at her, barely grazing the woman's broad hip. It was enough to confuse the larger woman. I slammed into her from behind. She hit the wall but remained on her feet. While she tried to regain her balance, I threw myself shoulder first, caught her square in the ribcage, and took her down. Her skull slammed against the floor.

I fell onto her with my entire weight. Francine was big and mean, but I was on the side of righteousness. I was also operating on animal instinct. I grabbed her by the hair and smacked her head repeatedly on the hardwood.

I didn't stop until someone lifted me, kicking and screaming, into the air.

CHAPTER 29

Out of Control

From the front porch steps, I watched as paramedics came by with a woman on a stretcher.

I tried to stand, but my legs wouldn't cooperate.

"Take it easy, there," a tall police officer held out her hand and pulled me to my feet.

The person on the gurney was much too large to be my mother. From beneath her bandage, a tuft of blonde hair stuck out like pieces of straw. Francine. She flung one arm across her face as she passed, signaling she wasn't dead.

Another pair of emergency workers appeared. I immediately recognized Barry on their stretcher. They shot past me and loaded him at such an efficient speed, I had no time to assess his condition. Within what seemed less than a minute, the driver of his ambulance tore down the driveway, siren blaring.

"Is he okay?" Taillights disappeared as the vehicle rounded the corner.

"Sorry, but I didn't get a good look at him. Is he your father?"

"He's my—that's right, my dad." A wave of dizziness came over me, and I leaned against her for support. "Oh, God. Where's my mother?"

"She's fine. Raised hell when they wouldn't let her ride in the ambulance."

Desperate to confirm her words, I turned toward the doorway, but she took my arm and stopped me.

"Please Officer, I have to be with her." As my head cleared, I realized I needed to be with her for more than the obvious reason of making sure she was okay. I had to find out exactly what she might tell the police. Or if she would keep up the pretense of not being able to talk at all. After her traumatic experiences today, it was possible, even likely, Mom wouldn't be pretending.

She introduced herself as Officer Wilson and promised I could check on Mom shortly.

My eyes stung as I fought back the tears. "She's not well and needs me by her side."

The front door opened, and light from the foyer outlined a familiar figure. Still addled from leftover adrenaline, it took a few seconds for me to recognize Carmela. By the time I did, she was already pulling me into an embrace.

"Gracias a Dios, you are all right." Her voice was loud enough for the neighbors to hear. But her next words were whispered. "If they ask, tell them you do not remember what happened. You do not know why those people wanted to hurt your family." She loosened her grip and moved back, holding me at arm's length. "Understand?"

I nodded. "Is Mom okay? They took Barry away, and nobody will let me go to her."

"Your mother is fine but unable to speak," she said to me, then glared at the cop standing next to us. "She is very tired. Luis and Sergio are helping her upstairs to bed."

One of those men must have dragged me off Francine. Although it infuriated me at the time, I recognized he saved me from serious criminal charges. I wanted to ask for details, but a car roared up the driveway. Blinded by the headlights, I didn't realize who it was until April sprang from the driver's seat and sprinted up the path. Like Carmela, she wrapped me in a viselike hug. Unlike our housekeeper, however, she was sobbing.

"It's okay," I murmured into her shiny hair. "Everybody's fine." *At least I hope they are.*

After several seconds, her sobs subsided into sniffles. She swiped her hand across her eyes, leaving trails of mascara in her wake. "I came as soon as Sergio called. He said Daddy's hurt."

Carmela put an arm over her shoulder. "He suffered an injury to the head. They have taken him to the hospital."

"Is it a concussion? Was he conscious? Please, say he's all right."

She pulled my stepsister out of earshot of the police officer. They whispered while I tried to piece together what commenced after I lost it with Francine. All I remembered was her look of shock as I smashed my fist into her face and being removed from the scene by an invisible source. My hands throbbed with the memory, and I held them up to the light. The red, swollen knuckles belonged to a stranger.

I was still staring at them when my stepsister approached. "Carmela said the police are talking to Sergio. If they want to talk to you, just say you're confused, can't remember anything. If they push, tell them to call your attorney." She reached into her purse and took out a business card. "This isn't really my specialty but, if necessary, I can set you up with someone in the firm. For now, I represent you. I'm going to the hospital but will check in later."

She was halfway to her car before I thought to ask exactly what special area I qualified for. Shouting from inside the house saved me from further consideration of my legal peril.

The woman who'd been keeping me from Mom rushed through the door, and I followed her. Two policemen stood in the foyer with Glen loosely wrapped in mother's pink silk kimono.

"You can't take me in like this," he whined. "At least let me put on my pants."

"Where the hell did you find him?" Wilson asked. "Jesus, man, close the robe before you cuff him." She shielded her eyes, while an officer tried to tighten the belt that refused to stretch around Glen's belly.

"He was upstairs, locked in a closet. Had to bust in the door. According to the security guy, he's an ex-con trying to rob the Winters."

So, Sergio was passing it off as a home invasion.

Glen shouted when he saw me. "That's the bitch who took my clothes. She's the one you should be arresting."

"I don't give a damn who stuck you in there, you fat fuck," the policeman to his right said. His partner scowled and tilted his head in my direction. "Sorry, ma'am. I didn't see you standing there."

Glen kept sputtering that I'd falsely imprisoned him and was a pervert for leaving him buck naked. They stiff-armed him down the walkway. With his skinny legs sticking out beneath Mom's fancy robe, he looked like a peacock whose feathers had been partially plucked. He was still yelling about the violation of his rights when they shoved him into the back of the cruiser.

Carmela joined me in time to see her nephew coming down the hall. A tall, thin man in a suit accompanied him. When they reached us, Sergio stopped and said, "Miss Liz, this is Detective Holloman. I explained to him that you were disoriented after the Larson woman attacked you. That your memory is not so good right now."

Well over six feet, he gazed down at me with frightening intensity before extending his arm.

"Eugene Holloway. Miss Tucker, isn't it? Obviously, you've had a rough night, and I sure don't want to make it any rougher. If you could answer a few simple questions, we can straighten out this mess." His voice was warm, almost friendly, but the fact that he knew I was a Tucker, not a Winter, indicated he'd researched me.

Sergio reinserted himself between us. I squeezed his arm, then turned to the detective.

"The attack really rattled me, but I'm willing to try. Let's go into the living room where it's quieter." Choosing the location for my interrogation made me feel more in control.

Holloway quickly dispelled that illusion. "About that." He removed a small spiral notebook from his jacket pocket. "Can you tell me how that went?"

"What do you mean?"

"I ask because the paramedics took Mrs. Larson to the ER. Seems like she's pretty banged up. Might have a slight concussion, they're saying. And you, well." He raised an eyebrow.

"Excuse me. What exactly was the question?"

"You seem to be in fairly good shape compared to the woman who allegedly attacked you. Can you explain that?"

"My memory of the entire event is very hazy. I'm afraid I might misremember the details."

"What *do* you actually remember, Miss Tucker?"

"Hmm." I touched my fingertip to my upper lip. "Well, I know that I came home and found Mom and Barry in the sunroom. He was slumped against the wall, bloody and pale, and she was shaking in terror. After that, I'm not sure."

I shouldn't have been surprised at how easily the lies flew from my lips. I'd been lying to myself most of my life. But I considered this performance one of my best.

The way he snapped his little notebook shut and jammed it into his pocket, along with the expression on his face, indicated Detective Holloway was less impressed.

"In cases like yours, it's not unusual for memories to return. Could you stop by the station tomorrow around eleven for a chat? By then, you may have recovered some of yours?"

"I can't commit to anything until I see how my folks are doing. But I will most definitely give it my best shot." I gave him my sweetest smile.

"I suggest you try really hard." He stood abruptly and strode from the room.

• • •

After we got my mother settled in bed, Sergio explained what he told the police.

"I said my aunt alerted us that someone had broken in. When I arrived, she was very confused and upset. Luis and I ran to the house where we found that woman attacking Miss Liz. We separated them and called the policía."

I admired the simplicity of the story. He made it easy to fill in details to support his account of a home invasion. I could even stick to the truth about how Glen ended up naked in the closet.

It was after midnight by the time he left. Carmela and I were at the table when we heard the garage door opening and closing.

Barry dragged in, his face whiter than the bandage encircling his head. April bustled in behind.

"Daddy, please sit before you fall down." She pulled out a kitchen chair and stood next to it with her arms folded in front of her. "He's so stubborn. They wanted him to stay overnight, but he insisted on coming home. Wouldn't even let me help him out of the car. I had to fight him to keep him from driving."

"I'm fine." Rather than sit, he said, "I need to check on Ginny."

"April's right." I walked to him and gently put my arms around him. "We just got Mom tucked in. Carmela talked to Doctor Stoneface himself."

I'd been shocked when he showed up shortly after the police cleared out. He still lacked warmth and personality, but it had been reassuring to see him. And he'd been cautiously optimistic about the trauma not causing any significant setbacks.

"Maybe I will sit down for a minute."

Carmela had already begun making his favorite—hot chocolate with a shot of Kahlua.

April took his arm and tried to guide him, but he shook her off and sat on his own. "Baby, you know what a hard head I've got. Besides, a drop in my blood sugar's the problem, not the knock on my noggin."

She dismissed his analysis. "You have to rest, and you shouldn't be drinking alcohol."

"I'm too keyed up to slow down, honey. Come on; sit with your old daddy and have a drink."

She eased into the seat next to him. "Make mine a double, please, Mela. And hold the hot chocolate."

"Doc said your momma's okay?" He asked.

"Yes, but he urged us to keep her calm."

He chuckled. "Calm? Have you met your momma? That's a tall order."

I smiled at the image of Mom ramming her wheelchair into Francine.

My stepsister slapped her hand on the table. "Enough. It's time for somebody to be honest about today. What happened and why?"

I started with finding Francine at Coral's house and following her. Unsure about her knowledge of Mom's history with the Larsons, I explained they'd been involved with Tommy Lee in a questionable deal that landed Glen in prison. And that, when he got out, he wanted to find his partner to settle the score. In the meantime, Francine discovered Mom was doing well financially and decided to hit her up for information and to rob her.

"Their business must have been pretty shady to warrant a ten-year sentence." April shot me a questioning look. Then she shrugged. "I guess it doesn't really matter."

She walked to the cabinet and removed the Kahlua, then poured a generous amount for herself, a smaller portion for her father, and handed the bottle to me. I filled mine to the top.

"Did the police question you?" she asked.

"The lead detective tried, but I told him I wasn't sure about anything."

"Good." She nodded her approval. "And Daddy, you don't remember either, right?"

"In and out of consciousness. No memory of a damn thing." He grinned and slurped from his cup. "Best in the world, Mela."

She beamed at him.

I looked at my stepfather, a foamy mustache forming on his upper lip, and wondered how involved he'd been in what had happened that night, and if he knew about the mysterious bag of cash. But it was much too late to request a private conversation with him.

My own cup became almost too heavy to lift, and I tried, unsuccessfully, to suppress a yawn.

"Lizzie, you need to get to bed. I can't be certain, but during one of my very brief moments of clarity," he cut his eyes toward April, "I believe you got quite the workout when Francine attacked you."

He reached across the table and held my hands palms up. Very gently, he turned them over and touched his lips to my discolored knuckles.

I rose, walked to the back of his chair, and patted his shoulder. "You should get some rest, too. Mom will pitch a fit if she finds out we didn't take care of you."

"Don't worry," April piped in. "I'm staying overnight to make sure he behaves."

On the way up the stairs, it occurred to me that not too long ago, the thought of spending a night with my stepsister in the house would have been like having a pebble in my tennis shoe.

I slipped inside Mom's room and tiptoed to her. It was unnaturally dark. Outside, a shroud of clouds covered the sliver of moon.

I waited for my eyes to adjust. After a few seconds, my mother's face floated into focus as if emerging from deep water. Her eyelids fluttered open, startling me with the sharpness of her gaze.

"Hey, sweetheart."

She patted her hand on the mattress, and I climbed in beside her, closer than I'd been in a long time. I had so many things to ask her, but it all could wait. I stroked her hair and drifted off to sleep. Or maybe she stroked mine. At that moment, like the answers to my questions, it didn't matter at all.

Around 3:00, I woke to the sound of Barry's gentle snorting snore and found him curled on the loveseat in the corner. I crawled out of bed.

In my room, I burrowed under the fancy comforter, but every time I closed my eyes, I saw myself smashing my fist into the Viking woman's face. I'd never been in an actual physical fight, never hit anyone. Other than the usual middle-school girl sniping, I steered clear of emotional altercations as well. I suppose growing up with a barrage of strangers and never getting emotionally involved as an adult made me an expert on conflict avoidance.

In the past week or so, my behavior escalated from causing a scene in a fancy restaurant to breaking my ex-lover's nose. And although I barely recalled it, taking down a dangerous home invader.

Strangely, I didn't feel the least bit guilty or sorry for any of it. When I pictured Russ's face—first humiliated, then bloody—and what I remembered of Francine's battered one, I experienced a jolt of pure satisfaction.

It was as if I were a new person, and while I kind of liked this kick-ass version of myself, I was also more than a little afraid of her. Because I wasn't sure if my behavior meant I'd become stronger or if it had simply awakened that girl in the truck.

CHAPTER 30

Taking Control

I plowed through the next morning in a sleep-deprived haze. When the doctor returned to evaluate Mom's condition, April was on the phone. I tried to process his comments but found myself missing my stepsister's superior ability to pay attention to details. My main takeaway was that we needed to keep a close watch on her for any signs of regression.

At the mention of regression, my mind returned to my own troubling emotional state, and I planned to discuss it with Barry as soon as he was able.

That turned out to be more difficult than I expected. Whether from the stress of worrying about Mom or residual effects from his injury, he became dizzy while the doctor examined my mother. He tried to talk my stepfather into checking into the hospital, but he refused.

"Being with this little lady is the best medicine for me."

Carmela promised she would supervise their recovery.

"You're all the most hard-headed people I've ever met," the doctor muttered as he left the three of them tuning into one of Carmela's soaps.

"Should we be worried about him?" I asked, leading him to the door.

"Who knows? It's probably more from stress than the head injury. At his age, though, we need to be cautious. And I suppose being with his wife is better than being laid up in a hospital bed."

I wandered to the kitchen where April stood at the refrigerator.

"I'm starving. How about an omelet?"

"Sounds great. How can I help?"

"You sit and fill me in on how everyone's doing." She took a bowl from the cabinet and started cracking the eggs. "I checked in and found Daddy and Ginny lying in bed seemingly absorbed with *Days of Our Lives*. Carmela told me I just missed the doctor, but not to worry. So, now, I'm more worried than ever."

I summarized the visit while April cooked. I was at the part of him agreeing Barry being with Mom might be the best medicine. She turned off the stove and passed out omelets.

"I hope he's right," she sighed. "But I don't care what either of them says. I'm getting the night nurses back."

"I hadn't considered that. When did you get so smart?"

She grinned. "Aw, shucks. But seriously, I've always been highly intelligent, gifted even. Case in point, my recent conversation with Benjamin Weinstein."

"Who?"

"The firm's expert in criminal law. He's already been in touch with the police. And guess what?" She paused a second but continued before I had time to venture a guess. "You are completely off the hook for whatever it was you did to those horrible people."

"Whatever I—"

"Don't tell me. The less you say, the better. The important thing is there aren't going to be any more police interviews in your immediate future. The Larsons accepted a plea deal. Rather Francine did. He was dead in the water when he violated his parole. And by the time she gets out, she'll be too old to mess with you. Although from what I heard about the way that nasty woman looked when they booked her, I doubt she'll ever agree to be in the same room as you."

"That's great news. It pays to have a lawyer in the family."

"Right. But please don't make a habit of needing one."

I smiled and promised to abandon my outlaw ways.

"I hate this whole crazy setback thing happened. I understand you're anxious to get out of here, but it shouldn't be long before Ginny's back on track. And I'm thinking about taking a leave of absence myself to hang out here until they're both better."

I stood up and took my plate to the sink. "Why don't you put that on hold? I can handle most of my work remotely for at least a few more weeks. After that, who knows?"

•   •   •

I didn't check in with Andrea until after two. I told her about Mom's setback and gave her an account of our home invasions, turning Glen into a disgruntled ex-employee and leaving out most of our history with the Larsons.

"My God, Liz!" she exclaimed when I finished my story with crooks in prison. "Who knew the South was so exciting?"

"Yeah, well, I could do with a lot less excitement. But I don't want to leave until Mom's more stable. Can you explain this to Russ?"

She laughed. "He doesn't seem too worried about the office right now. Especially not since Denise, Mrs. Young the third, discovered our boss in a very interesting position with his yoga instructor. Apparently, her timing couldn't have been worse for him. It seems Viagra and downward dog are a terrible combination, much worse when the dog is being smacked with a tennis racket."

"I didn't even know she played tennis."

"Well, she's playing now. Playing like she's planning to take him for everything, now that he's out of the hospital."

"She beat him badly enough to send him to the hospital?"

"No, those wounds were superficial, but he got his money's worth out of the Viagra. You're aware of the four-hour rule?"

"Yikes!"

"Right. Plus, he had some kind of heart issue while the ER doc was working on little Russ. Just palpitations, but it laid him up for a few days."

"I doubt his heart is big enough to cause him too much pain. Is Denise causing problems for you?"

"That's the good news. She doesn't want to be tied down running the business, so she put me in charge."

"And Russ is going along with it?"

"He and Miss Yoga Pants are somewhere in the Himalayas, tapping into each other's chakras."

After recovering from a bout of severe giggling, I thanked her for being so understanding and assured her I'd keep up with my accounts from home.

"I know you will. But, Liz, don't forget what's real. This business you and I are in? It's built on illusion. Your family—that's what really matters."

When I came back to Georgia, I was certain I'd be as out of place as before I left. The odd girl out around Whitney and Grant. A social embarrassment to my stepsister. The reminder of the one thing from Mom's past that would never stop haunting her.

But I was wrong about all of it. Whitney's pregnancy, Grant's betrayal, April's resentment—all of them were results of my own insecurity. As for reminding my mother about what we had done, with or without me, she could never forget it.

And now, more than ever, I had to determine the truth about that awful night. Maybe that was the reason for my reluctance to return to LA. Once I learned all I could, would I be ready to leave Georgia?

I put that question aside and fulfilled my promise to Andrea to make sure my accounts were in order. After two hours of answering emails and making calls, my lack of sleep caught up with me. I was on the way to the kitchen for coffee when the doorbell rang.

I looked through the peephole and drew in a quick breath.

"Grant," I said, wishing I'd taken the time to put on makeup. "It's—"

He cut me off by grabbing me and pulling me close. "Liz," he whispered. "You made the first page of the paper, and it scared the crap out of me."

I missed the warmth of his arms when he released me. Taking his hand, I led him to the kitchen, fixed coffee, and asked him about the newspaper account.

"The reporter says a woman your mom worked with and her ex-con husband broke into your home and had been captured. Other than reporting Barry's injuries, he didn't provide a lot of details. I called the hospital, and they told me he hadn't been admitted. I started to call you but had to see you in person. And here I am." He smiled and became the same sweet boy I met my first day on campus.

Of course, neither of us were the same people we'd been. But that could be a good thing.

"I'm glad you're here. We have a lot to talk about."

• • •

We talked well into the morning hours. When I told him about Whitney and the baby that wasn't, he seemed hurt at my low opinion of him. I accepted the blame, adding that growing up with a love-struck, self-centered mother could screw any girl up. My level of neurosis, however, required a more drastic reason. Something like running over your mother's boyfriend and then forgetting about it for the next twelve years or so.

I needed to make things right between Grant and me. Not to pick up where we left off—although that wouldn't have been bad—but to undo the way my actions spoiled memories of the happiest moments of my life.

The bigger problem was how much to reveal about my past. I doubted the knowledge he was dating a murderer would contribute to a solid relationship.

So, I asked him for time to discover who we'd become. Of course, he might not be thrilled with the newly evolved me. But the risk was worth it.

"I'd say ten years qualifies as pretty damn slow," he said, pulling me closer to him. "But if you want slower, then slower it is.

That wasn't what I wanted at all. I wanted to make up for all the time we'd been apart by getting as close to him as possible as quickly as possible. I wanted his hands on my body and to hold his face in mine. But even though we saw each other every evening for the next week, I resisted.

My days were filled with helping Carmela and April care for Mom and Barry. The doctor had been painfully accurate in his prediction that my mother might regress after her ordeal. Her speech became more slurred, and she tired easily. Rudolph said stroke victims frequently suffered from depression. He suggested we consider medication if she didn't improve in the upcoming weeks.

Barry had the most trouble accepting Mom's setback. He blamed himself for sending Sergio and Luis to check on the office fire. Apparently, Glen had been working on his electrician's certificate in prison and had learned just enough to rig a timer to cause a short in the wiring to trigger an electrical problem. Nothing we said eased his guilt, and I worried he, too, was slipping into depression.

Whitney called daily and stopped by with magazines and wine. Unlike Grant, I didn't feel as if I had to explain myself to her. She always seemed to accept the idea that there were things I had to keep to myself. Also, I doubted she would blink an eye if I told her I killed someone. She would have assumed he deserved it and offered to provide an alibi if needed. That was the kind of friend she was.

But not even my renewed friendship, nor April's relentless determination to be cheerful, nor Carmela's gentle caretaking made things easier. By the time Grant arrived in the evening, we were all running on empty.

He knew exactly what to do or say or bring to lighten the ever-darkening mood in the house. The peach-colored roses Mom loved, a tedious article from some financial journal Barry found fascinating, fresh cilantro for Carmela, gossip about one of April's rival attorneys.

As I observed him working his magic, it became harder not to break my own rule about insisting we move at a snail's pace. After seven sequential days of dinners followed by teenage-style make out sessions at my house, I suggested we have an after-dinner drink at his condo.

"There won't be any adult supervision at my place." He raised an eyebrow. "Are you sure you can trust me?"

Heat rose from my chest. "It's me I'm afraid I can't trust." My favorite go-to line from high school came to me out of nowhere, but I had a different follow-up. "Forget I said that. I'm not afraid at all."

CHAPTER 31

Unsinkable

Making love with grown-up Grant transformed me into two totally different people. I was the young girl so shocked by the urgency of desire she'd been unable to keep a safe distance from her emotions. That girl's skin had a memory all its own. But when he trailed kisses from her lips to her breasts, it was my flesh that burned. I knew exactly where to touch him, yet the power of his reaction startled me. Just as desperate for me as that first time, now he understood how to bring me to the same level of passion—to tease me until I no longer feared losing control—until I lost myself in him.

He imprinted his body on mine like one of those beautiful old maps with the spidery writing and subtle shading. But as we grew closer physically, the harder it became for me to keep my secret. I wanted to tell him about what happened the night Tommy Lee left. But how could I when it remained unclear to me?

Etched in my mind, his expression when he flew over the hood haunted me. My intent still puzzled me. Had it been an accident when I shifted into drive instead of reverse? And had that injury killed him? I don't remember pressing the gas before I hit him. Would the jolt of popping into gear have been enough to kill him? What about that second sound? More of a sensation really, a sudden bump. Had I been at the wheel then?

Almost as troubling was Mom's part in his death. Was our departure about escaping an abusive asshole or more about that canvas bag? If anyone found out we killed Tommy Lee, that kind of cash might seem like a motive. She had been so determined not to leave it behind she risked going back for it after she knocked him over with her car. But if he'd already died, how risky was it?

If I was honest with Grant, I wouldn't only be incriminating myself and my mother. Somebody—probably Barry and Sergio—had done a great job of getting rid of the body. Worse, I'd be making him an accomplice of sorts.

So, I didn't mention that night at all. I told myself it was because I needed to be sure about the events first. And since my stepfather promised to let Mom tell the story, I would have to get the truth from my mother.

I recounted my life before Barry showed up. It was on the second week of our new beginning, and we were in his bed with tangled sheets. Steel bands tightened around my heart as I began cataloguing all my mother's transgressions. Then a strange thing happened. Every time I shared a hurtful detail, something in my chest fluttered. When I got to the part about Glen, my breathing was light and easy.

Later that night, I dreamed I was at the ocean. I came across a bucket some child left behind. Inside it, dozens of tiny starfish floated. I took the pail to the water's edge, tipped it on its side, and watched each little creature scurry to the sea.

• • •

After three weeks of watching Mom fade deeper and deeper into herself, the doctor prescribed an antidepressant. He warned us not to expect overnight results. I spoke with him privately about Barry's increasingly gloomy mood, and he suggested we wait to see if an improvement in my mother would have a positive effect on him.

"It doesn't seem right not telling your mom we're dosing her with mind-altering drugs." Barry said, sitting across from me and April at the kitchen table.

"I wouldn't call them mind-altering, Daddy. And if she knew, it might put pressure to pretend to be better."

"I'm not crazy about it either." She would be seriously pissed off if she'd found out we were slipping happy pills to her. "But if they work, it'll be worth it."

I excused myself to check emails and send a weekly progress report. I could no longer put off making some difficult decisions. My new boss had been great about my working from home, but she would eventually need me in LA. Mom's recovery wasn't going to be a quick one, and I was beginning to fear she'd progressed as far as possible.

And then there was Grant. Logically, it was too early in our relationship to consider him a factor in my decision to return to California. But with our fuzzy timeline, logic played a small part. I didn't want to pressure him into a discussion about our future—assuming we had one. But I couldn't ignore his role.

Frustrated at the way I seemed to be going in circles trying to make up my mind about when or if I would return to LA, I noticed the newspaper on the dresser and picked it up. Then I turned to the source that, while it almost always let me down, never failed to amuse me. My daily horoscope. Only today's forecast gave me nothing to smile about. It raised the hair at the back of my neck and covered my arms with goosebumps.

Life has been hitting you with gale-force winds. Your sails are battered and massive waves are thrusting you into treacherous territory. But just because you're taking on a little water, doesn't mean you'll sink. Not if you remember to turn to the one source you can count on—your anchor in every storm.

Despite the cheesy nautical analogy, this astrologist spoke to me. The weight of unanswered questions and impossible decisions threatened to sweep me away. But was Mom supposed to be the anchor in this extended metaphor? Didn't anchors drag you down, hold you back?

I kept looking for something a little lighter to share with my mother and moved on to Libra. More straightforward with a less frightening, it offered a more land-locked message.

You have many openings and opportunities. Choosing them is like choosing a stop on a subway or an exit on the highway.

I wondered if she really had a choice or if her own "gale-force winds" had swept all her openings and opportunities away. I decided to stop mixing terrible metaphors and assess her mood before making my selection. If necessary, I could always improvise, my area of expertise.

I heard nothing in her room, so I knocked lightly, then entered. She stared at the view outside her window.

"Looks like it's going to be a beautiful day."

Without looking in my direction, she mumbled something I accepted as confirmation of my weather report.

"Feeling any better this morning?"

She shrugged and moved her hand in a "so-so response.

"I brought your horoscope." I sat on the edge of the bed, intentionally blocking her view. "Yours is quite interesting."

I used Virgo as a jumping off point since Jupiter aligned with Virgo's moon, which aided in finding balance between enabling and empowering. Then I came up with some crap about the planets being in perfect alignment, creating optimum conditions for meeting both her needs and desires. I added "and knowing the difference," which made it sound a little too much like the AA pledge, but she seemed to buy it. Or maybe she needed to believe it.

Whatever the reason, the conversation and her spirits improved. She managed to ask me about Grant and appeared content to listen while I gave her the PG-rated version of our relationship.

When Barry arrived, I switched the topic to the weather. After a few minutes of speculating on whether we'd break the current record high, I left them and went to my room to speculate on how the hell to spend the rest of my life.

• • •

Two days later, still unsure about what my next steps should be, I used the excuse of being slammed with work and taking care of Mom to avoid seeing Grant, hoping a little distance from him would clear my head. It occurred to me I might be reverting to my old habits of weaseling out of relationships.

When he didn't ask to reschedule, I rushed to the conclusion he'd tired of me. I slogged through the day, miserable, and was drinking beer in the den, watching *Outlander* when the doorbell rang.

"I should have called first," he said, running his hand through his hair. "But I was afraid you'd make an excuse not to see me, and I need to talk to you."

Overcome with an unfamiliar sense of dread, I held the door open. I used the same line myself right before slipping out of a relationship. All the leaving behind I'd done was about to catch up with me.

"Can I get you something to drink? Beer? Wine? Some of Barry's super expensive Scotch? Still tastes like iodine to me, but he loves it." If I pretended everything was the same with us, maybe it would be. He declined my offer and ignored my attempt at humor.

We sat together on the sofa. I braced myself for his next words.

"Remember what you said about taking it slow?"

I started to deny it but nodded.

"Well, you were right. It probably is a good idea to give ourselves time to figure out what our next steps."

It's a terrible idea, I screamed silently. But I kept my face neutral.

"The problem is I know exactly where I want to go, and, more important, who I want to go with me. We've wasted years already. I'm not trying to push you into anything. It's enough to be with you."

"I feel the same, but—"

He placed his hands lightly over my mouth. "I understand you love your job, so if you need to go back to LA, all I ask is that you consider letting me go with you. We don't have to get engaged or even live together. But I can't lose you again. I—"

Before he finished, I covered his lips with mine.

•   •   •

On the soft chenille sofa with a lap full of Frenchie, I laughed as Charles filled me in on his latest dating adventure.

"I thought we might be on to something until I found out that he," he reached over and held his hands over Truman's big ears, then whispered, "has cats, five to be exact. Truman can never find out." He scratched the sweet spot on the little dog's belly.

"More wine?" He poured Chablais into my glass.

We spent the day packing up the few belongings I planned to ship to Georgia and were waiting for Chinese food.

"I can't believe you're deserting me. I'm going to be desolate." He made a silly, sad face, but his glum tone elicited a little groan from Truman.

"I'll miss you, too. But you can come visit anytime."

It had been surprisingly difficult to say goodbye to California.

Andrea brought me to tears with her promise to supply me with all the freelance work I could handle. That, along with working Whitney's foundation, would provide a steady income while allowing me to help take care of Mom, who defied the doctor's expectations and made a remarkable recovery. She still relied on the wheelchair and occasionally struggled to recall words, but she was almost her old self again. I hadn't been confident enough in her resilience to press her for the whole truth about Tommy Lee's death.

Both Mom and Barry were disappointed when I moved into an apartment not far from them. But they'd been too thrilled with my decision to return to Georgia to push the issue. Grant and I stopped pretending we were taking things slowly, but we hadn't made any life-altering decisions—not yet anyway.

"I may just take you up on that offer. I hear the film business is booming down there. Hell, Truman and I might up and move, too." At the sound of his name, he hopped from my lap to his. "Would you like that, buddy?" He held the dog up far enough from his face to avoid his manic licking. "You might fall in love with one of those slow-barking little Southern dogs."

My phone vibrated. It was April.

"Hey, sis."

"You need to come home as soon as possible. Mom's had another stroke."

CHAPTER 32

Gale Force Winds

It came as no surprise that Mom planned her funeral down to the shoes she wanted to be buried in. They were red Jimmy Choo stilettoes, so high and uncomfortable she had only worn them twice.

"They shouldn't bother me much now," she wrote on the first page of the instructions. "And I don't hate anyone enough to leave them to."

"I remember them," April said as we opened one unlabeled shoe box after another. "They kind of matched her hair." She put her hand over her mouth, an expression of horror on her face. "God, Liz, I'm so—"

The sound of my laughter drowned out the rest of her apology. She giggled along with me for several seconds before we both began to cry.

Carmela found us collapsed and sobbing in each other's arms and took over Mom's fashion detail. She put April in charge of watching Barry and sent me downstairs where Whitney helped with the never-ending supply of condolence casseroles and phone calls.

Sometime before the viewing, she pulled me aside. "It's Xanax," she said, holding a little peach-colored pill in the palm of her hand. "Take it."

I hesitated for a moment. Didn't I owe it to my mother to suffer through it all—the pain and guilt, the what-ifs? Then I realized I had the rest of my life to experience it all, and I dry-swallowed the tablet.

I glided through the evening in a cottony haze, Grant by my side then and during the service the next day. He guided me down the aisle of the packed church and stepped up to support Barry when he stumbled on his way to kiss the closed casket. He stood with the family as an endless line of mourners shook my hand or pulled me into an awkward embrace. And he held me in the back of the limo as we followed the hearse to the graveside.

A warm May breeze drifted over us in front of the rose-covered coffin. The drone of bumble bees vying for a spot among Mom's flowers muffled the minister's words. Barry sat between April and me. I felt his stillness but couldn't look at him—not then and not when we walked away from the grave, leaving my mother behind.

When we returned to the house I once thought would never be home, a smaller group of mourners waited. Mom had instructed us to "party like Catholics," and we gave it our best shot. Barry brought out the good bourbon, and even a few of the church ladies got a little tipsy.

"Ginny would have liked this." Whitney sat beside me on the sofa after the guest had gone home. "It's a shame she had to miss it."

"I wish I'd been able to see her, to tell her it was okay. That I loved her and knew she loved me." My throat tightened, but the tears refused to shed.

"She knew. I'm sure of it."

I accepted her statement in the spirit it was given. For me, there would never be certainty, only the torment of words unspoken.

• • •

The morning after Mom's funeral, I woke up in an Ambien daze. I found a note from Grant telling me he'd see me for lunch. We sent Carmela home to be with her family, so I fixed a cup of coffee and carried it to the sunroom.

Three tiny hummingbirds hovered over the feeder attached to the glass. At the sound of barking, they burst away in streaks of blue and green and purple. A familiar black shape galloped down the hill, skidding to a stop at the edge of the pool. Buster sniffed the water before plunging in, his owner close behind him. She waved to me before wading in up to the bottom of her shorts and grabbing him by the collar. I stood and called out to her from the open window.

"It's okay. He's welcome anytime."

As a reward for his timely distraction of Francine, Barry gave Buster carte blanche.

"Thanks, but you don't need to be bothered today." She clipped on his leash. "I'm so sorry about your mother."

She scurried off, dragging the reluctant pooch behind her. My first thought was how funny Mom would have found it to see her neighbor sloshing into the pool after Buster.

My stepfather came into the sunny room. He shaded his eyes against the glare of the morning sun. On his way to the wicker loveseat, he brushed against Mom's favorite chair, and it rocked between us.

"Your sister drugged me," he said.

"You have to watch that girl." I smiled, only a little concerned he seemed to have forgotten giving in to April's suggestion that he take something to help him sleep. It's hard to keep track of incidentals when grief encases your mind in a heavy cotton-like coating.

"Your mom and I spent a lot of time out here."

His use of the past tense crushed me.

"Mostly, we spoke of ordinary stuff. What we were going to have for dinner or whether to plant a garden on the other side of the fence.

But lately, she brought up more and more about her background." He stared into the distance.

"She talked a lot about you, Liz. She blamed herself for the way things were between the two of you. Having you home these last few months..." He cleared his throat, then continued. "Well, honey, she was happier than I've ever seen her."

"You made her happy." Truthfully, I never thought much about her happiness. I assumed getting what you wanted was the same as being happy. It seemed Mom had finally gotten everything she always wanted.

"I hope so. Your mother was a complicated woman. But not when it came to loving you. That was the one uncomplicated thing about her."

My throat closed, making it impossible to sip my coffee.

"She bragged about you to anybody who'd listen. How smart you were, how successful, how pretty. But she worried about you, too. We both did. About six months before she had the stroke, we had a long discussion. We went back to that horrible night and what it did to you."

To me? Wasn't the issue more about what I had done to someone else?

"Anyway, she decided to have a sit-down with you the next time you came home. Get everything out in the open. Only things didn't turn out the way we planned." He rose from his seat and said, "Stay here."

He shuffled from the room. A squirrel hung over the edge of the pool, studying his reflection in the smooth surface. An overhead shadow sent the furry creature racing for cover. I walked to the window in time to see a hawk land in a tree by the fence. Wondering how he could be both so regal and deadly, I caught my breath when he pointed his beak in my direction. For a few seconds, we locked in a staring contest. Movement from the other side of the property distracted him, and he flew away.

I began to worry Barry had wandered off and forgotten all about me. Just as I was about to give up and go search for him, he returned with a slender packet in hand.

"Your mother left this for you." He dropped it on the coffee table, picked up his cup and walked inside.

The creamy envelope exuded the same air of elegance as my regal hawk. And what it held was potentially as deadly. Like the cloth napkins Mom insisted on using, expensive personalized stationery became accepted protocol in her home. For a woman accustomed to scribbling messages on sheets torn from one of my spiral notebooks, this new habit had seemed especially pretentious to me.

On the gleaming glass tabletop, the letter floated in time and space. It promised to shed the light I'd been demanding to those dark questions from my past. But was I ready to be illuminated? If Mom had the strength to write it, the least I could do was read the damn thing.

CHAPTER 33

Anchored

Dear Liz,

If you're reading this letter, it most likely means I chickened out about talking to you in person. Or that I kicked the bucket, but let's go with the first option.

It's a sure fact I haven't always been the best mother. And even though the day you were born was the happiest of my life, I made a lot of mistakes along the way. Despite everything, you turned into a strong, beautiful woman. That doesn't let me off the hook for my many screw-ups.

Tommy Lee was by far my worst mistake. People fantasize about finding your soulmate, the person who completes you, makes you want to be better. But they never mention running into someone who brings out the blackness in your soul. You turn into a worthless lump and believe him when he says nobody else will ever want you. Instead of building you up, he tears you down and remakes you in his image. That's what that man did to me.

You saved me, baby, by shining light into my darkness. But I let you down. What happened that night was so terrible I tried to bury it, to purge it from memory. When you were so quiet the next day, I was relieved. Yes, someday we'd deal with it, but not until our wounds weren't so bloody. I took your silence to mean you succeeded where I failed. You really didn't remember the ordeal.

I called that a good thing, one less burden for you to carry. But I benefited the most from it. At least, that's what my therapist says. (Yes, your mother has been seeing a counselor. And no, not Carmela's psychic aunt.)

Barry and I discussed it, and we planned to tell you everything. Somehow, that never happened, and while it still might, I'm writing this letter as a "jic." (Remember how we always had a "just in case"? Like candles if the check to the electric company bounced.)

So here goes. The morning after I burned the meatloaf, when you left for school, I drove to work pretending everything would be okay. I imagined him sweeping me off my feet with candy or roses or tickets to the fights. A grand romantic gesture. More likely, he'd walk through the door acting as if nothing happened, be real sweet for a while until something else set him off.

The empty house mocked me for my weakness, and a quiet fury filled me with bitterness and determination. No more black eyes and bruises or trips to the emergency room. No more Tommy Lee. I celebrated with a glass of wine, finished the bottle, and passed out. I woke a little after midnight. You had already gone to bed, leaving me alone with my rage.

I gathered bags and packed up his crap. Ragged t-shirts and work pants and dirty magazines. I pictured him when he discovered it waiting for him on the porch. I remembered he had more junk in the storage shed. That's where I found it.

I'd been worried he was into some bad stuff, but I stuck my head in the sand and pretended I imagined it. When I located the satchel, I had to recognize facts.

You were never a fan of having Barry in our lives, but he was a really good friend to me. He never hit on me. He only listened.

Anyway, I called him, and he booked a room at the Holiday Inn. He wanted to come get us, but I told him I didn't expect Tommy Lee to come home and insisted we would meet him at the hotel. Then I packed up a few of our things, woke you, and started loading up the car.

That's when everything went to hell in a hand basket. Tommy Lee pulled in behind us. I knew if he saw the money, he'd kill me, so I shouted for you to run to his truck. I planned to rush past him and pick you up. When I looked in the mirror, he was almost on top of me. I didn't realize I was still in reverse when I tapped the gas. I bumped him with our car hard enough to knock him down. I should have hit him again. Instead, I jumped out and tried to get to you.

I would have, too, if I hadn't gone back for the money.

You were behind the wheel when I finally got there. I screamed for you to back up. But we slipped out of gear the same moment he appeared. If he hadn't been moving so fast, we would probably only have grazed him. His sick determination sent him flying onto the hood.

I ran to the driver's side and shoved you over. With no idea where he was, I cut to the right and gunned it. That's when I heard it. He must have landed there. I'll never forget the sound. A thick, wet thud. I got the hell out of there.

Barry waited at the hotel. I told him the whole story, and he promised to take care of it. He called Sergio. When they found him, Tommy Lee wasn't breathing. It was an accident, but they were afraid the police might not see it that way, so they took care of it.

I had a lie ready for you. Tommy Lee found somebody else and ran off with her. That Barry made sure he was gone for good. But you didn't remember anything except me waking you up to go to the hotel. So, why stir the pot?

Then I started going to that damn therapist. She said you might be repressing what happened. That when it surfaced, you'd be trapped in a limbo where you wouldn't be able to distinguish reality from what was tangled up in your unconsciousness. (I had to look up limbo.)

Baby, the truth has set you free. No more fear or confusion. Let go of guilt and pain. Like Barry said, it was an accident, self-defense even, and you were nothing more than a bystander.

You have been the best gift I could ever have hoped for. Please accept this letter and the freedom it offers as my gift to you.

• • •

"You okay?" My stepfather sat by me on the loveseat.

"Not really." My hands were shaking, but I remained dry-eyed. "Did you read it?"

He nodded. "She wanted me to explain how she hated risking your lives and planned to make up for all the things she got wrong. She instructed me to explain the letter wasn't the only gift and to turn the portfolio over to you."

No heiress, I was in very good financial shape. But I questioned Barry about the contradictory details in our stories. He shrugged.

"I don't know what to tell you. Her version makes sense, and it's consistent with what Sergio and I found at your house."

When I asked why he hadn't just put Tommy Lee in the truck they pushed over the mountain, he explained Sergio said the injuries didn't look like the kind you get from going over a cliff.

"Wow," I said. "He's good." Maybe too good, considering his Colombian background. "Where did you end up, uh, putting him?"

"Let's just say we gave him a proper send-off."

I had no problem letting Tommy Lee rest in whatever peace he'd been able to find.

Later, I reread the letter. Her account didn't completely align with my unrepressed memories. How had she managed to run around and push me out of the driver's seat, making her responsible for that awful 'wet thud'? And she had forgotten or omitted when the truck rolled over Tommy Lee a second time as we pulled away from the house.

My mother said I knew the truth, but was there really such a thing? Weren't intentions as crucial as action? We hadn't planned on inflicting violence; we'd been running from it. And did any of that make any difference since we couldn't change the past?

What I would do next did matter. I could keep doubting myself and refusing to be happy. Or I could allow myself to believe I was worth loving—that Grant loved me, and it was safe to love him.

Taken in a more fragile moment where I wore a grim smile, and Mom's lips are unnaturally stretched into an awkward grin, the picture no longer propelled me to a dark, unforgiving place.

Someday, I would reveal the events of that night to Grant, confident in his unchanging love. But for now, I wanted to hold the secret between me and my mother close to my heart. Once a link to all that was wrong with my past, it had become a lifeline, a gift from the woman who, despite her mistakes, had loved me unconditionally. And I would accept it with joy.

The End

Acknowledgements

Navigating relationships between mothers and daughters can be difficult. Often, the intent is overshadowed by the struggle to survive. Today, over half of marriages end in divorce. When my parents divorced, it was much less common. Single moms seldom had the support necessary to get by. My mother was a nurse who worked double shifts to ensure my brother and I had all that we needed and more. Through her example, I learned what real strength was. She instilled a steely determination that kept me believing I could be or do anything I wanted. After years of work in other fields and raising my own family, I proved her point by becoming an author.

I thank her and all the single mothers who overcome despair, exhaustion, and criticism so that their children will have better lives. She got it right more often than not and shared her strength with me and my sweet brother, Bob Stagner.

I'm also thankful for the Roswell, Georgia critique group for their encouragement and kindness. A special thanks goes to my beta reader, Brian Lohmuller, one of the nicest people I know.

Most of all, I'm grateful to my husband for his patience in the face of a madwoman who sets herself unrealistic deadlines and makes him suffer through the process along with her.

I would never have been able to write this book without the support of my own daughters, Kate and Laura. They enriched my understanding of what loving mothers and daughters can be.

About the Author

Katherine Nichols is an award-winning author of seven novels. A vice president of The Atlanta Writers Club, she has also served on the board of Sisters in Crime Atlanta. In keeping with her decades long interest in empowering women, she co-hosts the inspirational *Wild Women Who Write Take Flight* podcast. Katherine lives in Lilburn, Georgia, with her husband. When she isn't reading, writing, or traveling, she enjoys spending time with her grandchildren and hanging out with her two rescue dogs and two rescue cats.

OTHER TITLES BY KATHERINE NICHOLS

Lucy Howard Mysteries

False Claims

Canceled Policies

Sisters Forever Series

The Sometime Sister

The Substitute Sister

Trust Issues

The Unreliables

NOTE FROM KATHERINE NICHOLS

Word-of-mouth is crucial for any author to succeed. If you enjoyed *Imperfect Alignment*, please leave a review online—anywhere you are able. Even if it's just a sentence or two. It would make all the difference and would be very much appreciated.

Thanks!
Katherine Nichols

We hope you enjoyed reading this title from:

BLACK ROSE writing™

www.blackrosewriting.com

Subscribe to our mailing list – *The Rosevine* – and receive **FREE** books, daily deals, and stay current with news about upcoming releases and our hottest authors.
Scan the QR code below to sign up.

Already a subscriber? Please accept a sincere thank you for being a fan of Black Rose Writing authors.

View other Black Rose Writing titles at www.blackrosewriting.com/books and use promo code **PRINT** to receive a **20% discount** when purchasing.

www.ingramcontent.com/pod-product-compliance
Lightning Source LLC
Chambersburg PA
CBHW030021200726
48283CB00012B/706